Eloise di

As yet he had not noticed her. His gaze was searching the faces of the crowd now lining the path between them. Occasionally he inclined his head in acknowledgment of a joyous greeting.

Then a steely gray stare locked with hers. Her heart hammered frantically. She stared back into a bronzed, lean face, as handsome as a dark angel. Eyes bruised with fatigue regarded her with glacial coldness....

Unmistakably Alaric's eyes.

PAULINE BENTLEY

Penruthin's Wife

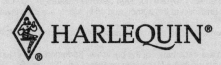

HARLEQUIN®

TORONTO • NEW YORK • LONDON
AMSTERDAM • PARIS • SYDNEY • HAMBURG
STOCKHOLM • ATHENS • TOKYO • MILAN • MADRID
PRAGUE • WARSAW • BUDAPEST • AUCKLAND

ISBN 0-373-30385-8

PENRUTHIN'S WIFE

First North American Publication 2001

Visit us at www.eHarlequin.com

Printed in U.S.A.

PAULINE BENTLEY

has long been captivated by history. Born in Essex, she trained as a legal secretary, but always came away from visiting castles or manor houses with the desire to write about them. She now lives in Sussex, is married with two children, has a growing menagerie of dogs, and finds inspiration walking over the South Downs.

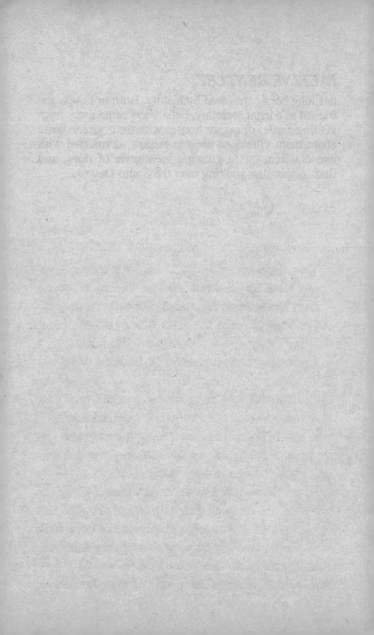

Chapter One

It was the summer of 1453 and the saintly King Henry VI of England had just been declared insane.

Lady Eloise Penruthin stared in disbelief at the pedlar who had brought the news which further rocked the foundations of her already uncertain future.

Dismissing the pedlar, she left the solar of Penruthin castle. Accompanied by her maid, Winifred, she set out to walk the short distance to the priory on Penruthin land. Too many events were taking place which were beyond her control. By marriage she was mistress of Penruthin, yet her authority was overridden by her brother-in-law, Sir Stephen.

When Eloise saw a guard detach himself from the group of men cleaning their weapons in the courtyard her temper rose. Nowadays she could not even walk within the castle precincts without being followed. And it was not for her protection. It was to ensure that she did not try to leave without Prior Ignatius or

Sir Stephen knowing of it. She was virtually a prisoner in her own home.

Any petitioner who intended to waylay her that
morning held back at the troubled look in her vivid
blue eyes. A breeze lifted her gossamer-fine veil, revealing a thick plait of ebony hair which reached to
her waist. Several villagers watched her progress with
concern. They all adored the lovely young bride of
their absent lord. During the seven years she had lived
at the castle her maturing poise and generous heart—
as she turned from self-conscious child-bride to an
assured and beautiful woman of seventeen—filled
them with pride.

It was time their lord returned and made her truly
his wife. It was time their lord returned...and that was
a simple fact. Sir Alaric Penruthin had been absent
from his lands and wife too long.

Rumours abounded from nearly seven years of
their lord's absence. Other knights had long returned
from the fighting in France to safeguard their ances-
tral lands. Five years ago word had reached Penruthin
that Sir Alaric's father, Lord Edgar Penruthin, had
been slain when his castle in Normandy had been
besieged by the French. It was said that Sir Alaric
had been filled with remorse that his men had not
arrived in time to save his father. To atone, he had
donned pilgrim's robes and, with only his bastard
half-brother Roland for company, had made pilgrimage to the Holy Land. Nothing had been heard of the
two brothers until a year ago, when a pilgrim had

passed through Penruthin on the way home to his village in Somerset. Was the news he brought true? Had their lord been captured by the Moors? Was he dead or alive? How much longer must the young bride remain a virgin in her marriage bed?

Troubled and defiant, Eloise faced the prior of Penruthin Priory. The room she had been shown into was more sumptuously furnished than her own chambers. A large gold cross dominated the far wall, and on each side of it hung a painted silk hanging showing one of the miracles performed by Christ. A glance showed her the remains of the prior's meal. The gnawed bones from four pheasants and two hares were piled on the silver plate. A half-eaten honey and apple pie accompanied the meat. The portion devoured would have satisfied three men. The sauce from the pie had dripped in a greasy trail on the prior's grey habit, and ran down over the immense girth of his twenty-stone figure.

The fleshy jowls of Prior Ignatius wobbled as he ineffectually tried to suppress a belch. It was not just his coarse manners which turned Eloise's stomach whenever she was in his presence. For a man of God, he emanated a coldness, a sly cunning and cruelty from black eyes in a round, fleshy face.

"What troubles you, my child?" Prior Ignatius asked, plastering a condescending smile on to his thin lizard lips.

"The repairs I ordered to the villagers' houses have

not been carried out.'' She eyed him stonily, controlling her loathing. ''If the work is not started immediately it will not be completed before winter. Several of the cottages were flooded during last night's rain.''

In her agitation Eloise began to pace the room. Winifred kept her head bowed, but Eloise could see her maid's fingers moving over the beads of her rosary. Like most people of Penruthin, Winifred was terrified of the prior. The maid's fear strengthened Eloise's resolve to protect her people. She was the only one who could speak out.

She halted her pacing to confront Prior Ignatius. ''Why did you insist that the carpenters and thatchers continue their work within the priory? Surely that can wait?''

''Work for the glorification of God can never wait, my lady.'' His pompous tone rang with righteous condemnation.

''I do not believe God would wish his children to suffer cold and deprivation,'' Eloise retorted.

The prior's black eyes snapped with anger that she dared to question his rule. Fleshy lids dragged down over their malevolent glare. ''It is not for you to judge what is God's will, Lady Eloise. In Sir Alaric's absence, I must consider the needs of my flock. Their spiritual needs are more important than those of their bodies.''

''I don't agree.''

The reptilian lips compressed. ''Those are the devil's words, my lady. Have you become a heretic?''

A coating of ice touched Eloise's spine. Prior Ignatius had condemned several heretics to the stake in recent years. They had been God-fearing people who had dared to question the wealth of the church, while they themselves starved during winter. She had been too young and inexperienced to help them. That was no longer the case.

Unfortunately, Penruthin was isolated in a remote Somerset valley. It was an arduous three-day ride to the Diocese town of Wells. The letters she had written to the Archbishop and to the Abbot of Shergrove, the prior's superior, had not been answered. Eloise suspected they had never reached their destination, the messenger stopped by Sir Stephen. He would want no investigation into the injustices committed on his absent brother's land. Prior Ignatius ruled supreme.

"You do not answer," the prior pronounced darkly. "Ever since the witch Clothilde was burned for her crimes last year, you have challenged my rule. I remember well how you begged mercy for the woman—a condemned fornicator and witch."

Eloise's blood ran hot at the prior's hypocrisy. Clothilde had been the most beautiful woman in the village and she had refused to enter the prior's bed. He had never forgiven her that insult.

"Clothilde was the mother of Sir Alaric's half-brother Roland," she responded tautly. "When Sir Edgar rode out to France and Clothilde returned to live in the village, many men courted her. She refused them all. She loved Sir Edgar until the day she died.

She doted on Roland, her only child. Her loss and her fear for him made her act strangely. She was not a witch.''

"She was seen praying to the trees. A pagan ritual."

"Her whole day was spent praying that her son was alive, irrespective of whether she was in a church, field or wood."

Eloise bit her lip to control her anger. It was an argument they had covered many times. She had never believed Clothilde to be evil. She had become the beloved mistress of Sir Edgar when his first wife died after ten barren years of marriage. From the villagers Eloise had learned that Roland was an adored son, even though he was born out of wedlock. When Lord Penruthin had remarried a year after Roland's birth, he had put aside his mistress. During the years when Roland had lived close to his mother, Clothilde had acted normally enough. Only when news had reached them that her son had been captured by the Moors had she started to act strangely.

Poor Clothilde had loved her child's father. Her loyalty had been repaid when Alaric's and Stephen's mother died giving birth to a stillborn daughter and she was reinstated as Sir Edgar's mistress. The villagers had told Eloise that Roland had remained Sir Edgar's favourite child. The boy had been brought up in the castle and educated with Sir Edgar's other sons, Alaric and Stephen. There had been no love lost between the brothers.

Roland had been destined for the Church, although he had evaded taking his noviciate vows. When Sir Edgar had gone to fight in France, Roland had begged to accompany him. Sir Edgar had agreed. On his father's death, it was said that Alaric had insisted on Roland's becoming his squire, forcing him to be subservient to the new Lord of Penruthin. From Eloise's own brief encounters with her husband, she sympathised with Roland. Sir Alaric was not a man to suffer a bastard brother appearing his equal in intellect or status.

Knowing that further discussion with the prior would achieve nothing, Eloise left him.

"Pray for the return of Sir Alaric," Prior Ignatius called after her departing figure.

Eloise's eyes narrowed. All at once the years of frustration and uncertainty overwhelmed her and she lost her temper. Rounding on the prior, she declared, "No one prays harder for my husband's safe return than myself."

She stopped herself in time before adding that in the past year she had come to realise that only Sir Alaric's return could save Penruthin from the plunder and tyrannical rule of Prior Ignatius. It was obvious Alaric's younger brother, Stephen, would never have the courage to stand up to the prior's rule. There were times when Eloise began to wonder whether Sir Stephen were not in league with the prior to bleed the estate dry of its wealth—the wealth brought to it by her dowry.

Prior Ignatius regarded her balefully, his cold eyes impaling her with their contempt. "Tender sentiments, when only six months ago you begged to be released from your marriage vows."

Eloise's head came up, her eyes flashing blue fire. "My marriage was never consummated. There has been no word, or messenger, from Sir Alaric in five years. I am a prisoner in a marriage which is no marriage. I am neither a true wife nor a widow. The Church must have laws governing such matters. All I asked was that my case was put before them. You refused me that right."

The prior sneered. "If your marriage does not please you, Lady Eloise, you may enter a nunnery. It is believed that your husband and his squire were taken prisoner by the Moors while on pilgrimage to the Holy Land. He is in God's hands."

With difficulty Eloise bit back her sharp rejoinder. A pilgrimage of guilt. According to rumour, Sir Alaric had been carousing with the English troops some thirty miles away when the French laid siege to his father's castle in Normandy. He arrived too late to save his father, who had died in the fighting.

The prior glowered at her. "False pride is a sin, my lady. You have never forgiven your husband for abandoning you a month after your wedding. He was not then to know that he would be prevented from returning by the time you reached an age to take your place in his bed."

His crudeness flicked at her raw nerves. A month

of living in the same castle as Alaric had revealed many unpalatable facts, not least that her husband despised her. He had only married her for her dowry. She let none of her pain show as she held the prior's condemning glare.

"The anniversary of my wedding is in three months. If there is no news of Sir Alaric by then, I will seek audience with the Archbishop of Wells, to ask that an Ecclesiastical Court declare my marriage annulled and that my dowry be returned to me. I have no intention of entering a nunnery." She was breathing heavily as her indignation rose. How dared this man continue to treat her like a witless child? "It is my right to marry and have children who will inherit my own lands at Whytemead," she went on. "I will even petition the King if I must."

"The King is a pious man. He believes in the sanctity of marriage." The prior regarded her with open contempt. He believed she was firmly in his power and that goaded her anger. She would be no man's pawn, least of all a man as evil as this one.

"King Henry is ill," she flung at him in chilling tones. "The war in France and the loss of so many of his dominions there are said to have broken his spirit. He has been declared mad. I will address my case direct to the Church, even to the Pope if necessary."

The prior's eyes gleamed and Eloise felt the first stirrings of foreboding. The prior's family were supporters of the Duke of York who would remain the

King's heir until the birth of the Queen's child in October. If the Lancastrian king was deposed and the Duke of York gained the throne, the prior's power would increase.

She did not want to think of that awesome possibility and turned on her heel, defiantly ignoring the prior's command that she return. She'd had enough of his lectures; she'd had enough of being told to wait like an obedient wife for her husband to return. It was likely that Alaric was dead. While she complied with the prior's wishes her dowry was rapidly being squandered. Why should she wait? It wasn't as though she even liked her husband.

Her mind seared with the humiliation of those first weeks at Penruthin. Alaric had not even glanced at her during the wedding service or the banquet following. Yet she had been aware of him. His strength, his tall, lithe figure and darkly handsome looks were all a maid dreamed of in a husband. He was ten years older than herself. A man already, while she was still a child. Despite her youth, she had been drawn by his masculine attraction. There had been a tournament to celebrate their marriage and Alaric had won every joust, although he had refused the challenge from Roland, who had also emerged from the lists undefeated.

She had been so proud of Alaric that afternoon, but her euphoria had begun to fade as soon as the wedding banquet began. Her husband had spent the evening dancing with a cousin, the beautiful Lady Isobel. The bride had been neglected.

Only Roland had come forward to honour her, and even in her gratitude she had seen pity in his expressive grey eyes. As she'd stared into his lean, angular face, which was so like Alaric's—even his hair and eyes were the same colouring—she had fleetingly wished that he were her husband instead of his haughty legitimate brother. She'd known instinctively that Roland was sensitive to other people's feelings. As his father's eldest son, but barred from inheriting Penruthin by his bastardy, he must have suffered many insults. Yet he had learnt to bear them with fortitude. When he'd drawn her on to the dance-floor and smiled at her, she'd felt her heartache ease. The pressure of his hand on hers as he'd led her through the stately steps had sent a pervading warmth through her young body, and her heart had fluttered strangely. Why couldn't Alaric have shown her such kindness? Her husband's neglect had lacerated her pride. It had also kindled a deep debt of gratitude towards Roland.

The next day she had been drawn by laughter towards the rose garden. Going to investigate, she'd seen Alaric embracing the Lady Isobel as they sat partially hidden in the rose arbour. Eloise had stood frozen with humiliation as she'd watched her husband ardently kiss his mistress, his hand caressing the heavy breasts he had freed from her bodice.

With a languorous sigh, Isobel taunted, ''How does it feel to be married?''

Alaric threw back his head, his dark hair shot

through with copper glints in the bright sunlight. His teeth gleamed whitely against his tanned skin.

"Shackled, don't you mean? By the rood, but the child is ugly! As dark-haired as a gypsy brat and just as graceless." He flicked imaginary fluff from the scarlet silk hose which encased the sleek muscles of his shapely thighs.

The coldness of his tone flayed Eloise. Thrusting a hand in her mouth she began to back away.

"Your wife is not to your taste, then." Isobel leaned forward, her pale golden hair a shimmering crown above her pale flawless complexion. She laid a hand on Alaric's thigh, sliding it towards his groin in a way Eloise had once seen a village harlot caressing a prospective customer. "At least she's young and malleable," Isobel went on slyly. "She won't interfere with our pleasure. And her dowry will enrich Penruthin."

Sir Alaric chuckled and caressed Isobel's heavy breast. "It's the only reason I was persuaded to wed her. Thank God I don't have to bed the wench for several years."

Isobel's reply was lost to Eloise as she bolted, her face flaming with embarrassment. From that moment she had hated her arrogant, unfeeling husband.

It was a hatred she had tried to come to terms with during the intervening years. She'd tried to make excuses for his conduct: he was so much older than herself, he was a passionate man who needed a woman's love, not a child's adoration. Yet still his insults rankled and festered. Although she dutifully prayed for her husband's safe return, her prayers always included Roland—that he also had been spared.

Whenever she thought of Roland, the same glow of warmth he had engendered during the dance returned to sustain her. It was his voice she heard encouraging her to confront Prior Ignatius and defend the villagers' rights. It was his self-assured dignity in the face of the adversity of his bastardy that she emulated when she was frightened by the future. Over the years the images of Roland and Alaric had become so confusingly intermingled that she could not separate one from the other.

Memories of her wedding-day rekindled her loathing for her husband. With indignation flaring through her, she observed to her maid as they strode back to the castle, ''I will not let Prior Ignatius continue to dictate my life. If my father were still alive he would help me to escape. He saw this marriage as a way to protect me. He could not have foreseen the mockery it has become.''

She realised now why her father had been so adamant that she wed so young. He'd known he was dying from the wounds he had received in France two years earlier. His punctured lungs had never recovered after his horse had thrown and rolled on him when a cannon-ball had exploded at its side. Her only brother had died in that same battle and Eloise had become her father's heir. The land she had brought with her dowry was prime farmland and with several rich copper and tin mines. It was the income from them that had made her acceptable to Sir Alaric as a bride.

The castle of Whytemead, her family home, was little better than a ruin. For too many years her warrior father had served as a mercenary in the King's army in France. His home had been neglected after her mother died from lung-fever a year after she was born. Eloise had been brought up in a convent until she was eight. She had hated the rigid discipline, the unquestioning obedience. Yet so much of the nuns' teaching had become unconsciously ingrained in her. Inwardly she had rebelled against her fate while outwardly she'd followed the nuns' dictates, obeying a higher will which had kept her subservient for so many years to the prior's tyranny.

"I'm not standing for it any longer," she vowed fiercely. "Am I not mistress of Penruthin? I am a voice to be heard."

"My lady, the people adore you," Winifred said with unaccustomed passion. "They have no love for Sir Stephen. They resent the way he gives in to the prior's demands and has no control over his wife's greed for jewels and gowns, when the money should be spent on repairing the castle's defences."

The maid fidgeted with her plain brown homespun skirt, scratching at a dried stain with a fingernail.

Eloise looked at her askance. Clearly her maid was disturbed. "Pray continue. You know I value your opinion and prefer you to speak openly. If I did not have you to confide in I think I would go out of my mind.''

Winifred blushed. ''And I would die before I betrayed you, my lady. Be patient. Your time will come. If Sir Alaric is dead...''

Eloise sighed. ''His death would free me, but it would condemn the people of Penruthin to still greater misery. For then Sir Stephen would be their legal lord. I do not wish that on them.''

She gazed round at the familiar battlements and high round keep. It was an impressive fortress, but its charm for her lay not in its structure, but in the villagers and servants who so openly gave her their devotion. She cared for them deeply and wanted to protect them from the prior's evil.

''Only Sir Alaric can save Penruthin from the weakness of his brother and Prior Ignatius's tyranny,'' Eloise continued tautly. ''Prior Ignatius is too wily to leave himself open to investigation in his dealings here. And Sir Stephen is his pawn. He is weak and ineffectual.'' Her eyes flashed with grim determination. ''How can I abandon the people while they need me? Things cannot be permitted to remain as they are. I will not allow the people to suffer another winter with inadequate food or shelter. Penruthin, which once was so proud, has become a place of shame in its neglect.''

''My lady, the people love you,'' Winifred declared. ''They will follow you in anything you ask.''

Eloise clasped her hands together, her heart fearful.

"I would not ask them to rebel against the Church. That way would lead them to the gallows or the stake."

She stared into the narrow face of her maid, which beneath its white wimple appeared even thinner. Winifred was only four years older than herself and they had always been close. Now she was comforted by the compassion and understanding in her maid's brown eyes.

"The people's hope lies in Sir Alaric's return. For their sakes let him not be dead."

"But what of your hopes, my lady?" Winifred questioned with a frown.

Eloise smiled with false conviction. "Seven years is a long time. Who knows? My husband may have changed. If he has indeed been a prisoner of the Moors, he may have learned the value of humility instead of arrogance. I would hope for that much at least."

Winifred sighed, her expression wistful. "You mean he may become more like Roland?"

Eloise did not answer, but that was exactly what she meant. She tilted her head proudly as she surveyed the bustling activity within the crowded courtyard. A castle was never still. Forty men-at-arms were garrisoned here, many of them recruited since Sir Edgar's departure. It was disquieting to look into the hard faces of the mercenary soldiers and know that their loyalty was to Sir Stephen, not to herself. When Sir Alaric returned it would be with his own large band of loyal retainers. She did not trust Stephen meekly to hand over his power.

Frowning, she studied the soldiers around her. Those not on duty lounged in the sunshine, cleaning their weapons and armour or rolling dice. Two men were stripped to the waist and wrestling, urged on by cheers from their companions. A wheelwright crouched over the broken wheel he was repairing was knocked to the ground as the two wrestlers fell against him. Her regard moved to the far side of the courtyard where an elderly fletcher seated on an upturned barrel was teaching his apprentice how to align arrow-feathers in their shaft. There was noise all around Eloise as grooms exercised horses and children ran and laughed among the foraging pigs and poultry. The castle dogs barked and strained at their chains. The washerwomen carried their laundry baskets to spread the linen sheets on bushes to dry, and several women from the village were waiting to bake their bread in the castle's communal oven.

Any villager who saw Eloise watching tugged his forelock in respect, the women bobbing curtsies. Eloise knew every villager by name and her breast tightened with emotion as they shyly paid her homage when she passed. How could she abandon them— even if her own happiness depended on it? She must be their champion. Her resolve was firm. She would no longer allow Prior Ignatius and Sir Stephen to bleed Penruthin dry. It was no good waiting for her

absent husband to return; she must fight for the people
and for herself. She would start today.

Eloise was too disturbed by her interview with the
prior to settle. She paced through the castle, needing
to be busy to still her anger. She ordered fresh rushes
to be cut from the river-bed. The old ones, which
smelt musty, were swept from the floor and burnt in
the courtyard. When the new rushes were laid they
were sprinkled with fragrant herbs and she went to
the garden to gather what she needed.

Two hours later she regarded the Great Hall with
satisfaction. The silver tableware on the dais table
gleamed and the cobwebs had been swept from between the oak beams of the arched wooden roof. Even
though it was August, a large log burned on the central stone hearth, its smoke curling up to the ceiling.

In a moment of rebellion she had ordered four extra
pigs killed and roasted, to be dispensed to the poor
of the village. Her extravagance was bound to cause
an argument with Sir Stephen, but she did not care.

She glanced disparagingly up the staircase where
Sir Stephen had his rooms. It was long past midday
and he still had not made an appearance. A sultry
female laugh caused Eloise to lift a brow in exasperation. The Lady Isobel had wed Sir Stephen a year
after her own marriage. Rarely a day went by when
Isobel did not show her contempt for Eloise. She was
jealous that Eloise was mistress of Penruthin and

never missed a chance to deride her youth and inexperience.

Eloise's eyes glittered. Her youth was now behind her and so was her inexperience. She ran the household better than Isobel. A year ago she had faced her sister-in-law who was seated in the central chair on the dais. That chair was Eloise's place by right. Before the gathering of retainers, Eloise had demanded that Isobel vacate the mistress of Penruthin's chair. Isobel had sniggered and was joined by Stephen.

"Deny me my rightful place on the dais and you deny my marriage to Sir Alaric, Lord of Penruthin. Sir Stephen, you may be the custodian of Penruthin until Sir Alaric returns, but deny me my rights and you will find it the poorer by the repayment of my dowry."

A cruel smile twisted Isobel's scarlet lips. "I do not fear Sir Alaric, should he return."

The challenge in her eyes said that she had been his beloved mistress, while Eloise had been an unwanted wife.

The insult stiffened Eloise's spine. "You remind me often that Sir Alaric married me for the wealth I brought to Penruthin," she returned with false sweetness. "He coveted my fortune enough to make me mistress of Penruthin. As Sir Stephen's wife, you may be a lot older than I, but you are not my superior in this castle."

Lady Isobel's face bleached of colour and her lips

curled back to form a scathing reply. Stephen stopped her with a hand on her arm.

"Do as the Lady Eloise commands." He smiled thinly at Eloise, though his grey eyes remained cold. Like Alaric and Roland he had the Penruthin grey eyes and dark hair of his father, though his resemblance to his older brothers ended there. He was of medium weight and slightly built; a narrow brown beard and moustache concealed the weak line of his jaw and mouth. "Lady Eloise is now a woman, not a child," he continued. "She must take her rightful place and the responsibilities which go with it."

He leaned across to unhook the gold chain of the chatelaine around his wife's waist. The household keys jingled as he rose to come to the front of the dais and held them out to Eloise. Then, offering Eloise his hand, he escorted her to the central chair. Isobel remained seated, staring in frozen-faced silence along the lines of trestle-tables. She clearly expected some support from the men-at-arms. Eloise knew that Isobel had taken several of the guards as lovers to appease her voracious appetite.

Silence fell upon the Great Hall; not even a knife scraped against a plate as every face turned towards the dais. No one challenged Eloise's right to take up her duties as mistress of Penruthin. With a harsh grating of her chair, Isobel rose, trembling with anger.

"I won't forget this," she whispered harshly to Eloise. "You'll regret crossing me."

Then, deliberately turning her back to her, she

flounced to a vacant place on the other side of her husband. A loose board on the raised dais creaked under her weight. Since Alaric's departure the Lady Isobel's excesses had begun to strip away her beauty. The once lovely face was lined beneath the thick layer of rice powder from her debauchery, and her curvaceous figure was now becoming gross from indulging in too much honeyed wine and sweetmeats.

Eloise was aware that in her need to establish her rights at Penruthin she had made a spiteful enemy. Even so, she had not expected her triumph to be so easily accomplished. It had proved to her how frightened Sir Stephen was that he had squandered her fortune. She also realised that it was a conciliatory gesture to appease her. From that day she had begun to feel as though she was a prisoner in her own home.

Still restless after supervising the morning's work, Eloise's thoughts festered on the interview with Prior Ignatius. There was little she seemed able to do to help the villagers improve the quality of their lives. At least neither Sir Stephen nor Prior Ignatius stopped her tending the sick. Last winter she had sold several pieces of jewellery to pay for stonemasons to build an infirmary in the village.

Cutting short her reverie, she gestured for Winifred to accompany her. As they walked through the archway of the outer bailey and over the drawbridge to the village, she announced, "We will visit your mother, Githa. She is working in the infirmary today.

I promised her I would help with preparing the comfrey unguent.''

"You are almost as proficient as my mother in making up the herbal remedies," Winifred said. "I never was any use to her. I could never tell one plant from another. Hen-witted, she called me.''

Ahead of Eloise, Samuel the swineherd was shouting. The pigs, startled by pounding hoofbeats, had scattered, grunting noisily as they ran for cover into open doorways and gardens. A grin of amusement spread across Eloise's face at the antics of several youths and men as they ran hither and thither to shoo the pigs out of their gardens before their precious crops were trampled underfoot. The smile died as she saw who had caused the disturbance. Prior Ignatius trotted past, his horse's hooves flailing out and nearly knocking down a toddling child.

Unmindful of the danger to herself, Eloise darted forward and snatched the child out of the horse's path.

"Have you no care for the safety of your flock?" she stormed as she glared up at the prior.

The look he shot her was one of pure venom. It made her skin rise like gooseflesh, chilling her blood. He did not halt his pace, or deign to answer her. Where was he going in such haste? He rarely stirred himself from the comfort of his priory to journey abroad. The chill of unease turned to frosty alarm as she recalled their last conversation. Hadn't she threatened to seek audience with the Archbishop of Wells to annul her marriage? If she succeeded, her dowry must be returned to her. That would impoverish Penruthin. A man as avaricious as Prior Ignatius would not allow such wealth to be taken from his grasp.

She cursed her wayward temper. For years she had been curbing it. In a moment of ire and frustration she had been indiscreet and revealed her plans. Her stomach contracted with fear. She had no doubt that Prior Ignatius would make a vindictive and dangerous enemy.

Through the thinning trees the ragged traveller could see the keep of Penruthin Castle. Against an azure sky the gold standard with the black lion rampant billowed in the breeze.

He closed his eyes, drinking in the long-remembered smells of these woods. The charcoal-burner's fires, the scent of meadowsweet, jasmine and wild garlic. In the distance he could hear the waterfall and in another direction the rhythmic thud of the woodman's axe.

With a shudder of disgust, he opened his eyes and stared down at his dirty ripped tunic and torn hose. Weeks ago his boots had fallen to shreds and his bleeding feet were bound in rags. He leaned heavily on his staff, weariness and the aches in his body diminishing as he realised that he was finally home.

He rubbed a grimy hand across his bearded jaw. How could he approach the village looking like a vagabond? His pride would not allow it. He turned towards the waterfall. He could at least wash away the dirt. The landscape blurred and the pounding in his head warned of a return of the fever that intermittently smote him since his capture. He gritted his teeth and pressed on. He would not return to Penruthin weak and near the point of exhaustion. He would rest first, then stride proudly through the village.

Still he hesitated; the lure of his home was strong. He edged closer, concealing himself within the shoulder-high ferns and wild flowers at the edge of the wood. He could hear the excited voices of children, the steady clang of Saul the blacksmith's hammer. Geese honked as the young swineherd guided them back into their pens. They were familiar sounds, long denied him.

Through the foliage he scanned the village for sight of a remembered face. But it wasn't the people he saw that boiled the anger in his gut. Could this run-down village, with crumbling daub on the wattle walls and gaping holes in the thatch, be Penruthin? What had happened in his absence? The people looked leaner, some even gaunt. Only the children laughed. He heard disgruntled muttering from the women gathered by the well. He frowned. Not a single man was visible in the village, or at work on their own strips of land. When he saw the score of tiny figures in the distance working on the church land, which bordered the lord's demesne, his knuckles whitened on the pilgrim's staff. Prior Ignatius was up to his old tricks.

Speak of the devil and it was said he would appear.

The pilgrim glared at Prior Ignatius riding into view on a magnificent grey Barbary mare, its trappings of gold embossed red leather. The prior had doubled in size in the past seven years. It was obvious what had happened here. The people had starved whilst the Church had prospered.

A child ran across the path of the prior's horse. The pilgrim opened his mouth to shout a warning. It was never uttered. He saw a woman dart forward. She scooped up the child and he heard her berate the prior, although he was too far away to catch her angry words. Her courage caught his interest and he studied her. She was tall, slender and from the way the sunlight caught the sheen of her gown it could only be made from the finest silk. When the breeze lifted the edge of her veil, he saw an ebony plait. He frowned, unable to place to her. Then his eyes widened in surprise. It could only be the Lady Eloise. She was too far away from him to see her clearly, but he was impressed by her regal dignity as she confronted the prior.

When the prior rode on, ignoring her anger, outrage ripped through him. Its intensity made him sway. The fever struck with ferocity, his starved body unable to combat it. He did not want to be found like this. He must reach the reviving waters of the waterfall. He must be strong when he returned to Penruthin. There was a battle ahead. It was no easy task to take on the Church and win.

He swayed, his body burning, every limb aching as

somehow he found the strength to reach the waterfall. He plunged into the icy water, its coolness reviving him. The water felt good. Standing on the bottom of the pool, he began to scrub at his clothing and body with his hands, wishing he had even the roughest of soaps. Several times he ducked under the water and rose to massage the dirt and travel grime out of his hair, clothing and skin. When his teeth began to chatter he hauled himself dripping on to the grassy bank. He flopped on to his back, unable to keep his eyes open. The sun caressed him, not with the fierce tormenting desert heat he had endured after his escape from the Moors, but with a gentle warmth. Then he began to shiver. Perhaps bathing had not been such a good idea with the fever about to reclaim him. The pain was growing behind his eyes, throbbing mercilessly. Above him the circle of blue sky interlaced with tree branches blurred. His eyelids were weighted, closing as exhaustion finally claimed him.

A babble of voices roused him. He opened his eyes and shook his head to focus his gaze. The pain in his skull remained. Absently he noted that the sun was lower in a sky now laden with clouds. He had slept for three hours or more. Edging towards him was a squint-eyed man with a red birthmark covering one cheek. It was Dickon, the woodcutter's son. He was older, taller, his thin face sprouting a straggly brown beard.

"It is his lordship," Dickon was shouting over his shoulder to other companions who were dim shadows against the bright sunlight. "Praise God, Lord Alaric has returned."

There was the sound of running feet disappearing towards the village. A cry went up. "Lord Penruthin has returned. Our lord is not dead. He will save us."

The words pounded through the traveller's brain. He had not been wrong. Penruthin was in sad repair, its people neglected in his absence. Prior Ignatius and Stephen had much to answer for.

Dickon pressed a water-bottle to his mouth and the warm liquid trickled between his lips.

He drank it gratefully, the cobwebs of fever receding from his mind. He looked around at the circle of expectant faces. No man stood; they all knelt in homage to their lord. As he saw the ravages that time and poverty had carved on their faces, his anger deepened. They had suffered no less than he in the years he had been away. They had suffered under the patronage of his family in a way which shamed his father's name.

The woodcutter frowned. "It is you, Sir Alaric, isn't it?"

Threads of the fever still clung tenaciously, making speech difficult as he strove to combat the feverish shivers which attacked his body.

"What's happened here in my absence?" he finally forced out.

"Nothing that can't be put right now you've come back to us, your lordship." Dickon was openly weeping with joy. "'Tis a miracle you've returned. The people are starving. Lady Eloise has done her best, but she is young. Her orders are countermanded by the prior or Sir Stephen.''

"The Lady Eloise." He recalled the dark-haired child from so long ago. It sounded as though she had escaped the corruption he suspected here. He put a hand to his head, wishing his brain were clearer of the fever. His thoughts were disjointed. The men were gazing at him as though he was their saviour. He saw Dickon scan the undergrowth.

"Have you returned alone, my lord? Is Roland dead?"

It was a long time before he spoke. Obviously the pilgrims he had asked to visit Penruthin and inform them of his brother's death had not journeyed so far. All his concentration was on absorbing what he had seen in the village. "My brother is dead," he said at last. "I must speak with the Lady Eloise. Help me to my feet."

The boulders around the waterfall spun as he fought to recover his wits. The water-bottle was again pressed to his mouth and he drank deeply. He cursed the weakness of his starved and fevered body, but pride made him stand tall. Wryly, he commented, "I would have wished to return to Penruthin looking less like a vagabond."

Dickon grinned. "My lord, the people will not see your rags. They will see only their lord who will save them from the prior's greed and persecution, as your father did before you."

A bald-headed man with bushy grey eyebrows remained kneeling and reached for his hand. He kissed it in homage, his voice hoarse. "God bless you, Lord Penruthin. We thought you were dead. We thought ourselves bound to misery and the evil which darkens this land."

Looking into the man's beseeching gaze, the pilgrim felt his anger turn to white-hot rage, and something more—a feeling of intense loyalty and the need to right the injustice perpetrated here. The emotion was so sharp, it clamped his chest in agony. He gritted his teeth against the unexpected pain. He knew then that he had been spared to save the people of Penruthin from the prior's evil tyranny.

Frowning, he said, "It's Peter, isn't it—my father's reeve? You had a cap of thick brown hair when I left."

"Ay, I lost it and my position the same day. Shock it were made it fall out overnight." It was not bitterness at losing his hair that made his eyes bleak with grief. "It was the day they burned my father, Lord Edgar's loyal steward. He was condemned as a heretic for declaring that after a failed harvest the people should be spared their taxes to a Church whose grainstores were overflowing."

"Would that I could have returned before this," he answered heavily.

Dickon grinned. "You are here now, my lord. Everything will change."

The pilgrim leaned heavily on his staff, his outrage at what he had seen and heard scalding through his body. "There will be no more burning of heretics and no more deprivation for the people. My father's name has been dishonoured by what has passed."

"It is a miracle you have come back to us, my lord," Dickon cried jubilantly. "And the Lady Eloise will be overjoyed at your return."

Remembering a long-ago wedding-day, he felt a spasm of unease. He doubted very much if "overjoyed" was the word the Lady Eloise would use on learning of her husband's return.

Chapter Two

"Sir Alaric has returned. Our lord is not dead. He will save us!"

The shout brought up Eloise's head and her hand stilled in pounding the comfrey leaves in the infirmary stillroom. A rush of blood to her head made her sway. Had she heard aright? Was Alaric back? Her throat cramped and a mixture of fear and elation flooded her. Sir Alaric would be Penruthin's salvation, but would he be hers?

Removing her apron, she walked into the sunlight. Villagers ran from the priory fields, still carrying their hoes and rakes. Women with babes strapped in shawls to their backs, others, with their forearms white with flour from their breadmaking, left their houses to stare towards the wood.

A group of men was approaching. Several she recognised as villagers. But the one at their centre was a stranger. Or was he...? Surely that ragged vagabond could not be Alaric.

She stood immobile as a statue, her heart pounding with anticipation. Her throat was dry and a nervous moisture coated her palms as she studied the man purported to be her husband. A green hood shadowed his features. She saw only a brown-bearded jaw and skin bronzed from long exposure to the sun. The height was Alaric's as she remembered him, but the build was more wiry. His stride held none of the swaggering arrogance she had so detested; it was weary. He stumbled, and she sensed the sheer effort of will and pride which kept him upright before his people. Reluctantly, she admired his unbroken spirit. She had expected that, when Lord Penruthin returned, he would arrive bedecked in silks and riding his black Arabian horse. Instead, she found herself staring at someone who could be mistaken for a beggar, except that no beggar would have so imperious a stance.

As she watched, his head came up. A wild cheering erupted from the villagers closest to him.

"God bless Sir Alaric, Lord of Penruthin."

The change in him was immediate. The broad shoulders squared, the head was tilted proudly and the stride lengthened.

Still Eloise did not move. Through her mind tumbled the derisive insults she had heard from him after their wedding. As yet he had not noticed her. His gaze was searching the faces of the crowd now lining the path between them. Occasionally, he inclined his head in acknowledgement of a joyous greeting.

Then a steely grey stare locked with hers. It was

as though she had been struck by a lightning bolt. Her heart hammered frantically. She stared back into a bronzed, lean face, as handsome as a dark angel. Eyes bruised with fatigue regarded her with glacial coldness… Unmistakably Alaric's eyes.

There was no warmth, no recognition, in that chill glare. A dark curved brow lifted in query as he continued to regard her, taking in the richness of her sapphire silk gown and simple gold fillet which held her veil in place. She wished now that she was wearing one of her fashionable hennin headdresses, instead of the plain veil and fillet she favoured as more practical for everyday wear. She must look like a child to him. The haughty Lord of Penruthin would expect his wife to appear before him in the extravagant court fashions as befitted her station.

Discomfited, she blushed.

Momentarily, the expression in the grey eyes softened. The change startled her, making her heart leap and her pulse beat erratically. It was now Roland's eyes which studied her: compassionate, understanding, recognising her. The impression was fleeting. He halted several feet from her, his stance imperious, chilling and commanding. Haughtiness was again evident in every line of his tall, lithe figure.

Which brother was he? Her mind spun in confusion.

Winifred nudged her elbow and whispered, "My lady, it is Sir Alaric. You must welcome him."

But was it Alaric? A doubting voice echoed in her mind. The people had accepted him and yet...

She hesitated. He did not move. He was waiting for her to come to him. Grey eyes silently challenged: impelling, self-assured and dangerous. Their steady glitter rebuked her that she did not at once acknowledge him as her lord and her husband.

Still she faltered. This was the Alaric she remembered. But even so there was something subtly different in his manner. It was almost imperceptible; transient, but it tugged at her conscience. *Could* this be Roland, his bastard half-brother? They were so alike; it had always been difficult from a distance to tell them apart.

And a distance of seven years—with only childhood memories, which she admitted were coloured by prejudice—played tricks with her instinct. Since he had apparently returned alone, deception could be easy to perpetrate, if he so wished it. She thrust that thought aside. The Roland she remembered was an honest man. He would never impersonate his brother.

She could feel the villagers' eyes on them. Several were chanting Alaric's name. They seemed so certain that it was Sir Alaric.

Her mind whirled. Alaric, or Roland...Roland, or Alaric?

"My lady, have you no greeting for me?" The deep husky voice was attractive. Yet its challenge rang with the arrogant authority she remembered with distaste.

"Sir Alaric?" she ventured.

The unspoken doubt lay like a trench between them.

He pushed back his hood so that she could see his face. It was Alaric's ruggedly handsome countenance, the cheeks thinner, refined by deprivation and suffering. It was Roland's face, chiselled by imprisonment, without its softness...

The grey eyes flashed, their glint alerting her to the danger of offending her husband. His full lips twitched, though whether from anger or amusement she could not tell.

"Have you forgotten me, my lady?" It was a rebuke, but delivered like a teasing caress that had the power to send a shiver of trepidation down her spine.

Then unexpectedly he laughed. The weariness behind its tone plucked at her heart. She hated to see anyone suffering, and his cut and bleeding feet must be agony to stand upon. When his lips lifted into a persuasive smile, Eloise mistrusted it. It did not reach his eyes. She could feel him assessing her reaction.

"I left a gauche young girl behind," he continued off-handedly, his piercing stare never leaving her. "And I return to find a beautiful and graceful woman." He looked down derisively at his ragged garments. "I fear I do not return the conquering hero, but a weary, tattered pilgrim."

The self-mockery was what she would have expected from Roland, not Alaric. Yet his words rekindled her humiliation at Alaric's words to the Lady

Isobel. It was still humiliating to admit she had been married for her wealth, and not because her husband had any fondness for her.

He turned to gaze at the castle. His expression harshened. "I saw Prior Ignatius depart. Is my brother Stephen here?"

"He's probably still sleeping off last night's excesses," a gruff voice from the crowd offered.

"Then he hasn't changed."

The disparagement in his voice relieved some of Eloise's fears. He was frowning as he looked around the village. Clearly, he did not like the neglect he saw.

"I will not disturb my brother from his slumbers." He staggered slightly and put a hand on the woodcutter's shoulder for support. "My journey has been long and arduous. I need to rest."

Another forthright stare was fixed upon Eloise. She had been neglectful in her homage and welcome to him. Doubts as to his true identity still shadowed her mind. But under that compelling gaze, she felt her spirits lift for the first time in years. This was not the pleasure-seeking, arrogant husband she remembered. The rags and his bleeding feet spoke of the trials he had endured to return to Penruthin alive. Would not seven years, of suffering as yet untold, have changed even Sir Alaric's arrogance? And the people—who knew the two brothers so much better than she did, for they had watched them grow up together—they appeared to have no doubts that this was their lord returned.

A flutter of expectancy quickened her pulse. Was this truly her lord, her master, her husband? Despite his rags, a masculine virility emanated from him, unlike anything she had perceived before. Her life at Penruthin may have been sheltered, but she was surrounded by men: villagers, servants, gruff men-at-arms and the priests. Although isolated, there had been occasional visits to the castle from passing noblemen. None had affected her so blatantly.

Again eyes that were both Alaric's and Roland's challenged her. Eloise felt her stomach tighten. He was so handsome—too handsome for her peace of mind. She must not let it affect her judgement. A tremor of expectation tingled through her body. He was waiting. He was judging her as she judged him. It was a poor wife who received her lord with cool disregard. How could she shame him before his people?

"My lord, forgive my shock, which leaves me witless as a mooncalf," she murmured. She walked forward, surprised to discover her legs were trembling. Yet they seemed to move with a volition of their own, drawn by an unseen force that compelled her to obey. With each step her heart thudded harder, until its frantic pace threatened to stifle her.

Mixed emotions beset the pilgrim as the Lady Eloise gracefullly sank into a curtsy at his feet. Her oval face was turned up, her loveliness striking him with the impact of a body-blow. Her skin was flawless, the high cheekbones blushed with faint colour were not those of conventional beauty, but far more breathtaking and sensual. Black brows winged delicately upwards. Thick black lashes enhanced the vivid sapphire blue of her eyes. The unremarkable cygnet had grown into a ravishing swan. As she walked towards him, the breeze moulded the folds of her gown to the slender shape of her hips and long legs. Desire quickened his blood. Her waist looked as though he could span it with his hands, and her high breasts were full and rounded. Her figure was as voluptuous as a siren's, her beauty like a breath of heady spring air. But it was the aura of innocence which struck him most forcefully.

After the pain and suffering of his imprisonment and the hardship of his pilgrimage, she was like an angel of mercy, a gift of pure enticement from the gods.

Seeing the uncertainty in Eloise's eyes, his own glittered in challenge. He could order her to acknowledge him as her lord, but such blatant force of will was not his way. The gaze holding his shimmered, then long dark lashes veiled her expression. She had no reason to welcome the return of a husband who had shown her no tenderness or kindness.

"My lord, I give praise that you are safely returned to us." Her soft musical voice spoke the appropriate words, but he sensed her tension. She might be pure and virginal and still young, but she was not a fool; nor would she be an easy conquest.

To his surprise, he discovered that was not what he

wanted. Too many women had succumbed to him with no effort on his part. The Lady Eloise was different. He had been shocked at the neglect of the estate. In the past his father had wagered bitter battles against the greed of the Church. Not all of them had been readily won. Prior Ignatius had influential relatives at court. It would not be easy to reclaim from him any wealth stolen from the Penruthin coffers.

That was in the future. Now he reached out to take Eloise's hand to help her rise. He checked himself with a grimace. Sighing, he stared at his broken nails, encrusted with dirt, which hovered inches from her white and slender hand.

''I am unfit to touch you,'' he said, gruffly.

His humility cast aside Eloise's anguish. Closer to, she saw the exhaustion and the tell-tale flush of fever on the sculptured leanness of his cheeks. He was drawing upon his reserves of strength to maintain his dignity before these people, and she was delaying him from his badly needed rest.

She smiled and covered his hand with hers. It was warm, too warm. She detected the first tremor of the chills that would soon accompany a raging fever. ''Welcome home, my lord,'' she said softly.

He withdrew his hand and she glimpsed an urgency and tension within him. Thoughts, fast and searing as comets, sped across her mind. He was close to collapse. Pride to appear strong before his people kept him upright. It would be humiliating for the Lord of Penruthin to be carried into his castle unconscious. Or was it something more sinister which made him fight to keep control of his wits? If she had doubted him, so would others. They had more at stake to lose than herself.

His gaze never wavered from hers. Its imprint branded her soul. Against her better judgement, she found herself willing that he was Alaric; that he had changed, that this handsome man would be all she desired in her husband. She netted her wayward thoughts. Time would reveal the truth. Until then, she must be cautious. Now he needed to rest and regain his strength. Compassion overlaid her doubts.

"Your return is cause for rejoicing," she said, recovering her poise. "Once you are rested, there will be celebration at Penruthin, the like of which has never been seen before."

His grey eyes sparkled. Was it triumph or fever?

A cheer followed her words. Sir Alaric was whisked from her side and borne on the villagers' shoulders into the castle. Eloise followed more slowly, her gaze fastened on his figure as it was carried beneath the portcullis, across the Outer and Inner Bailies and up the steps to the round keep. The people surrounding their lord cheered and threw their hoods into the air. To witness their joy momentarily warmed her. Yet away from his presence the doubts returned: was it Alaric, or Roland? The people saw only Lord Alaric, their saviour from Prior Ignatius' tyranny.

Doubts continued their stubborn whispers. If Roland knew that Alaric was dead, could he not deceive them by posing as his brother? For the people to accept him was only the first step. She frowned, her hand clenched against her breast. If he was indeed Alaric, then he had changed from the man she remembered. The arrogance she had hated appeared to have mellowed. Wasn't that what she had prayed for? Surely a man could not live a prisoner of the Moors and remain unscathed? Even so, she would keep her reservations.

For the good of Penruthin, she would outwardly accept him as her husband. However, he must prove to her, beyond doubt, that he was Sir Alaric. She would not dishonour her marriage vows and take a man other than her true husband into her bed.

Beneath her fingers she was aware of the nervous fluttering of her heart. She put a hand over it to still its nervous fluttering. Even unkempt and ragged, she had been inexplicably drawn to him in a way which was disconcerting.

She must remain on her guard against him. To protect herself, she would not forget the coldness of the man she had married. Whatever exposure of character lay ahead in the next days, there were bound to be storms rather than peaceful acquiescence.

Eloise strode purposefully up the steps to rejoin her husband. She did not believe that Prior Ignatius would welcome Lord Alaric without interrogation. And what of Stephen and Isobel? Isobel had loved Alaric. Would they again become lovers? Eloise had no intention of allowing her husband's mistress to continue living under her roof. But Stephen was the greater danger. He would lose his control over the estate and would be accountable for the neglect of the estate and the squandered revenue.

Yet, even as her resolve was set to remain on guard against the pilgrim, an insidious doubt burrowed at its foundations. A part of her already believed that he was Alaric, that her husband had changed for the better. The people would not have been deceived: he must be Alaric and not an imposter. Too many people knew them both.

Penruthin is a rich prize, cautioned an inner voice. A flare of heat scalded her cheeks. It was not only the land of Penruthin which he would claim as his own. Was she not also part of that prize?

A quiver of apprehension swelled in her breast. She could already sense the change in the atmosphere since Penruthin had returned. There was a brightness of spirit where earlier there had been weighted burdens. Laughter, so long absent in the resentful villagers, had been resurrected. Winifred, together with several young women, had begun dancing an impromptu reel. The maid spun back to Eloise's side, her face flushed with pleasure. She sobered on seeing the shadows still clouding her mistress's eyes.

"Why do you look so troubled, my lady? Has not your husband returned? And is he not still the most handsome of men? Even in his rags I could see that every woman present wished his gaze to fall on her. He had eyes for no one but you."

For once Eloise did not confide her feelings to her maid. She was disconcerted at the way her heart was pounding as she watched Alaric being carried into the castle. Belatedly, remembering her role as Mistress of Penruthin, she picked up her long skirts and hurried to the castle. Herbs must be collected and prepared to restore Sir Alaric's health and combat the lingering fever she saw in his eyes. Lavender-scented sheets must be laid on the great bed in the lord's chamber to aid his rest.

The thought made her stomach clench. She had seen his appraising stare turn to desire as he watched her approach him. Would he expect her to share the marriage bed immediately? Her lips clamped shut in a fierce line of determination. Her husband's neglect at their wedding still had the power to wound her. Her pride rebelled. A pallet would be made up for herself in the small ante-room where Winifred usually slept. If Alaric wanted her as his true wife, he would first have to woo and win her. For nothing yet had convinced her that she wished to remain wed to him.

She reached the Great Hall as Sir Alaric was being lowered from the shoulders of the villagers. Even from a distance she could see the flush of fever was more pronounced. He swayed and managed to recover himself. As the throng of people parted to allow her passage to her husband's side, she saw Sir Stephen and the Lady Isobel descending the stone stairs which joined the hall to the family chambers above.

Both were dressed in their most costly finery. Sir

Stephen's reedy figure was disguised by an emerald brocade floor-length tunic, belted low over his hips. Long fur-trimmed sleeves swept the floor. A gold satin cap with a trailing scallop-edged scarf was adorned with a large diamond and ruby brooch. A large gold cross studded with emeralds hung from the heavy gold chain draped across his shoulders. The Lady Isobel wore a high-waisted gown of scarlet velvet encrusted with thousands of seed pearls. Her two-horned headdress was of gold filigree and measured nearly two feet across. Word must have reached them of Alaric's return and they intended to greet him with ceremony.

Stephen's thin lips curled back as he studied his brother. His eyes were bloodshot after his excesses of the previous evening and his narrow face, above his wispy beard, had its usual unhealthy pallor.

"So you have returned alone," Sir Stephen snorted, his manner at once antagonistic. "I'm surprised you have the audacity to show your face here. Where is Sir Alaric, Roland?"

Eloise's heart did a somersault. Stephen's attack threw her again into confusion.

An uproar broke out among the assembled villagers.

"He *is* Sir Alaric," several men shouted. "God bless Lord Penruthin!"

"What knavery is this, Roland?" Isobel declared. "Did you think Stephen wouldn't recognise his bastard brother?"

People surged forward. There was a shocked gasp. Alarm clutched at Eloise's throat. Why had Alaric not answered? As she fought her way to his side, she saw the reason. The fever had claimed him. His face was hotly flushed, his frame visibly shaken by the chills. The heavy lids drooped, fluttered, lifted vainly, as he fought to stay conscious.

"Damn you!" he rasped. "I am...am..."

His knees buckled. Eloise cried out as he fell to the floor unconscious.

"He's an impostor!" Isobel ranted. "Guards, arrest him."

Stephen's face was devoid of colour. Isobel glared at him, until he finally followed her lead. "Guards! Take him away. Throw the impostor in the dungeon."

"No." Eloise sprang forward. She sensed the dangerous mood of the people. They were murmuring ominously. The atmosphere in the hall was charged with menace. They would not allow the man they believed their saviour to be imprisoned. Neither would she.

"You have no proof that this is not Lord Alaric." Eloise quivered like a willow branch, so great was her fury. Stephen wanted to destroy Alaric before he could find out how he had abused his position here. She could not allow that to happen. She drew a steadying breath before continuing, "I have acknowledged him to be my husband. Until I am given proof that this man is not Sir Alaric, I will stand by my decision."

A growl of approval rose from the assembly. Several guards had entered the hall at Stephen's angry shout. They hesitated with halberds raised, hands on their sword hilts.

"I say he's an impostor!" Stephen raged. "He is the bastard, Roland. Arrest him."

The guards surged forward, knocking to the ground several villagers who tried to prevent them. Once Alaric was locked in a dungeon, Stephen would gain the advantage over his brother. He would ensure that he was discredited without being able to defend himself. If Stephen believed that it was Roland who had returned, why did he fear to confront him in public? Surely right would be on his side. Eloise knew that Stephen was lying. He had no more idea than she which brother had returned. This was his ruse to seize the Penruthin lands for himself.

"Halt!" Eloise commanded as she ran to place herself before the figure on the floor. "Any guard who lays a hand on the Lord of Penruthin will be hanged for treachery."

It was enough to make the soldiers pause. She knelt and took Alaric's head into her lap. Through the thin silk of her summer gown she could feel the heat of his body as the fever mounted. She guessed that only sheer strength of will had enabled him to walk the last few miles to his home. Her glare was blistering as she turned it upon Stephen.

"With respect, Sir Stephen, you forget your place," she warned. "I am Mistress of Penruthin.

You have countermanded my orders too often. I cannot permit you to continue to do so upon so important a matter.''

A sneer contorted Isobel's scarlet lips. "You were no more than a child when you married Alaric. How could you possibly recognise him? From what I recall of that time, you spent more time in Roland's company than in your husband's. Whilst I..." Her eyes narrowed spitefully. "I was very close to Alaric then. That man is not Sir Alaric. I am better qualified to recognise him than you."

Isobel threw back her head, the horned headdress giving her the appearance of a bull about to charge. She raised her voice so that it carried throughout the hall. "The bastard, Roland, should rot in the dungeon for daring to usurp Sir Alaric's place."

"You are quick to condemn him," Eloise accused. "You cannot possibly know that he is not Alaric until he is questioned."

The burly blacksmith, who was always outspoken, stepped forward. "He is Lord Penruthin. You want his wealth for yourself."

"Aye. Aye!" Others chorused. "God bless Lord Penruthin!"

Two guards raised their halberds to strike the blacksmith. Appalled, Eloise shouted. "There will be no violence. This should be a time of rejoicing. Any son of the late Lord Penruthin who has returned from captivity by the Moors should be welcomed in his father's castle. He will be honoured, not reviled.

Whether he is Alaric or Roland, he will be allowed to recover and speak for himself before judgement is passed upon him.''

The people stopped their angry murmuring and looked expectantly towards Eloise. She glared at Isobel. The older woman was looking insufferably smug.

''It would suit you if he was Roland, wouldn't it?'' Isobel said venomously. ''It was me that Alaric loved, not you. You're in league with Roland to steal Penruthin for yourself.''

Eloise's temper boiled. She could no longer check the humiliation which had festered since her marriage. Too often in the past the Lady Isobel had turned her spiteful tongue upon her and she had not retaliated, unwilling to stoop to the pettiness of the other woman's conduct. The nuns had brought her up to believe that a lady does not wrangle like a fishwife. Now she felt justified in venting her scorn.

''Everyone here knows you were Sir Alaric's mistress before you wed his brother.'' Her voice hardened with recrimination. ''You seek to safeguard your own interests by denouncing the man who rejected you to wed another—myself.''

Eloise had no qualms about using ruthless methods to protect the pilgrim. Whichever brother he was, her sense of justice demanded he be allowed to prove his identity.

Turning her back on Stephen and Isobel, she appealed to the middle-aged captain of the guard who was staring down at the unconscious figure. ''Captain

Maddock, you have served at Penruthin castle for more than a score of years. In your opinion, is this man Sir Alaric?''

The captain scratched his stubbled chin, his expression grim beneath his domed steel helmet. With a sigh he shook his head. "Couldn't say for sure, my lady. Both inherited their father's features, and with seven long, hard years gone by... Once he's able to speak for himself, then it could be a different matter.''

"Exactly," Eloise declared. "Until then, he will be treated with respect as a son of Lord Edgar Penruthin. He is ill and needs care. When he is free of this fever he will answer any doubters for himself.''

Stephen snorted with contempt. "I still say he's Roland. And shouldn't I know my own brother? Guards...''

Eloise wrapped her arms protectively around the pilgrim's body. "I will not permit him to be taken.'' She could feel his body shivering with chills. She was determined not to back down. She remembered the debt of gratitude she owed Roland. Defending him now would be her repayment for his kindness. Yet deep in her heart she wanted him to be Alaric, for he alone could put an end to the tyranny of the prior over his people.

She decided she would act as though she were convinced this brother was her husband. Defiantly, she insisted, "Sir Stephen, now that Sir Alaric has returned, it is not for you to summon the guards to lay hold on him. I repeat: any man who lays a hand on this man will be hanged for treachery."

She regarded Captain Maddock. "Do you and your men acknowledge me as the Mistress of Penruthin?"

"You are indeed, my lady."

She looked down at the figure in her arms. Her heart twisted as she regarded his lean, handsome face. Her caring heart was moved that such a strong and vibrant man could be brought so low by a fever. Many lesser men would never had survived imprisonment with the Moors, or the obvious hazards of his long journey home. Beneath his rags she could feel the firmness of his muscles even though he had lost weight on his travels. It was a cruel blow that illness had robbed him of strength at the very moment he most needed it. Racked by fever, Sir Alaric was not the arrogant tyrant she remembered. He needed her support and she would not fail him. Her sense of justice demanded it.

A rush of tenderness overwhelmed her as she clasped him close. She was determined to protect him from harm until he was well enough to defend himself. If he was Roland, then he would have to pay for attempting to impersonate his brother. That was an issue which would be resolved later. Now all that was important was to return him to health.

She commanded, "Captain Maddock, until this matter is resolved no guard will lay a hand on Sir Alaric. Your orders in future come from me, not Sir Stephen."

Captain Maddock shuffled uncomfortably and cast a nervous glance at Sir Stephen, who had come from the dais.

"The guards remain under my orders, Lady Eloise," Stephen proclaimed. "The instructions given by my father when he rode out with Sir Alaric were clear. I am your guardian and the custodian of Penruthin until Alaric returns. Clearly this man here..." he pushed the bloodied foot with his toe and wrinkled his nose with distaste, before continuing "...whether he is Sir Alaric—or Roland, as I believe—is in no fit state to rule Penruthin. Therefore the guards remain under my control."

Keeping her voice low so that only Stephen would hear, she replied, "Then I advise you to think and act very carefully. If you denounce this brother as an impostor, and have him thrown into the dungeon, you will have a riot on your hands. The people have suffered much under your guardianship. They have waited for justice at Sir Alaric's return. Deny them at your peril."

"You dare threaten me?" Sir Stephen blustered, but she could see he was uneasy. His gaze kept searching the hall. Clearly, he was looking for support from Prior Ignatius. It was easier for her that the prior had ridden out earlier. With luck he might not return for some days.

Behind them the people had started to chant Sir Alaric's name.

"What's happened to our lord?" an insistent voice

from the back asked. "Is he ill? Why isn't he being cared for?"

Further rumbles of discontent gathered momentum. Perfectly composed, Eloise brushed a tendril of matted brown hair back from Alaric's hot brow and clasped one of his hands. Again she felt shock waves of emotion pass through her. Even unconscious, this man had the power to affect her deeply.

Looking up at Stephen, she said quietly, "I am sure you will not wish me to inform the Sheriff of the County that you condemned your brother without proof of his identity. If, as you say, this man is Roland, then I shall be demanding the return of my dowry. Also, if he *is* Roland, then we must assume that Alaric is dead. I am thus a widow and free to marry again."

"God bless Sir Alaric!" The chanting grew louder. "Long live Sir Alaric! Long live the Lady Eloise!"

Sir Stephen was breathing heavily. Eloise could imagine how his devious mind was working. He was wrestling with his desire to declare his brother an impostor. With Alaric proclaimed dead, he would be Lord of Penruthin. Yet her declaration had disturbed him. If he were forced to repay her dowry, Penruthin's coffers would be empty. Also, he would have to answer awkward questions about how her dowry had been misused. The long months he spent at Court were expensive, as were the rich clothes, jewels and entertainments he and Isobel favoured.

Stephen scowled down at her. He was always a bad

loser and this now showed in his truculent expression. He would relish seeing her humbled.

Ignoring him, she turned to Captain Maddock. At forty, he was stocky, his pockmarked cheeks further puckered from a sword wound he had received as a young man fighting in France. The most trusted retainer of Sir Alaric's father, he had been left in charge of the garrison. From what she knew of Captain Maddock, he was loyal. Honesty had made him hesitate in identifying the pilgrim. She could trust him to do what was right. The guards respected him and would follow his leadership.

"Have Sir Alaric taken to the lord's chamber," she ordered. "Perhaps, as a precaution, one of your most trustworthy men can be placed on guard outside the door." She paused before adding meaningfully, "For Sir Alaric's protection, as well as for security reasons."

"I shall have the honour of guarding him," the captain replied. Turning to his men, he barked out his orders. Alaric was lifted up and carried out of the hall to the chambers above.

Eloise stood on the dais and held up her hands for the anxious and angry whispers to fall silent. "Your lord has returned, and as you see he is sick of the fever. I shall tend him myself. Let us pray that within a few days he can take his rightful place as Lord of Penruthin."

"Or pay the price for his infamy!" Isobel declared malevolently.

"Lady Eloise, beware the consequences of your actions," Stephen warned. "When my brother is proved to be an impostor, you will be implicated in conspiring with him. May you both burn at the stake for your crimes."

Eloise suppressed a shudder. That was no idle threat. Had she by trying to give Alaric the benefit of the doubt, unwittingly played into Sir Stephen's hands? If she was put on trial for abetting Roland, Stephen would have both Penruthin and her dowry. Whilst she and he would die horribly at the stake.

Chapter Three

On entering her chamber, Eloise ordered everyone but Githa to leave. Alaric—for that was how she must regard him—lay on the sheets. Sweat streaked his dark hair and peppered his upper lip and brow. Every few moments his limbs twitched, and he began to rave an unintelligible stream of words. The fever was advancing rapidly and with a virulence which alarmed Eloise.

"He is much weakened," Githa said with concern. "Let us hope that it is just a fever he suffered from and not the pestilence contracted in foreign lands."

Eloise's throat dried with alarm. "There are none of the tell-tale marks of the pestilence. I don't want the people frightened."

Githa gave her a closed look and did not reply. Eloise remembered that Roland's mother, Clothilde, had been the orphaned child of Githa's friend and, as she had no living relatives, had been reared by the wise-woman.

The two women worked quickly and for the most part in silence. Eloise took up her scissors and began to cut away the ragged clothes from Alaric's body. Githa prodded the fire that had been lit in the fireplace and sprinkled some herbs into a goblet of wine. Eloise held up Alaric's head as Githa patiently forced a few drops of the liquid between his parched lips. At first it trickled out and down into his beard. Then finally he swallowed and, satisfied, Githa stood back.

Returning to her work with the scissors, Eloise cut away the tunic and shirt. A blush crept up her neck and into her cheeks when she peeled back the clothing to reveal a sun-browned torso. Her throat became tight and dry as her hand brushed against his body. His flesh was hot from the fever and her breath snatched at her throat as her gaze roamed over the broad shoulders and the dark tangle of hair on his chest.

She paused before tackling the torn hose. There was little privacy within a castle even for the lord's family. With a garrison of forty men, she had become used to seeing half-dressed men washing or being caught making love to one of the women. She took it in her stride as part of daily life. But she felt strangely embarrassed at having to strip her husband, especially since she had held him in such awe for so many years.

"Check him for injuries," Githa suggested. "Pilgrims are often attacked by robbers on the road. Internal bruising could be the cause of his fever."

Eloise could feel her cheeks flushing with darker colour and her fingers tingled as they travelled skilfully over his ribcage. His stomach was flat and his hips slender. His body was lithe and magnificent. She tried to view him with the dispassion of a healer as she gently examined the firm flesh for any broken bones or sign of internal injury. There appeared to be none. Yet as she worked the muscles in her stomach clenched, and a sweet warmth pervaded her senses.

Githa chuckled. "You blush, my lady. He is a man many women would look on with desire."

Annoyed by her own awareness of this man's masculine potency, she replied more sharply than was warranted. "He is indeed handsome. But a manly figure or a handsome face does not necessarily make an attractive man. It is what is inside which matters."

"Aye, that could once be said of Sir Alaric." Githa nodded. "He was arrogant and pleasure-seeking, but he always cared for Penruthin and its people."

Eloise paused in her work, her voice crisp, "Which is why he married a child he had no time for, so Penruthin could prosper from her dowry."

"That was a long time ago, my lady. He'd have to be blind not to want you for his lady now." Githa pointed to two long white scars, one on his shoulder, the other below his ribs. "Sword cuts, from the look of them. He didn't have them before he left here. Battle can change a man. So can experience."

Eloise finished her examination, uncomfortably aware that her movements had become slow and dreamy as her hands skimmed over the muscles and contours of his figure in what was almost a caress. She could not stop her gaze from returning to his face. Even with the unkempt beard, the handsome, rugged contours of high cheekbones and strong jaw were evident. In repose the angular lines were softened and just to look upon him brought a curious fluttering to her breast. She pushed a damp lock of hair back from his wide brow, noting the thick crescent of his dark lashes. The slender nose was imperious, the line of his lips full and sensuous. With a start she collected herself. She had vowed to keep her emotions guarded. The effect he was having on her was frightening in its unexpected intensity. She had not realised until now how much she wanted a man to love and care for.

"Githa, help me turn him so I can pull his clothes from beneath him." She dragged her concentration back to tending him as a healer, forcing herself to shut her mind to the powerful magnetism of his body.

A low groan broke from him as they gently turned him. When Eloise saw his back, she gasped. Raising her hand to her mouth, she felt tears sting her eyes. It was scored with whipmarks, which criss-crossed like a nest of silver snakes across his shoulders and ribs.

Githa sucked in her breath. "Make sure his back is kept covered, my lady. Roland was whipped when he was seventeen by Sir Alaric."

"So he *is* Roland, then." Eloise whispered.

"Perhaps. Perhaps not," Githa said, staring down at him. "I've heard whippings are common punishment for the slaves of the Moors. Sir Alaric was too proud to acknowledge a man other than his King to be his master. To break him, they would have beaten him. Doesn't look like they succeeded. Or he would not be here."

Eloise ran a finger along a silvery scar. The heat from his flesh licked at her own like a candle flame. "Why was Roland whipped?"

Githa shook her head sadly. "Alaric as a young man had a wicked temper. All the squires had been practising at the quintain. Even though Roland was a bastard, Lord Penruthin insisted that he was taught knightly skills. He could ride and fight better than any of the squires. He often bested Alaric and the young heir resented it. Alaric had been drinking heavily the previous night and he performed badly at the quintain."

The old woman paused and stared for a long moment at the unconscious figure. Her expression was unreadable, but her voice was sharp with censure. "His horse was skittish and he was thrown. In a fit of temper Alaric ordered Roland to have the animal destroyed, declaring it had a vicious nature. Roland refused. The two were always at loggerheads. This time Alaric had him whipped for his insolence. Roland almost died. Lord Edgar was furious when he learned of it on his return from court. Struck him across the face in public and ordered him to tend Roland whilst he was unable to leave his bed. Alaric hated Roland after that.''

Eloise digested these words in silence. Her emotions were in turmoil. She no longer knew what to believe.

Githa glanced at her mistress and added darkly, ''Sir Stephen would seize on those marks to have him imprisoned, if not killed as an impostor.''

It was not until the man was turned again to lie on his back and a clean shirt pulled over his head to hide the incriminating scars, that Eloise spoke. ''Who do you think he is, Githa?''

The wise-woman gazed at the figure for a long moment, refusing to meet Eloise's searching stare. ''Look into your heart, my lady. It will give you the answer you need when the time comes. Whichever brother he is, he's not the same man who left here seven years ago.''

Clearly Githa would not be drawn further. And with her own life in danger, Eloise knew that she must be cautious. She eased the covers over his figure, her hand drawn to touch the side of his bearded cheek.

''Do you wish me to shave him, my lady?'' Githa enquired.

''Let him rest without disturbing him further,'' she answered.

''Rest is the best cure,'' Githa declared. ''I suspect he has the Tertian fever which he contacted in the Holy Land. Such a fever comes and goes. They can be free of it for months, even years, then without warning it will return.''

"How long will it last?''

"In that he is in God's hands. Sometimes it can leave them in a few hours. Or he could be raging with the fever for days.''

"He won't die?'' Eloise felt her heart contract in sudden dread.

"He's exhausted from his travels. But he is strong. He will recover, my lady.''

For three days Eloise did not leave the chamber, and no one except Githa and Winifred were allowed in. Every morning and evening she sent a report through Winifred to Sir Stephen.

A loud knocking on her door jerked Eloise awake. She winced at the crick in her neck where she had fallen asleep on a stool by the bed. In the night Alaric had been restless; the fever had been high and she had fought for hours with his unconscious figure to keep the bedclothes in place. If his body chilled, he could contract a lung infection and die.

"Who is it?'' she demanded. With the fire banked high, the room was stiflingly hot. She had removed her outer gown and stood in her diaphanous kirtle. Lack of sleep had made her head throb and she had loosened her hair from its thick confining plaits so that it hung like a sable mantle to her hips.

"Prior Ignatius. I demand to see the prisoner.''

Eloise stiffened. The prior's absence since Alaric's

return had been a welcome reprieve. Stephen was too weak to face a confrontation. The prior was not.

"There is no prisoner here," she informed him coldly, refusing to be browbeaten. "Only Lord Penruthin, who is sick of the fever. He will see you when he is well."

"If he is so ill that I cannot see him, then perhaps he should be given the last rites. Would you have him die unshriven?"

The bullying tone angered Eloise. He was trying to trick his way into seeing Alaric.

"Lord Penruthin is in no danger of dying. All he needs is rest. Pray for him, Prior Ignatius. His fever is abating. He will be as eager for you to answer his questions about the neglect of the estate as you are to question him."

"I demand to be admitted." He banged louder, the door creaking alarmingly on its hinges.

His pompous tone roused a stubborn streak in her nature. She'd had enough of being dictated to by the prior. "I will not have Lord Penruthin disturbed. Please leave."

"You are alone with a man who Sir Stephen believes is not your husband," the prior accused and rattled the door latch to punctuate his threats. "You bring shame to the name of Penruthin. The punishment for adultery is…"

"Careful how you threaten me, Prior Ignatius," Eloise cut in. She faced the door, her eyes snapping with anger. "I am not alone. Githa sleeps in the ante-room. I will not have my honour unjustly maligned, even by a man of God. You will see Lord Penruthin when he is strong enough to receive visitors. No amount of threats will change my mind.''

There was a furious growl from the prior.

''You heard her ladyship,'' Captain Maddock spoke sharply. ''Do I have to escort you, Prior? Or will you leave quietly?''

Eloise relaxed. She trusted Maddock to obey her orders.

''I will not forget this, Lady Eloise,'' the prior gritted out.

Eloise folded her arms across her breast and breathed heavily. She could feel danger pressing in on her. Prior Ignatius would exert all his influence with his relatives at Court to wriggle out of facing any charges of corruption at Penruthin. To save his own hide, he would not hesitate to denounce Alaric as an impostor and herself as his whore and accomplice. She feared they were now both in grave danger.

She turned to the silver cross set into a niche in an alcove. Clasping her hands together, she was about to kneel in prayer when a hoarse voice made her pause.

''You have great courage, Lady Eloise.''

She whirled and moved slowly to the foot of the bed, not sure if she had imagined the words. Alaric's eyes were open. Their grey stare was bright and free of fever. She let out her breath in a relieved sigh.

''They wanted to imprison you. They say you are Roland, not Alaric.''

The grey stare deepened in intensity. He lifted a hand and beckoned to her to come closer. Last night before retiring, Githa had shaved him. Without his beard he was even more handsome, and those grey eyes were both commanding and compelling. Tending him in such close proximity had increased the initial attraction she felt for him. Throughout her nursing vigil she had wondered about the scars on his back. Her hand was often drawn to smooth back a wayward brown curl as it fell forward over his brow. She had tried to resurrect her old distrust of Sir Alaric, but watching him fight the fever had destroyed much of that hatred. Several times he had cried out incoherently, his hands clenched into tight fists, his throat corded as he relived some past horror. At such times she took his hand and held it firmly between hers, her softly spoken words of reassurance eventually soothing him.

Now as she studied him, her heart pounded treacherously fast. She was aware that they were both half naked and to all intents alone. Githa, whose hearing had dulled in recent years, was snoring as she slept in the adjoining ante-room. She had not even stirred when the prior banged on the door. Eloise reminded herself that she must not let those handsome looks distract her. As she continued to hold his gaze, she sensed a threat in that uncompromising grey stare as menacing as storm clouds.

His expression betrayed nothing of his thoughts.

"The prior will cause trouble," he said. "Yet you do not appear afraid."

"If you are Sir Alaric, I have nothing to fear. Not from the prior," she hedged. Instinct warned her that it was him she must fear. He was too self-contained, giving none of his emotions away. That containment chilled her. Since the death of her father she had felt herself an intruder in this castle, unwanted by the Penruthin family. The thought of spending the rest of her life with a man incapable of loving her filled her with dread.

Alaric's nostrils flared and his mouth hardened. "Do you doubt that I am your husband?"

She sensed the dark threat behind his words. Inwardly she flinched. This man was still a stranger to her and she could feel the danger he presented to her future and her happiness. She conquered her unease to face him defiantly.

"In truth, my lord, how can I know? I saw you so briefly after our marriage." She smiled tremulously to soften her words, aware that she would be foolish to antagonise him unnecessarily. "I had you brought to my room to stop Stephen throwing you in a dungeon. He says you are Roland."

He heaved himself upright and rested his head on the silk hangings above the carved wooden headboard of the four-poster bed. A muscle pumped along his lean bronzed cheek. "That would be in my brother's best interests, would it not? He has had his own way here too long."

The lethal edge to his voice made the hairs at the back of her neck prickle. He was dangerous—the cultured voice and manners were only surface deep. Power emanated from him; not just the power of a man born to rule, but power honed by experience, both as a warrior-knight and a survivor from one of the harshest prisons on earth.

She strove to control an inner shivering. She must not let him see her fear or uncertainty. He would be ruthless in using it against her. Defiantly she held his stare. A flicker of interest brightened his eyes. His gaze was now insolent, slowly inspecting her from the bare toes peeping out from beneath her kirtle, sliding upwards over her thighs, hips and breasts to the ebony crown of her head. She suppressed the urge to cover her figure with her hands, aware that the diaphanous kirtle revealed the outline of her figure.

"Do I pass your inspection, my lord?" she said, tautly. "I was a sad disappointment to you at our wedding." Turning aside, she snatched up a crimson velvet robe and wrapped it around herself.

A wicked gleam sparked in his eyes. He lifted a dark brow, his eyes mocking as he continued to survey her. "I am not disappointed." He folded his arms across his chest and continued to study her. "But what of you, Lady Eloise? Where do your best interests lie? Without a husband at your side, you have little power in Penruthin."

The lazy indolence of his voice was the one which all those years ago had delivered the insults about her.

The sheer arrogance of the man astounded Eloise. Did he think that marriage to him was the answer to her prayers? Her eyes blazed as she remembered the humiliation he had subjected her to. "I have long believed that my best interests lay in you being declared dead. I could then be released from a marriage you never wanted to an ugly gypsy brat of a child. For that is how you described me to the Lady Isobel."

Not even an eyelid moved to betray his emotions. His handsome face could have been carved out of ice. Then the full lips quirked and merriment sparkled in his eyes as he continued to appraise her. "I would certainly never refer to you as such now, my lady. You are very beautiful. And desirable."

"And we must not forget wealthy." Her temper flared. Did he think her a naïve fool to fall for such easy flattery? Though every one of her senses warned her that this was not a man to cross, pride made her call him to account for those insults. "It was my dowry which filled Penruthin's coffers. That was why you wed me. You neglected your bride in favour of your mistress."

He laughed unabashed. "And as I recall the bastard Roland played the gallant to the bride. Did you expect me to fall in love with a child of ten? But we have our time again, my lady. You will not find me inattentive to your wishes now."

"Because it is in your best interests to humour me," she accused heatedly, mistrusting his taunting. "Do not misunderstand my motives for supporting you. I did it out of a sense of justice. Whether you are my husband or Roland, you should be given the chance to recover your strength before you face Stephen's and the prior's questions.''

His goading had destroyed the image of the more compassionate knight she had begun to believe had returned. She was certain now that this was Sir Alaric. Roland would never have been so brutal.

''Then I am indebted to you, my lady. You have restored my strength...and my ardour.'' His eyes darkened as he moved, quickly capturing her hand in his.

Suspicious of his motives, she tensed and drew back. Her hand was held fast.

''What are you afraid of, Eloise?'' The amusement had left his face. ''Do I not deserve a welcoming kiss?''

She glared at him in outraged silence, her face pale but proud.

His bark of laughter was so unexpected it stunned her. Then with a twisted smile he jerked her towards him. The suddenness of the action overbalanced her, and when her knee connected with the side of the mattress, she fell forward to lie beside him. With her free elbow she levered herself up to glare her fury.

''Release me at once!'' she commanded.

''A wife's duty is to obey her husband, is it not?''

Her eyes narrowed. Her heart hammered wildly at being treated so disrespectfully. ''If you *are* my husband. That has not yet been proved.''

"Not only beautiful, but spirited also. Do you not fear my wrath?"

Even with her temper simmering, she was aware of the tension in his figure. He was testing her. Why? Did he doubt her virtue that she had taken him so readily into her chamber?

"I fear dishonour more. Neither will I jeopardise my own case in a court of law. I am a maid. A virgin bride, as you will remember."

His grip remained firm and she put out a hand to fend him off. It was trapped against his hard chest as he pulled her to him. Trembling seized her. His arms slid around her like fetters pressing her against him in an embrace so intimate that, through the thinness of her robe, she could feel every powerful muscle subjugating her softer curves.

Her mouth opened to cry out a protest. The sound was smothered by his lips covering hers in a kiss that left her gasping for breath. Outraged, she struggled. He was treating her like a whore. Such behaviour was what she would expect from Alaric and, even though she was his wife, she would not be treated in this fashion. Frantically, she twisted to be free of his hold. The pressure on her mouth changed; no longer plundering, but softer, more tender. With masterly precision, it enticed her surrender. Her resistance was webbed in a mesh of betraying emotions. Thrilling spirals of heat whirled through her veins. Her pulse raced. She had never been kissed by a man before, and was unprepared for the devastation it could inflict upon her senses. She felt as though she had been suddenly tossed into a millrace of tempestuous sensations. Her head reeled dizzily. The drumming of her heartbeat vibrated through her body so loudly she thought it would burst. A warm glow which had ignited deep within her was radiating outwards to encompass her entire being.

Again the pressure on her mouth changed; it was coaxing, subduing, magical and all-pervading. She was encompassed by the pleasant male scent of him, her limbs moulding to his hard form, no longer obeying her instinct to resist. When his hands slid slowly down the length of her spine, her own responded of their own volition, entwining around his neck. She had not been aware until then that he had released his imprisoning grip on her. But she had no will to escape. The intoxicating kiss was all-consuming and she revelled in the new and glorious sensations awakening in her body.

A soft moan rose to her throat. The sweetness of his lips was now pure beguilement, moving tantalisingly over her mouth, causing her body to pulsate with hitherto unimagined pleasure. They blazed a trail of delicious sensation as they buried themselves in the hollow of her throat. A flame of longing seared her whole being.

A snore louder than others jolted her back to the realisation of what she was permitting. From the anteroom where Githa slept, the wise-woman grunted and muttered to herself as she came awake, and there was the sound of the pallet bed creaking as she heaved herself out of it.

"No!" Eloise gasped in horror as she pushed back from him and rose to stand over the bed. She was breathing heavily, her sable hair tumbling about her shoulders and breasts in wild abandonment. "I will not be tumbled with the lack of respect you would show a serving wench."

Her anger was directed at herself for the ease with which she had responded to his deliberate attempt to seduce her. She was careful to keep her voice low enough for only him to hear. "How dare you treat me in this manner? Our marriage was not of your choosing, or mine. Since I am still a virgin after seven years of marriage, that is ground enough for an annulment. And there are other wealthy heiresses you could wed."

No emotion showed on his shuttered features. "There are indeed, madam. Yet for the moment there will be no annulment. But you, like my brother, will learn that I will not be thwarted in my will."

The threat was typical of what Eloise expected from Alaric. It roused all her old antagonism and with it an obstinate resolution that she did not want to remain married to him.

She squared her shoulders, her haughty expression matching his. "I am no longer a child of ten to be bullied by your arrogance, my lord. I have had to fight to win my status here and protect the interests of your people. By so doing, I have made enemies. But I will not back down upon a matter which I believe to be right.''

The grey eyes appraising her smouldered with an indefinable light. She would not believe it was admiration, preferring in her outrage to interpret it as resentment that she had defied his will. The shuffling gait of Githa entering the bedroom prevented her from adding anything further.

''Lord Penruthin!'' Githa exclaimed with delight. ''Your fever has left you.''

He turned to the wise-woman and smiled. It transformed his austere countenance and, despite her anger, Eloise found her heart skipping a beat. She spun on her heel, despising herself for the way her body responded to such blatant and manipulative charm. She plucked a gown and veil from their pegs in the garde-robe and, with all the regal dignity she could muster, swept through into the ante-room to dress. A treacherous irrational part of her mind regretted that he had not bestowed such a genuine welcoming smile upon herself.

As she dressed she heard the conversation in the bedchamber. Alaric sounded relaxed.

''It is thanks to your wisdom with herbs, Githa, that I have recovered so rapidly.''

''Nay, 'tis more to the care which the Lady Eloise tended upon you. She's not left your side for the three days you were taken by the fever. And she kept Sir Stephen from throwing you into prison.''

There was a pause and Alaric's voice was guarded

as he clipped out, "Go on. Tell me what happened after I passed out. I remember arriving in the hall and Stephen accused me of being Roland. Then the fever took hold and I can remember nothing until this morning."

Briefly Githa explained what had happened and how Eloise had defended him, placing her own safety under threat if he proved not to be Sir Alaric but Roland.

Eloise was dressed now. She had heard enough praise from the old woman. It was unwarranted. All she had done was protect a sick man until he was well enough to defend himself.

"You may leave us, Githa," she said as she returned to the main chamber. "Have a maid bring food for Lord Penruthin."

She followed Githa to the door.

"My lady, please stay."

Alaric's tone was imperious and it brought up her head. She bit her lip to hide her resentment as she turned slowly to regard him. He had risen from the bed and stood tall, sleek and commanding, his shirt covering him only to mid thigh. His stance was authoritative and unmistakably that of the predatory male.

"My duties within the castle have been neglected whilst I tended you, my lord," she reminded him. "I will send a manservant to tend you and assist you to dress once you have eaten. The people of Penruthin will expect to celebrate your return with a feast. Preparations must be made.''

''It is more important that we talk.'' His tanned knuckled rested on his slim hips, apparently unconcerned at his state of undress, which was bringing a rise of colour to her cheeks. ''I was shocked by the neglect in the village. Stephen has failed in his guardianship. And what hold has Prior Ignatius over him and the villagers?''

Eloise called over her shoulder to Githa, who had paused to speak with Captain Maddocks. ''Githa, I will also break my fast in my chamber.''

She again regarded Alaric, keeping her gaze fixed firmly on his face and away from his half-naked figure which was having such a stifling effect on her breathing. She had not believed it possible that just the sight of a man could make her own body flush with heat. Neither did the way his cool, grey eyes held her gaze transfixed help her composure. He was breathstealingly handsome; being close to him caused her body to tingle as though fireflies danced upon her flesh.

To regain her composure she nodded to a battered, wooden coffer decorated with brass bands. ''I had this brought up from the storeroom. It contains some old clothes of yours. You thought them too unfashionable to take with you to France. At least they are more fitting than the rags you arrived in.''

Did she detect a quirk of amusement on his full lips? If so, it was fleeting. Alaric was already crossing to the chest and he flipped back the lid. He held up a scarlet velvet doublet with gold lining in its long, floor-length scallop-edged sleeves.

"No wonder I was called the Peacock of Penruthin, with such gaudy plumage," he said with a grin. "The vanities of youth."

His words surprised her. Alaric had taken his fashionable dress too seriously ever to mock it. He tossed the scarlet velvet aside and another of emerald and gold brocade, to choose one of dark sapphire velvet trimmed with silver braid. Continuing his search, he scattered brightly coloured hose on the floor in his impatience and finally straightened, holding dove-grey hose in his hands.

When he sat on the bed and began to pull on his hose, Eloise turned away, her cheeks again growing pink. The intimacy of the scene increased the prickling heat on her skin. It was absurd. She had spent the last three days bathing him and had become accustomed to the sight of his body. But that was when he lay immobile. Alaric on his feet emanated masculinity like a threat.

"You will need boots," she said, annoyed that her voice sounded so thick and tight. "They are in the second coffer by the fire."

She busied herself picking up the discarded hose and bright-coloured doublets from the floor. Then she fidgeted with the box of herbs and potions by the bed, needing to do something to distract her mind from the movements of the man dressing in such close proximity.

"Tell me what my brother has been up to in my absence?" he asked as he went to the second coffer to rummage for a pair of boots.

She began to explain the extravagant entertainments; the months Sir Stephen and Lady Isobel spent at Court. She spoke with growing anger of the neglect and the extra work-days the villagers were forced to perform on Church lands.

She watched his expression as she told him that Isobel was his brother's wife. He paused in pulling on a leather pointed-toed boot.

"They are well suited," he commented drily.

With both boots on he stood up, and she saw him wince. "The devil, my feet seem to have spread. These will cripple me." He pulled them off, tossing them aside with disgust. Marching to the door, he wrenched it open and spoke to the serving-boy who waited outside for orders. "Fetch the cobbler, lad, and be quick about it."

He was frowning as he strolled back into the room and caught Eloise's troubled stare upon him. Did a man's feet change in shape at Alaric's age? she wondered. The leather of the boots he had discarded had been of the finest quality and soft as silk.

Two maids arrived carrying bread, cold chicken, cheese and a silver flagon of wine. They both cast admiring glances at Lord Penruthin as they placed the food and drink on a coffer by the dying embers of the fire. One, who was blonde and buxom, was disposed to linger, her gaze riveted to Alaric's handsome figure. She picked up a poker preparing to stoke the fire.

"Leave it," Alaric declared. He seemed less at ease and as soon as the two women had left the room he snapped the bolt into place.

"I don't want Prior Ignatius bursting in here just yet."

That he had explained his action alerted Eloise further. Alaric never justified anything he did—or he hadn't in the past. Even as heir to Penruthin, he had considered himself above vindicating his motives.

Her appetite deserted her as her suspicions that he was not her husband returned. Covertly she studied him as he ate his meal. His manners were impeccable. But then, as the son of Lord Edgar brought up in the castle, they would be. He was clearly ravenous, yet he ate delicately, although with the impatience that governed so many of his movements. Alaric had always been so reserved and nonchalant about everything he did, almost as though it was too much trouble for him. It was the way of many noblemen, affecting boredom when their lives were surrounded with richness and ease.

"We heard you were a prisoner of the Moors," her curiosity got the better of her. "Is that true?"

"For five years." He stopped eating and stared down at his wooden trencher. "Five years that I would not wish upon my worst enemy. It is not something I wish to discuss.''

"I doubt you can avoid it, my lord. Sir Stephen and Prior Ignatius are demanding that you answer to them. They would prefer to believe that you are not Lord Penruthin returned to us.''

He shot her a piercing look, his lean cheeks taut. "Prior Ignatius is the man who rules here, is he not? I doubt Stephen had the guts to stand up to him.''

"A substantial amount of my dowry has been used to refurbish the priory chapel and the prior's private quarters,'' she replied heavily. "The people fear him. He burnt several at the stake as heretics. That was how he stopped his actions being challenged. When the last victim was accused, I sent word to the Archbishop of Wells and the High Sheriff to investigate his persecution. The prior wriggled out of it. He has an explanation for everything. He convinced the archbishop that the woman was a heretic, when she was no more than worried out of her mind for the safety of her son.''

This was an opening to test him. She hated to be brutal about such a matter, but surprise would give her the advantage she needed to gauge his reactions. "The last heretic he burned was Clothilde.''

Beneath his complexion, nut-brown from months of exposure to the sun, she could see he had paled. A muscle ticked along his cheek and he swallowed. Every line of his body was tense. A piece of bread crumbled between the white joints of his stiff fingers.

"Then I have failed her," his voice was hoarse. "I have failed my father. He made me swear that Clothilde would always be revered if he did not return from the French campaign. She was to have a place of honour at Penruthin." He thumped the table with his hand, venting his frustration. He leapt up and was darkly silhouetted against the mullioned window. "I cannot believe any of the people were heretics. The man's evil."

Eloise hardened herself against a wave of compassion. If he was Roland, he must be aching inside at the brutal death of his mother. Yet she dared not be lenient. Too much depended on her knowing the truth of his real identity. "That vow to your father must have cost you dear, my lord. I recall you had no love for Clothilde. You refused to have her attend our wedding celebrations. Did you not declare that if she entered the Great Hall you would walk out of it?"

He planted his legs apart and with hands on hips glared at her. "It was said to anger Roland. It was no secret that I hated my brother in those days." There was an edge to his voice which betrayed an inner anguish. "That was before I was taken prisoner. My brother opened my eyes to many things in the years we were captives together. I owe my brother my life. It was his sacrifice when he was wounded during our escape that enabled me to reach safety."

A sharp rap at the door broke the tension. Captain Maddock called out, "My lord, Samuel the cobbler is here."

Alaric strode to the door and opened it to admit the villager. Securing the bolt again, he sat down on the edge of the bed, saying tersely, "Those damned boots no longer fit me. I need a larger size."

The cobbler shuffled forward on spindly legs. He was a hunchback and had suffered many cruel taunts from Alaric when he was a youth. "Them boots were made of the finest leather. They fitted you well enough when you left 'ere."

"Do you question me, serf?" Alaric did not raise his voice, but there was a dangerous edge to it which made Eloise flinch. "They don't fit now. And I need a pair which do."

The cobbler visibly quaked. "Aye, my lord." His expression was sullen as he knelt to measure Alaric's feet. When he had finished, he drew back and it was several moments before he spoke, his squinting eyes wary as he studied the lean face of his lord. "'Appen Roland's boots may 'ave fitted you, had he not taken them all wiv 'im."

"Since he did," Alaric snapped, "they will be of no use, will they? So don't talk nonsense, man."

Alaric stood up and paced the chamber. His bearing was pure arrogance. He showed no sign that the cobbler's words could have a deeper meaning. By implying that he could fit Roland's boots, was the hunchback inferring that he believed him to be Roland and not Alaric?

Eloise felt the hairs of her neck tingle with unease. First, there were the scars on his back, and now his old boots did not fit. Prior Ignatius would seize on such obvious facts to prove that the man proclaiming to be Lord Penruthin was an impostor. Yet the man's haughty manner was so like Alaric... Her thoughts raced in confusion. Hope mingled with dread as she assessed the vulnerability of her own position. She wanted to believe he was Alaric: the people needed their lord to save them from the prior's tyranny. Her own marriage and fate were of secondary importance.

A thread of reasoning discomfited her. It would be too cruel for Roland to have returned from his captivity, only to be hanged or burned as an impostor. If this man was Roland, he was deliberately duping not only Stephen but herself. That rankled. She eyed him stonily. If he was indeed Roland, did he not deserve to be punished for attempting to steal an inheritance which was not his? Her suspicions again roused themselves and jostled to be heard. He'd had a lifetime to study the way his brother acted. From the mummers coming to the castle on festive days to entertain them, she had seen how some people were able to copy the exact mannerisms, even the voices of another.

"Are there boots for me to wear, or not?" Alaric demanded, cutting short her deliberations.

The cobbler had not taken his eyes from him. He nodded slowly. "'Appen you're man enough to fit Sir Edgar's boots. They'll fit you. He hated new boots and kept his for years. There were two pairs needed new heels when he left. They were put in the storehouse with the rest of his clothes."

"It is fortunate that nothing is ever thrown away at Penruthin," Alaric answered, less stiffly.

When the cobbler left, Eloise faced Alaric. He had shown himself capable of guarding his thoughts and emotions too well to be easily tricked into revealing whether he was Roland. She took a deep breath.

"Are you Alaric or Roland?"

He laughed easily. "You have acknowledged me to be your husband."

"That does not answer my question," she persisted. Her expression matched his in hauteur as she held his stare. "I gave you the benefit of the doubt. I ask in return the courtesy of your honesty."

Her words apparently struck beneath his guard. His eyes crinkled, their grey depths winter bleak and uncompromising. Was it from anger that she had challenged him, or unease?

"Why do you now doubt that I am Alaric?"

How deftly he avoided a straight answer. Was it out of guilt? Then she remembered the tales that Alaric had a perverse way of testing people's loyalty. Those who failed suffered his displeasure. Her eyes flashed blue fire. How dared he test her loyalty? Hadn't she already risked much to help him?

She began to circle him as a wolf circled its prey before closing in for the kill. "The cobbler doubted you," she parried. "He as good as said that Roland's boots would fit you. I've also seen the scars on your back. Roland was whipped on his brother's orders."

A muscle pumped along his jaw and his full lips

compressed. "You dare to remind me of my shame," his voice crackled as he turned to keep on a line with her circling. A dangerous gleam entered his narrowed eyes. She had the distinct feeling that she was the impending victim, not himself. His voice harshened, "My brother and I were reconciled before his death. I expect loyalty from my wife."

She halted abruptly and flung at him, "If I am your wife."

She braced herself to ride his anger. Instead he grinned, his expression as wicked as a satyr. "You are mine, Eloise." He closed the gap between them and gripped her shoulders. "That was proved before the old woman interrupted us."

A smile of enticing intimacy transformed his austere features. Beguilement sparkled in his eyes, his gaze both a caress and a challenge. She reared back from him, her body rigid in his hold.

"Nothing was proved, least of all your identity." Her eyes flayed him with contempt. "Prior Ignatius and your brother will demand the truth from you."

"I have not lied to you, Eloise."

He admired her spirit. Who would have suspected that the quiet, awkward child-bride would turn into such a fiery beauty? Her sense of honour was impeccable. She was also intelligent and sharp-witted. He had forgotten about the significance which could be placed on his scarred back. He'd had many whippings when a Moorish slave. Bile rose to his throat as humiliating memories returned. He wanted nothing more than to forget those days.

He appraised the woman who did not fear either to defend him before the prior, or question his motives. That took courage. There was a graceful dignity about her which aroused his interest. Despite the dilemma in which she found herself, she was too proud to surrender without a fight. And he had unexpectedly enjoyed their verbal sparring. It had excited him as her easy submission to his will never could have done. She was a worthy mistress of Penruthin.

He could only guess how badly the people would have suffered had it not been for her intervention in recent years. Each battle would have been won at a cost to her pride. He knew the vindictiveness of the prior. And with Isobel as her sister-in-law, there must have been many humiliations for her to bear. The woman was as vindictive as she was voluptuous. Isobel had resented the marriage. She had wanted Penruthin for herself.

The thoughts were rapid as an arrow's flight. He was aware of the danger to himself and to this lovely woman. He should never have returned to Penruthin without a troop of guards at his command. There had been no money to pay them. A ragged pilgrim did not inspire confidence in moneylenders. The lure of home had been so strong that nothing else had seemed important. He had seen no shame in returning to his home in pilgrim's garb. The fever had been an unexpected curse. He had thought himself long rid of its lingering effects.

Through his fingers he could feel the tension in the woman's body. This was not the homecoming he had envisioned. The fever had robbed him of the element of surprise. From the angry tones of Prior Ignatius, it was obvious he had made his judgement. The man would denounce him as an impostor to suit his own ends. Anger clenched his stomach. The prior was too ambitious to wish the Lord of Penruthin to return. And Stephen would side with the prior. His only ally was Eloise, who was as strong-willed as she was lovely.

And he needed an ally. The truth could be twisted and distorted. Without men to command he could not be overpowered and imprisoned. If he was declared to be Roland, then what would be Eloise's fate? Chivalry, which was something he had often play-acted at a tournament, rose in his breast. He did not want to see her hurt.

Eloise felt pinned like a hare in torchlight as his grey, calculating stare held hers. His touch burned through her clothing and her pulse raced treacherously. Close to him, it was difficult for her to breathe. It took all her willpower to break that spellbinding stare. She swallowed hard and jerked her body free of his hold. She was breathing heavily, but her mind was clearer now that he no longer touched her. Even so, his gaze seared her soul.

"Must I prove to you again that you are mine?"

he taunted. He was being deliberately provocative.
Alaric at his most aloof yet all-commanding.

She lifted an ebony brow and regarded him archly.
"You would be better served proving to Prior Ignatius that you are Lord Penruthin. Upon that outcome
much depends."

Their conversation was interrupted by the return of
Samuel the cobbler. With him was Githa. She carried
a bundle wrapped in sackcloth.

"What have you there, Githa?" Eloise asked, puzzled by the wise-woman's nervousness.

"The guards have just been issued two months'
wages as incentive to obey Sir Stephen. He informed
them that Sir Alaric is an impostor. There'll be trouble. I thought his lordship might need these."

She unwrapped the sacking and held out a broadsword in a plain leather scabbard, together with a belt
and a dagger.

"God's blessings on you, Githa," Alaric said, taking up the sword and buckling it around his hips. The
dagger he thrust into the top of the sword-belt.

"I recognised Maddock's voice outside the door,"
he announced. "I thought him loyal to my father. Is
he no longer to be trusted?"

Eloise hastily assured him, "I have faith in Captain
Maddock. But he is no one's fool. He will pass his
own judgement when you confront the prior and your
brother."

"How many men will follow Maddock's orders?"
Alaric rapped out, rubbing his chin as he totted up

the men upon whom he could rely if it had to be put to the test.

Eloise shrugged. "Maddock has influence with the guards. But they are mostly mercenaries. Few were here in your father's day. Most are loyal only to their paymaster."

Samuel shuffled uncomfortably and blurted out, "My lord, you're condemned as an impostor in the prior's eyes. But the people are with you. Say the word and they'll rise up and take on the guards if need be."

"It has not come to that," Alaric said stiffly. "Nor, I pray, will it. The law is brutal against villeins who rebel against their masters."

"But you have right on your side," Eloise protested. "Stephen and the prior have judged you out of their own self-interest. They cannot act against the true Lord of Penruthin; if they do, they must answer to the law."

Alaric's tanned face was grim. "When did Ignatius ever care about right? Burning heretics proved how ruthless he can be. It's greed which rules him."

He pulled on his father's boots and sighed with satisfaction that they fitted. As he stood up, every line of his commanding stance was that of a natural leader. He tilted his head back and looked down his long slender nose at the cobbler. It was the manner in which she had seen Alaric address a servant.

"I'll have two pairs of boots made in your finest leather as soon as possible," he said as he walked with the hunchback to the door. Now properly attired and with his hand resting on the sword hilt, his mood was confident. "May I be worthy of Lord Edgar's boots."

Such humility from Alaric was not what Eloise expected. It brought a spread of warmth to her veins. The changes she had so far discerned in him were, in her opinion, all for the better. She had disliked the way that previously Alaric never lowered himself to be pleasant to servants.

"'Appen you will, my lord." All truculence was gone from the hunchback's manner. "'Appen you will."

As the door closed behind the servants, Alaric turned to discover Eloise studying him intently. He smiled. If he lost her support, his task would be fraught with danger. No one outside Penruthin knew of his return. The castle was isolated. He could be overpowered and arrested, even murdered. The prior, to vindicate his actions, would declare him to be Roland impersonating their lord. How safe would Eloise be? At the least she would be shut away in a nunnery, or forever silenced by joining him on the scaffold. Prior Ignatius would never permit her to accuse him in a court of law. There was danger ahead for both of them.

Chapter Four

"**I** have not thanked you for your intervention, Eloise." Penruthin bowed to her. The poised assurance was that of a man in command of his destiny. If he had any fears regarding his confrontation with Prior Ignatius, none of them showed in his demeanour. "It seems I would be rotting in a dungeon declared an impostor, if you have not spoken out," he went on. "It was not the homecoming I had envisaged."

"Prior Ignatius has become more powerful since Lord Edgar was not here to curb his ambition," she replied heavily. His gratitude and the admiring way he was looking at her was playing havoc with her breathing. He had a way of looking at her which held the confidence of seduction and the promise of untold pleasures. She should be annoyed at his boldness; instead she was excited by it. To divert her thoughts away from the attraction and sensual spell the man wove around her, she regarded him in his finery. The richness of his clothes and the imperious way in which he carried himself was irrefutably how she remembered her husband. Yet something was different, something which played at her conscience. She studied his face, framed by brown locks. It was his hair which was different. Alaric wore it cropped and fashionably short. Roland had worn it long to his shoulders, as the man before her wore his.

"You're frowning, Eloise. Do you fear to face my brother and the prior?"

"Certainly not! Whatever threats they have made to me, I have done nothing wrong. I was thinking that your hair should be trimmed. You always wore it short."

He grinned. "This *is* short." His tone was tinged with irony. "It reached my waist not so long ago. I looked like the wild man of the woods."

Again his self-mockery surprised her. He had indeed changed. There was no sign in his manner towards her of the pompous arrogance she detested. It made her voice soften as she suggested, "You should appear before your people as they remember you. Roland favoured longer hair than yourself. It is not wise to give rise to doubts. Will you permit me to cut your hair, or shall I summon a servant? Stephen will have learned of your recovery by now. I fear we have little time before you are summoned."

His full lips curved into a bleak line. He marched to the door and hauled it open, barking out, "Maddock, inform my brother and Prior Ignatius that I shall receive them in the Great Hall. At once." He paused and regarded the captain of the guard for a long moment before adding, "I hear the men have been paid extra wages and told that I am an impostor. My father trusted you to protect Penruthin in his absence. Are you in my brother's pay, or mine?"

"All the money comes from Penruthin's coffers. I am loyal to Penruthin and to its lord," the veteran soldier answered gruffly. His manner was respectful, but there was a wariness in his manner. "I was born in the village and rose through the ranks to become captain. It is a post I hold with honour. You'll be wanting an escort of six men to accompany you to the hall, I take it?"

"Escort or prison guard, Maddock?" Alaric countered.

"Escort, my lord. The people rejoice at your homecoming."

"There speaks a man who is reserving his judgement." Alaric eyed him coldly. "I could have you whipped for insolence."

"That would be your right as Lord of Penruthin," Maddock responded.

Eloise shivered. Why was Alaric deliberately antagonising the captain? He was one of the few guards she relied upon for their loyalty.

"And once would I not have had you whipped without compunction for such insolence?" Alaric declared. "Yet whippings do not win loyalty; only hatred. It is far better to rule by respect than by fear."

The scarred face of the captain remained dour, yet

Eloise detected less stiffness in his stance. "There's been too much fear instilled here. Unless it should be proved that you are not who you say, I give you my allegiance, Lord Penruthin."

"I accept it on those terms. But why?"

"There's been too many good people died at the stake. My brother was one. He spoke out against the prior's demanding extra work-days in his fields. There had been an early frost. The villagers needed to get their own harvests in, or they would starve that winter." He paused a moment then added, softly, "the woman Clothilde was no heretic."

Again he halted and Eloise glanced towards the two men as she finished pinning her headdress into place, looking for any reaction on Penruthin's face. There was none. Quickly the captain added, "She'd denied the prior her bed. Now, any woman he looks at complies with his wishes."

Penruthin put a hand on the captain's shoulder. "Your loyalty will not go unrewarded. I will take up your offer of an escort. My meeting with my brother is likely to be stormy. He has more to lose than I."

"They would have your life." Maddock grunted. "A man has a right to defend himself.

Alaric looked drawn as he came back into the room to face Eloise. In his absence she had dressed her hair into a coil high on her head and now wore a tall hennin headdress which matched her wine-red silk gown. A silver tissue veil hung from its point to cascade like a waterfall to the trailing hem of her gown.

Around her neck she wore a ruby and diamond neck-lace and the only rings she chose to wear were the plain gold wedding band and the Penruthin betrothal ring with its large blood-red ruby.

Alaric smiled as he noticed her rings. It reminded the world, simply yet effectively, that she was the wife of Lord Penruthin. He sat down and stared rigidly in front of him.

"You had better trim my hair."

He sat unmoving whilst she worked. When her knuckles brushed the nape of his neck, she felt the tension corded within. Again her heart went out to him. How he must have suffered in the last seven years! He must have dreamed of his homecoming, of receiving the homage of his subjects.

Having finished her task to her satisfaction, her hand lingered on his neck, drawn by his masculinity, yet instinctively wary of her feelings. Recalling that Stephen had been summoned, and surmising that Alaric would wish to gain advantage by taking his place on the dais in the hall, she withdrew her hand. It was re-taken by Alaric as he rose to his feet. His expression was enigmatic as he stared down at her.

"Do I pass your inspection?" he taunted, his gaze approving of the high-waisted gown she had donned, its floor-length sleeves lined with cloth of silver. It was a costly garment without any of the ostentation Isabel had displayed to try to impress her status upon him. Eloise needed no such showy grandeur; her nobility shone from her in graceful movements and magnanimous conduct.

When Alaric lifted her hand to his lips, their touch was like a liquid flame. "Penruthin has a worthy and beautiful woman as its Mistress."

Eloise heard in his voice the warning that she was his property as much as the castle and lands. The tenderness she had begun to feel for him withered. She was not part of the conquest. She had seen the easy charm which had won over the servants and the captain of the guards; she would not concede so easily. For too long she had dreamed of freedom from this marriage.

Alaric placed Eloise's arm over his and together they walked sedately to the door. Outside, the six men-at-arms fell into step behind them with Captain Maddock at their head. Eloise noted that they were all young recruits taken from the surrounding villages on Penruthin land within recent years. Her heart was pounding with trepidation as they descended the stone steps from the lord's quarters to the hall. To her dismay, she saw no villagers were present in the hall. Passing a window she glanced outside and saw them gathered in the courtyard. A double row of guards on the steps leading to the Great Hall barred their admittance. Stephen expected support for Alaric and was taking no chances. Deliberately, Eloise paused at the window and opened it.

"My lord, show yourself to your people," she suggested. "They await to greet you."

He had anticipated her gesture and was already at the opening, lifting his arm to the people below. A cry was raised when he was spotted.

"Lord Penruthin! God bless Lord Penruthin!" The cry was taken up and chanted. They were still chanting as Alaric and Eloise entered the Great Hall.

Stephen was pacing the dais. When he saw Alaric approach, he made a comical dart to the central lord's chair and sat on it, his expression wary as he glared at his brother.

Beneath her hand, Eloise felt the muscles of Alaric's arm tighten, but nothing else in his manner showed his anger. He continued to walk towards the dais and led Eloise to her chair. He bowed to her graciously as she smoothed her skirts, matching his calm composure; then he turned his attention to his brother. He did not speak; he simply stared at him, his tanned countenance rigid with disapproval. Beneath that steely glare, Stephen shifted, his cheeks first flaring with colour, then bleaching white. His knuckles whitened over the carved dragons' heads on the chair arm, and his gaze slid from Alaric's.

Eloise saw that Stephen's hand was shaking. The whites of his eyes were an unhealthy yellow shot through with red veins. He'd been drinking heavily since Alaric's arrival, no doubt needing to bolster his courage. There was a rustle of silk and Isabel hurried down the stairs to take her place behind her husband's chair. If Stephen's eyes did not hold Alaric's stare, his wife's did. They were black, viperish pools of hatred.

"Your place is out there with the peasants, Roland," she launched her attack.

"I know my place." He looked pointedly at the Lord's chair. "It is my brother who has forgotten his."

"Impostor!" shrieked Prior Ignatius. His grey robes flapped around him as he stormed down the length of the hall. His round face was red and stippled with sweat from having to push his way through the crowd, who were still chanting in the courtyard. "You may have fooled the villagers. But you do not fool us."

Eloise admired the calm way in which Alaric rode the insults. Her own pulse was frantic in its stifling pace and her nerves jangled with the strain. The moment the prior entered the hall, an icy chill played over her flesh. The man emanated malevolence and evil. She came to her feet and took her place beside Alaric. Her hand replaced on his arm proclaimed her allegiance. Fleetingly, there was a softening in Alaric's stare before it was turned with glacial coldness upon his adversaries.

"I have seen the neglect here," Alaric pronounced loudly. "You have both abused your positions. Do not add to your crimes by allowing your greed to make you careless. It is not for you to judge me. My fealty is to the King and he alone can pass judgement.

Too many people know of my arrival. I know you have bribed the guards.''

His gaze lifted to the men-at-arms standing stiffly to attention at the back of the hall. There was repressed power in his movements as he walked to stand before the prior, and Eloise found herself holding her breath, admiration rising through her concern for his safety. He showed no fear. He was a man confident of his status and his authority, although the odds were clearly stacked in the prior's favour. She gripped her hands tightly together so that she might appear composed. Inwardly, her heart was pounding with fear for Alaric. His courage proclaimed him worthy of her loyalty.

Alaric dropped his voice so that only those on the dais could hear him. ''You could of course have me declared an impostor and murdered. A dangerous path. Can you rely on the silence of all the villeins? They are chanting for their lord to go amongst them. I have their love. What do you have that will bind them to silence?''

''Don't threaten me.'' Prior Ignatius exploded with rage. ''I am God's instrument in this land. You are an impostor who would usurp his brother's place.''

''What proof have you of that? You've asked me no questions to prove my identity.'' Alaric raised his voice to carry to the guards lining the room. They were all thickset men, mercenaries of indeterminate ages, loyal to the highest paymaster; hard men, who would kill upon orders, their consciences untroubled.

He stood poised with one leg slightly bent in front of the other, every inch of his tall frame was the bearing of a nobleman and—more important to the men-at-arms—a warrior. Stepping down from the dais, he approached the menacing assembly of guards.

"How many of you have crossed swords with the enemy on French soil? Who of you have felt the bite of steel slicing through your flesh in defence of England's honour? I warrant at some time each man here has done so, as I have myself. I salute you. As I salute all brave and honourable men who have fought for England and King Harry."

Eloise held her breath. Even armed and a skilled swordsman, Alaric would be overpowered if he was attacked by so many. She was shocked to see that his expression was derisive as he regarded the soldiers.

Lord Penruthin paced slowly back and forth before them, inspecting each man with military precision. When his stare fell upon a tarnished domed helmet, or a rent in a tabard bearing the Penruthin coat of arms, Eloise saw each man shift uncomfortably. Alaric did not comment on their slovenly appearance, but the men began to look ill at ease. Several of the guards on duty outside, on hearing his words, had begun to drift into the hall.

"So we lost our lands in France," his voice rang out. "But we kept our pride. The French now know the terror of the English pike and sword. I did not spend my days growing fat on the labour of others; I fought beside my father's men, men who were brave warriors and gave their lives for the glory of England. They were proud to wear the Penruthin lion on their breasts. With the final battle lost, I took up the pilgrim's staff to pray for my father's soul and for the souls of the men who died with him.''

Already there was a subtle shift in the demeanour of the soldiers. The hall was now full of men-at-arms. Behind them the villagers, no longer held back, were jostling for places to hear what was happening. It was the guards who held Eloise's attention; they were the danger. Alaric was reminding them that, unlike Stephen, he was no pampered courtier, but a seasoned soldier like themselves. The allegiance of brothers in arms was more binding than any forged by silver. Was Lord Penruthin's speech winning them over, or had the prior's bribe retained their loyalty? These mercenaries were a surly breed and Eloise felt uncomfortable whenever she was close to them. With relief, she noticed how the guards were responding to Alaric's words. Many had straightened their shoulders, their expressions no longer sullen but respectful.

''I was taken by the Moors,'' Alaric continued, still addressing the men-at-arms, ignoring his brother and the prior. ''For five years I was a captive, the fate of many Englishmen fighting abroad. It was the memory of Penruthin which kept me alive. The vision of the Penruthin standard sustained me, its black lion rampant worn proudly by its men as they rode into battle and further glory. As we will again when King Henry rallies his army to teach the French that we are not beaten.''

Eloise saw the attentive expressions on the soldiers' faces. This was a language they understood.

The prior, aware of what was happening, was red-faced with fury. ''Enough!'' Ignatius roared. ''Your words are twisted to distort the truth. You are here to answer…''

Alaric ignored the command, raising his voice to carry over the prior's angry bellow. A voice used to shouting battle orders above the clash of steel and thunder of cannon was too powerful to be denied.

''I survived the Moors' captivity,'' Alaric continued, ''knowing that the Penruthin standard had always been at the forefront of any battle, that its soldiers were the envy of many of the greatest noblemen in England. Yet, on my return, I find that Penruthin has become a cesspit for the indulgent.''

Again his gaze swept over the guards, his expression scathing. ''Look at yourselves. Call yourself soldiers? God's blood! Your armour is rusty! There wasn't one of you practising at arms when I looked out at the practice yard this morning. What are you, fighting men or a troop fit only to protect milksops and old women? Where's your pride in your skill?''

Eloise's heart swelled with pride at the way he was rousing the men's fighting spirit. She had no need to assume an expression of false admiration as she gazed at Penruthin. It blazed in her eyes for all to see. The daughter of a noble warrior, her own blood stirred with loyalty.

The guards shifted with discomfort. One, known to Eloise as a troublemaker who was always starting fights, mumbled inaudibly. He was feared by many of his companions. Her heart jolted. Had Alaric gone too far? If he had turned the guards against him, all would be lost. They would be in the power of the prior.

Penruthin did not even halt in his ridicule. "I'll tell you what's happened to your pride. It's been smothered by apathy. Where's the pride in protecting a castle when its guardian is a lily-skinned despot? How can you hold your heads high when your master has no backbone to ride out into battle?"

Stephen leapt to his feet. But, before he could speak, Alaric rounded on him. He returned to the dais, standing taller than his brother by several inches. Stephen shrank from the contempt in Penruthin's face.

With a dismissive flick of his wrist, Alaric turned back to the guards. "My brother declares that I am an impostor. If he wants to challenge my right to be master here, let him do so by the sword in a feat of arms presided over by the King. Is that not the way of noblemen?"

Every guard nodded assent.

"If you accept me as your lord, kneel now and give me the fealty due."

Hands on hips, Penruthin studied the men before him. He had tilted back his head to look down his nose at the gathering. It was an image of the haughty Alaric Eloise would rather forget; that cold impersonal authority which surrounded men of noble birth, an authority that could not be crushed. Even as she resented the qualities which made him a respected leader of men, a more powerful emotion overwhelmed her. What woman could fail to be moved by this magnificent figure which showed no fear? She held her breath, marvelling at his bravery, or was it rashness? In that last command he would triumph or fail. For the space of several tortured heartbeats, the guards hesitated.

"Fine words," Prior Ignatius sneered. "But these men do not know you of old. The Peacock of Penruthin would never return to his people dressed in rags. You speak so grandly of warfare. Where were you when Lord Edgar needed the support of your men? In a bordello twenty miles away if rumour is true."

"When is rumour ever based on the whole truth?" Penruthin kept his temper, but his body was stiff with affront. "I was in a bordello, trying to persuade Lord Bellingham and Lord Southford to rally to my banner. I knew the French were close to our French demesne. Their men had been without rest for six weeks. They were drunk and we lost half a day trying to sober them up. That was why I arrived too late to save my father."

He disdainfully flicked an imaginary speck of dust

from his doublet. "As for my pilgrim's garb: what else would a pilgrim wear?"

Penruthin knew that he must bluff them, must never let them suspect that he had returned to England without the necessary support. "My old friend, Lord Kilgarron, thought my wits had addled when he recognised me on the road near Glastonbury some days past. He could not believe I preferred my pilgrim's robe and to travel barefoot. I made a vow when I was a captive, that if I escaped I would give praise to our Blessed Saviour at every shrine on the road to my home. My journey has taken fourteen months. Part of my vow was to travel as a humble pilgrim, without the privilege of rank or status."

The prior snorted in disbelief. "Why did not Lord Kilgarron send us word that you were in England? The man's a born gossip-monger. Your disappearance has been the talk at Court for years."

"I swore him to secrecy. He respects a religious vow." Penruthin grinned. "Besides, from our youth we both know secrets about each other that neither would want bandied abroad. Since his wife died last year, Kilgarron is eager to wed the King's ward, the Lady Margaret."

Eloise began to relax. Alaric had every answer ready. With each response her own doubts were being laid to rest. When, from the corner of her eye, she saw Isobel whisper in her husband's ear, her tension returned. There was a cruel twist to the older woman's carmined lips when she straightened. It sent a chill through Eloise.

Stephen puffed out his chest. "All very plausible, brother. But words are just words. Yours prove nothing. Both my brothers were alike in colouring, height and build, yet Roland was Alaric's underling. He was whipped for insolence. Show us your back, brother."

Penruthin stood his ground. "My back will reveal to you that I was whipped on many occasions by the Moors. It will prove nothing conclusive. I did not live in a Moorish palace. I was a galley slave during most of my captivity."

Eloise gasped, her hand lifting to her mouth with anguish. She had heard of the horrors of slave ships. They were hell-ships, the slaves starved and beaten mercilessly, many drowning when the vessels engaged in combat.

"You have an answer to everything," the prior pronounced. "The cobbler was with you this morning. A strange request, since the Lady Eloise insisted that all your clothes were brought up from the storerooms." He looked pointedly at the old-fashioned boots Alaric was wearing. "Aren't they Lord Edgar's boots? Alaric never wore anything but the softest leather."

There was a grunt of pain from behind them and Eloise whirled to see the cobbler being frogmarched into the hall, his arm twisted viciously behind his back.

"Let that man go," she commanded. "There is no need to hurt him."

The prior glared at her. "Your heart is too soft, my lady. All it takes is a hard-luck story and you will champion any beggar's cause."

"Compassion is not a sin." She turned his words against him. "I am not deceived by silver tongues which distort the truth to suit their own ends."

The narrowing of his eyes told her that he had not forgiven her for reporting him to the archbishop and that last year he had been forced to answer to his actions over the heretics. Folding his hands piously over his vast stomach, the prior turned his attention to the cobbler. "Why were you summoned by the impostor?"

The hunchback looked terrified. His eyes were huge and his thin, straggling brown hair was streaked with sweat. "To fit him with new boots."

"So those belonging to Sir Alaric did not fit this man?" Stephen interrupted, his voice rising with triumph.

"I'd not have expected them to in the circumstances." The cobbler was looking at Alaric and it seemed to give him courage. "His lordship, from the looks of the scars on his feet, had been barefoot as a prisoner. A man's feet will spread without the confines of leather."

Eloise swallowed against a lump of emotion rising to her throat. The cobbler in the past had had no cause to revere Alaric, though she had seen Roland stop the village boys from jeering at the hunchback. She thrust the thought aside. This was no time for doubt; she had to have faith in him.

The prior thrust his face up close to the cobbler, spittle spraying over the wretched man's face as he observed, "Feet may spread, but they would not grow in size, would they?" The prior was gloating, convinced he had trapped Alaric. "The guard was asked to bring the wooden lasts with him. Where are they?"

The guard replied, "There was no sign of either Lord Edgar's or Sir Alaric's last in the cobbler's cottage."

"There wouldn't be," the cobbler reasoned. "I burnt them two winters ago when the snow was so thick I couldn't get out for kindling. We had no woodpile. The prior had kept the villagers busy filling up the priory woodshed all winter. The snow came early that year. If we wanted firewood we had to buy it from the priory. I had no money."

"A craftsman does not burn the tools of his trade." Prior Ignatius shot out an accusing arm. Samuel the cobbler flinched and hobbled backwards.

Eloise wanted to intervene, but a warning glare from Penruthin stopped her. The prior was trying to intimidate the cobbler into betraying Alaric. To his credit the hunchback, though afraid, spoke out. "It was that or freeze. My daughter had the fever. She were shivering with cold. They weren't the only lasts I burnt. Several other old ones also went into the fire along with several pieces of furniture. A shoe-last can be recarved. The work is a small price to pay for saving the life of my only child.''

The guards and villagers in the crowded hall were becoming restless. Eloise knew the prior was capable of any trick to turn the balance back in his favour. She stepped forward, knowing that the people loved her enough to follow her lead.

''My lord husband has asked the guards for their fealty. It is his right as the Lord of Penruthin to receive the homage from every servant, villager and vassal on his lands.'' She turned to face Alaric, knowing that she was irretrievably committing herself to support him. Gracefully she sank to her knees, her head bowed, hands together and held towards him. When his warm firm fingers closed over hers, she repeated the ancient oath of fealty. As her gaze lifted to hold his, the admiration in his eyes set her pulse racing. Tenderly he raised her to her feet and lifted her hand to his lips. It was no perfunctory acknowledgement of her oath; his mouth lingered, the warm pressure ardent, promising, challenging, threatening her resolve.

It showed her a glimpse of what could be—a union founded on respect and, dared she hope, love? No, not love. The Alaric of old loved only himself; he could not have changed that much. She must not forget that he was a philanderer; a man who would flaunt his mistress at his own wedding was not to be trusted in matters of the heart. She steeled herself against the seductive charm he was weaving around her. She told herself that he needed her. Had she not just shown the people their duty?

It was one thing to school her heart and mind not to trust Alaric and another to maintain her resolve. He showed no fear before his accusers. He stood tall and proud, superior in courage, figure and spirit to any man within the hall, silently commanding the assembly to pay him homage.

Prior Ignatius' face suffused with choler. "He is not your lord. You will perjure your souls by swearing allegiance to an impostor."

"Yes, guards; listen to no more of his deceit," Stephen raged. "Arrest him!"

Captain Maddock stepped forward. "A soldier's oath is to his master alone. His soul is in God's hands." He went down on one knee.

To Eloise's relief, the guards who had escorted Alaric and Eloise to the hall followed the lead of their commander. Two others, both scarred war veterans, also knelt. Then with a creaking of worn leather and rasping of swords against flagstones, every guard knelt facing Alaric. With Captain Maddock taking the lead, they all recited the oath of fealty to the new Lord of Penruthin.

Alaric bowed his head in gracious acknowledgement as they rose to their feet. Yet there remained a tension in his figure Eloise did not understand. "Tomorrow all of you will assemble in the practice yard to resume your daily training," he declared. "Today

I would celebrate my return. Servants, break out the wine casks. An ox will be roasted.''

Hoods were snatched from the villagers' heads and tossed jubilantly in the air. The hall broke into chaos, cries of ''God bless Lord and Lady Penruthin!'' resounding high up to the oak-beamed ceiling.

His expression still imperious, Alaric swivelled to confront the prior. Ignatius sneered, his eyes slits of hatred.

''You think you've won. You haven't.'' His fat jowls wobbled in his fury. ''The matter will not rest here. You will be watched. One false move and you are undone. I *know* you are Roland. I shall prove it. You cannot impersonate your brother for ever. Your natures were too different.''

''Since you find my presence here such a trial, my Lord Prior,'' Alaric said silkily, ''I suggest you stay within the priory. I saw Brother Cedric in the village yesterday. He was my father's chaplain. He will perform the daily services in the castle chapel.''

The prior shook his head, black demons dancing in his cruel eyes. ''None of the brothers will set foot into this castle whilst you are its lord. There will be no services for the supporters of an impostor and usurper. By choosing you they have denied the Church.''

Eloise gasped. The prior was condemning the people to hell-fire if he denied them the Mass.

''Then I shall inform the archbishop of your decision,'' Alaric clipped out. ''I will lead the prayers as

I have often done on the battlefield. God will never renounce the innocent. If any soul is doomed to burn in hell, it will be yours, not mine, Prior Ignatius.''

With an angry snarl the prior pushed his way through the cheering crowd. Their shouts of joy had been too loud to hear the prior's declaration. Eloise's heart was heavy. How would the people react when they realised the prior had denied them the Mass and Absolution from their sins through the Confessional?

''The prior will not harm you, Eloise,'' Alaric murmured. ''Together we cannot fail to right the injustices done here.''

Taking her arm, he smiled at her. The warmth bathed her in a sensual glow. For once she did not fight it. Nor did she want her fears to show and alarm the villagers. Alaric deserved his moment of triumph. He was the strong and commanding figure that Penruthin needed to return to prosperity.

Alaric's smile faded as his gaze rested on Stephen and Isobel.

''You won't get away with this,'' Stephen threatened. ''You've duped the people and won over the guards, but not me.''

''When were you ever won over by me, Stephen?'' Alaric jeered with the vicious sarcasm of old. ''You were always jealous that you were not our father's heir, that the riches of Penruthin could never be yours. You hated Roland because Father doted on him and not you.''

"Penruthin will be mine when you hang, brother," Stephen jeered.

"Until then, you have forgotten your oath of fealty, Stephen." The challenge rang like a clash of swords in the air between them.

"Go to hell!"

To Eloise's astonishment, Alaric tipped back his head and laughed. "If you think your right to Penruthin is more just than mine, then meet me on the tourney field."

Scowling, Stephen marched away. Isobel shot her husband a look of disgust. She was studying Alaric in a way which made Eloise's hand itch to slap the salacious smile from her carmined lips. Isobel had not taken her eyes from Alaric all morning. Now she walked towards him, her hips swaying provocatively, her shoulders held back so that the outline of her heavy breasts strained against the thin silk of her gown in blatant invitation. Isobel craved power, which was why she had married Stephen. Did she now think to seduce Alaric back to her bed? Misplaced jealousy smote Eloise. The memory of her humiliation burned her cheeks. She would not endure such again.

"Stephen always was a fool," Isobel simpered.

The cloying scent of Isobel's heavy perfume stung Eloise's nostrils. The woman's lips were pouting provocatively, her eyes boldly appraising Alaric, not caring that she was observed by everyone in the crowded hall. Her smile was a sultry promise that nauseated

Eloise. Did that woman have no morals, no concept of honour? she fumed. She stood stiffly at her husband's side, observing his reaction. Isobel was still an attractive woman; she exuded wantonness as ripely as any tavern bawd.

Isobel curtsied low. "Have I need to swear fealty to you, my lord?" she said huskily. She pushed her arms together so that the low neck of her gown gaped and Alaric was favoured with a view of her splendid breasts, her nipples, thus blatantly displayed, were carmined. Her smile conveyed the secret knowledge of their shared intimacy. "Was the homage my body paid you in the orchard on the night of your wedding not proof of my undying devotion?"

Eloise dug her fingernails into her palms to control her outrage. When Alaric returned Isobel's smile, anger swamped her. She stood ramrod straight, deliberately erasing emotion from her ivory cheeks.

"How could I forget?"

Isobel laughed seductively, her hand brushing his thigh. "We were good together. You always said I had no equal. You never had time for virgins, did you, Alaric? When you tire of your wife's inexperience, my door will be open to you. Don't keep me waiting. We have so many nights to make up for."

Eloise did not stay to hear more. She spun on her heel and walked with her head held high to summon the servants. It felt as though a fist were squeezing her insides. *Damn* Alaric. He had not changed. A leopard did not alter its spots, nor a reprobate his lecherous ways. She was a fool to have been swayed by his charm. Wasn't that how he had always got his own way? He manipulated people to his will. She had seen how he won over the guards by playing on their sense of valour. Well, he would fail with her. For the moment he needed her support against the prior and his brother. And that would be all he got—temporary support. As soon as she decently could after his position here was assured, she would petition for an annulment to their marriage.

None of the pain she was feeling at Alaric's perfidy showed on her face as she instructed the servants to prepare a banquet to celebrate his return. She knew her duties as Mistress of Penruthin and she would not shirk them.

Summoning Winifred, she returned to the lord's chamber and ordered her maid to move all her possessions to the smaller chamber next door. An hour later she was arranging her silver-backed brushes and cosmetic pots on a coffer by her dressing-stool when the door opened without the customary knock.

"Put the last of my headdresses on the bed for now, Winifred. Some of my dressing-trunks will have to go to the storeroom, for the space is somewhat cramped. I had not realised how much clutter I had collected in the last seven years."

"You collected more than clutter." Alaric's deep voice startled her into dropping a silver ring-box. "You also acquired a husband. Have your possessions moved back to where they were."

"A husband in name only," she reminded him sharply. "I am your wife merely for so long as it takes for an annulment to be granted. You have Isobel to take to your bed, and that suits my purposes well. It is not uncommon for a lord and lady to have separate bedchambers; I will not share yours."

He regarded her sardonically. "There is nothing between Isobel and myself."

Her temper soared at his thinking her so naïve and gullible. "Don't take me for an innocent and a fool." She kept her voice glacial with contempt. "Isobel could not wait to humiliate me again in front of our people. I did not see you repudiating her claim to be your mistress."

"How do you know my response to her attempted seduction?" His tone was equally frosty. "You marched off, having formed your own judgement." His censure smote her; he was again putting her in the wrong. But was it possible that he had rejected Isobel's invitation? Her heart gave a treacherous leap. She crushed the rising hope, reminding herself that she was an innocent in the ways of love. He was an accomplished reprobate who knew every trick to coerce her to his will.

"Why should I care what Isobel is to you?" she countered.

Alaric lifted a dark brow, his manner superior, self-assured and clearly impatient at her conduct. "Isobel would make a dangerous enemy. It would be unwise for me to antagonise her at this moment. As you must know her so well, I should not have to explain that to you.''

She was about to retort when she realised that once again he had explained his motives, something Alaric never did. And he spoke the truth. It did not ease the pain she had experienced, nor did it lessen the guard she had erected against him. She knelt to pick up the fallen ring-box, scooping up a handful of scattered rings from the polished wooden floor. No rushes had as yet been laid in the room, which would have made her task harder. She kept her head bent as she replaced the jewels and shut the lid. When his hand slipped beneath her elbow to assist her to her feet, she flinched from its touch.

''I will not be humiliated as I was before,'' she announced, her eyes sparkling with warning. ''Neither of us wanted this marriage. I want to use my dowry to repair my father's castle.''

His face was shuttered. ''Your old home at Whytemead is in sad decay. I passed through one of the outlying villages. The people fared well. The cottages were in better repair than those here.''

''I sold most of my mother's jewels to ensure that my people did not suffer,'' she informed him. The memories of the battles she had fought with the prior made her sigh wearily, and her voice was heavy as she continued, ''The prior could not stop me from aiding my own people. But in other ways they are not so fortunate. Their cattle have been run off by thieves.

My orders for the guards here to protect my land were countermanded.''

A muscle pumped along his jaw, his grey eyes piercing the composure she was struggling to preserve. ''The prior has much to answer for. But, until he does, we have appearances to maintain. I have no intention of forcing myself upon you, Eloise. Or did you think I would add rape to the grievances you already bear me?''

Her cheeks flamed. How like Alaric to put her in the wrong, and himself above reproach.

He thrust his thumbs over the sword belt around his slender hips. ''I will give you time, Eloise. My return after so long is naturally a shock to you. We are strangers. I have enemies enough without adding you to them.'' He lifted a hand and stroked the back of his fingers along her soft cheek. ''Especially you.''

The words were a caress, a promise—a threat.

''I am not your enemy, Alaric.'' The breathless sound to her voice made her curse the effect he was again having upon her. She had no intention of being one of his conquests.

His self-confident smile roused her anger, which still smouldered from his conduct with Isobel. It helped her to harden her resolve. ''In fact, I am entirely indifferent to you,'' she responded. ''But I will not forget the role I must for the moment portray. I would safeguard the people of Penruthin. The prior would seize upon any obvious dissent between us to imply that you are an impostor.

Lord Penruthin tensed at the way she was freezing out his attempts to win her. It added to the pent-up anger and frustration he was experiencing due to all the neglect he had seen when he inspected the castle, and which now channelled through his self-control. Seeing the frigid contempt in her expression, the fragile leash on his fury snapped. He grabbed her waist, pulling her hard against him, so that she was held captive against his chest in a fierce embrace.

"Indifferent to me? I think not, my lady."

Eloise shivered, knowing she had struck some hidden demon. His mouth crushed hers, possessing her lips with savage dominance. Outraged, Eloise struggled, striking her fists against his body in a futile attempt to break free. The more she struggled the tighter he held her, and the greater the ravage to her lips. Her frantic squirming had only moulded their bodies closer. Every movement served to fuel the flame of his punishing passion. The soft flesh of her lips was bruised and a strangled cry rose from her throat. Then all at once the pressure of his mouth changed, becoming more gentle, although still demanding. He was teaching her that he would not be denied, that his will alone ruled at Penruthin.

"No!" The muffled protest wrenched from her was her downfall. That brief parting of her lips had allowed him to deepen his kiss, his tongue playing over the inner softness of her mouth. His hands were no longer gripping her roughly. They had spread out across her back and slid slowly down the length of her spine, spreading a trail of tingling awareness in their wake. Her skin was coming alive, budding with soft swirls of sensations that pirouetted across her flesh. All at once there was a delicious spiralling of her heightened senses. The musky scent of his skin assailed her, his breath tasting sweet and as heady as a love-philtre. Her body no longer felt earthbound, but transported to float sinuously, cloud-high. The practised caress of his hands as they slowly explored the hollows of her back and rose to tantalise the fullness of her breast made her tremble. And it was not from anger. Deep within her, feathery petals fluttered, exploding into glorious blossoms of exquisite sensation.

She was powerless to quell the passion unfurling within her. Reason was stilled as she surrendered to the rapture of the moment. Her hands slid over his broad shoulders, her fingers curling into the thick hair above his high collar. She was drifting, drawn inexorably into a vortex, where she had no control over her movements, no power to overcome the responses he had evoked.

Then, as abruptly as she had been pinioned in his arms, she was released.

He was breathing heavily, his lean face bleak with nothing so refined as desire. It was dark with lust. When he dragged a hand through his hair, she saw that it was unsteady. ''Perhaps you would have preferred it, if I were Roland,'' he taunted, caustically.

"Was he not your knight errant on your wedding day?"

She backed away, lifting a trembling hand to her mouth which still throbbed from the passion of his kiss. The fiery splinters died in his eyes and he sighed.

"Don't deny me, Eloise. And don't lie to me."

The kiss, which had roused such pleasure in her, meant nothing to him. It was punishment for rejecting him. She swallowed, despising herself that the tell-tale stinging in her eyes revealed how deeply he had wounded her.

"Get out!" she flared, blinking aside tears she was too proud to let fall. "You haven't changed. I hate you."

He shook his head, denying her words, and sauntered to the door where he paused, his expression no longer mocking. "You wrong me, my lady. Stop using the past against me. This is a new beginning. Fate has bound us together."

Chapter Five

Lord Penruthin was grim-faced when he continued his survey of the castle. There was a dangerous crack in the battlements of the north wall. A leaking gutter had not been repaired for years. Water spilling from it had seeped into the wall of the harness-room, ruining a score of bridles and several saddles now rotted with mildew. The corn store was empty, although he was informed that the priory store was bulging with grain.

But it wasn't the neglect he saw which ground through him. Eloise had not deserved the rough treatment he had shown her. Her beauty and poise were from a world he had almost forgotten. He had remembered her only as a child, but her kiss today had been all woman.

A tortured look shadowed his eyes and his fists bunched at his side. He cursed the circumstances which had shaped the demons haunting him. The wolves were after his blood. Eloise was a complication he did not need.

Let her go! an honourable part of him mocked. A wife was never in your plans. Yet somehow the words rang hollow. He had never envisaged a wife the like of Eloise.

He threw back his head and laughed, disturbing the doves from their roost in the dovecote. Penruthin had yielded many disturbing surprises upon his return, not least the Lady Eloise.

"Your eyes consign me to the devil," Alaric chided as he entered Eloise's chamber to escort her to the hall for the evening banquet. "Do I displease you so much?"

He was being deliberately provocative. He had changed into a short doublet of peacock blue with matching hose, and across his broad shoulders lay a heavy gold chain which had belonged to his father. At its centre hung a gold lion—the same shape as that in the family coat of arms. The chain was something which Stephen had taken much pleasure in wearing. Alaric had evidently won another round of the conflict with his weakling brother. Eloise suspected that the colours had been deliberately chosen to remind his brother that the "Peacock of Penruthin" had returned.

Unease whispered in her mind. Both she and Stephen would do well to remember that those rich garments of courtly fashion were carried upon a frame of honed precision. Alaric was a master of arms whose prowess was legion, and a champion of the lists. Gone also was the plain sword belt replaced by one of gilt and enamel. It was an ornate piece of craftsmanship which had belonged to Alaric's grandfather. He cut an imposing and prepossessing figure and, to Eloise's consternation, she felt her emotions stir. Just being in the same room with him brought an iridescent glow to her body and made her pulse race.

It was then she noticed the short sword in the scabbard at his side. She frowned, her sharp gaze inspecting it more closely. The hilt was chased with a design of two fighting dragons—her own family crest—and the gold hilt was set with a single diamond the size of a gull's egg.

"You wear my father's sword," she accused. She resented that another, so important, token of her family's wealth had been appropriated without her permission. Lord Penruthin was no different from the prior.

"As is my right." He looked puzzled at her displeasure. "Was it not part of your dowry? And, from the look of the coffers and castle account rolls, there is little else that remains of it."

Eloise's eyes flashed dangerously. She had long suspected that most of the money from her dowry had been squandered, but this pilfering of her private possessions was too much.

"The sword is mine. It is for me to bestow upon my son, or upon a man who I deem worthy of its heritage. Must that right also be stolen from me?"

Beneath his bronzed complexion, Penruthin paled.

Tight-lipped, he unbuckled the sword and wordlessly handed it to her. She clasped it defiantly to her breast as he strode angrily to the door. "A common soldier's sword will serve me just as well."

Suddenly her actions appeared petty. He was right. The sword was part of her dowry. He had no sword of his own, for his and his father's had both been lost in France. Yet, obstinately, she did not want to see her father's sword worn by any man who had not earned the respect and devotion she had always held for her father. She placed the sword lovingly into a coffer, concealing it beneath her gowns.

When Penruthin returned moments later he wore the sword Githa had smuggled to him. "Our people await us in the hall for the banquet to begin, my lady." Frost coated his speech and was reflected in his glare. "Does my attire now meet with your approval?"

She nodded. Just when she expected him to continue his scathing attack, his mood veered. "With so much of your dowry stolen from you, I did not seek to add further insult. I was honoured to wear your father's sword. He was a noble soldier, as also was your brother who lost his life on the battlefield."

"I have been churlish," she answered softly. "My father's sword is very precious to me. Please wait here a moment. There is time before we are expected at the feast."

She hurried from the chamber to the store-room and was breathless when she returned to find Alaric pacing the chamber. His expression was thunderous. He had disliked the delay and she felt a moment's qualm that he would take amiss the gesture she was offering him. Holding her palms upwards, she displayed an identical sword to her father's, with the two dragons carved into its hilt. The diamond was missing in this one; in its place was an oval ivory carving of the Holy Grail.

"It is not fitting that the Lord of Penruthin wear a common soldier's sword," she said, her tone reconciling. "This sword was my brother's. He was heir to Whytemead, but never its master. It was only ever wielded in honour."

Their gazes met. Penruthin's was as usual unreadable. He had not missed the warning in her words. She did not accept him as master of Whytemead, or master of herself. To her surprise, there was no longer antagonism in his posture.

"It is a fine sword, and I shall wear it with pride."

He slid it into the scabbard and, reclaiming her hand, smiled. Her throat became oddly dry, and her heart palpitated as she held his unswerving gaze. His long tapering fingers were brown against the paleness of her skin. Their touch was cool and assured, against flesh which took fire beneath that subtle pressure. When he raised her hand to his lips, a curious tingling spread through her overheated body.

"I would never knowingly insult you." His gaze caressed her, the admiration in his eyes placating her earlier antagonism. "Your lovely eyes betray you, sweet Eloise. They hold such fire, such passion. I would not have them spark with rebellion. You cannot fight fate, dear lady. For seven years you have borne the name of Penruthin. It is what our fathers willed.''

How easy it would be to surrender to the lure of his charm. She resisted, although she was disturbed by the effort it needed. ''I am no longer a child to be ordered into submission,'' she replied with barbed sweetness as he led her from the room.

''I had no time for a child-bride, if you remember.'' The self-assurance of his smile this time did not anger her. It also held another intimate message, one so poignant that only a blind woman could have resisted. He added, smoothly, ''But now, you are a beautiful, passionate woman who is also courageous...'' He paused, his gaze shimmering in a way which made her heart pound even harder. ''This is our destiny, Eloise.''

She knew Alaric to be a womaniser; she had not expected him to be a romantic. No wonder women fell for his handsome looks and charm. They were irresistible when he so chose. She braced herself against them.

''I would make my own destiny,'' she informed him.

As Alaric and Eloise entered the Great Hall, she was dazzled by the brightness from the burning cressets and flaming torches set into the stone walls. Four

long trestle-tables ran the length of the hall, the
benches on each side crowded with retainers and villagers. At their entrance, speech was silenced as the
chamberlain banged his official staff on the flagstones, announcing, "Bid welcome to Lord and Lady
Penruthin. God bless them both!"

The cheering was deafening as Alaric led Eloise to
their places on the dais. Neither Stephen nor Isobel
was present. It boded ill for the future, but meant that
for tonight, at least, there would be no double-edged
confrontations with which to contend.

The meal was served with grand ceremony. The
pages paraded the steaming silver salvers along the
hall from the kitchen. Wine flowed freely and the
carefree laughter, so long missing from Penruthin,
echoed to the rafters. The sound brought a lump to
Eloise's throat. As was customary, Alaric shared the
same cup and plate with his wife. He had been surveying the hall as the pages filled their plate and she
saw him nod approval.

"Our own differences aside, my lord—" Eloise began, wanting to make amends for demanding the return of her father's sword "—the people are overjoyed at your return. They need you." She lifted the
large goblet they also shared and raised it to him.
"May Penruthin and its lord prosper. Welcome home,
my lord."

She sipped and passed the goblet to him. He took
it, his gaze locked with hers over the silver rim as he

pointedly turned the goblet so that his lips touched where hers had lingered.

"To Penruthin, and may its lady find peace and contentment here." His eyes sparkled like sunshine on crystal water and his voice was husky with intimacy. "A truce, dear lady. I may yet prove not to be the ogre you fear. Will you drink to a truce?"

The goblet was pressed towards her. As she took it, their hands brushed, and Eloise's breath caught in her throat at the searing thrill which resonated through her arm. The pulsing within was perceptible in her fingers, which shook as she carried the goblet to her lips. He was trying to beguile and manipulate her as he did all people. It was all false, all for Penruthin's self-interest; he did not care for her as a woman. He must realise that his estate would be in debt for years if he were forced to repay her dowry…

…Yet, when he continued to look at her in a way which intimated that she was the only woman of any importance to him, she was reminded of the kisses which had robbed her of reason and revealed a world of forbidden pleasure. She knew his faults and should hate him. Perhaps it was a glimpse behind the mask to another face which so affected her. With tenderness softening the austere lines of his countenance, she was reminded of Roland. The same look, the same expression had been in his eyes on her wedding day when she had been so unhappy. Roland had understood her suffering, because he knew the pain of rejection by others. So many questions needed answers.

But the time was not right for them; tonight was for celebration not reflecting upon unhappy memories.

The minstrels were playing in the galley above them. Penruthin took the goblet from her trembling fingers and smiled. "Let us show our people that we are united. Come dance, Eloise. Tonight is for merriment and celebration."

She was tempted to deny him. But already his hand was upon hers, drawing her up. She resented the ease with which he had manoeuvred her and was about to protest, despite the curious eyes upon them. Then she saw Isobel enter the hall. Her low-cut gown had been dampened so that the saffron silk clung to every contour of her figure. Eloise was conscious that one or two of the guards were watching her speculatively. It brought an ache to her throat. Barrack-room gossip would have gloried in dragging up the liaison between Alaric and Isobel. So the guards had not been entirely won over: loyalty and respect were not won in a day. These mercenaries paid tribute only to silver. Had they been bribed again?

Anxiously, she scanned the hall, not seeing the drunken revelry, or the shadows thrown up by the torches. Tension had returned to the gathering. Her own thoughts were in disarray. Roland's face was clear before her mind and would not be banished. Roland, whom she knew to be capable of the tenderness Penruthin had shown her this day; not Alaric.

She twisted her head to regard him. A muscle had throbbed along his angular cheek at Isobel's entrance.

There had been dislike in his stare. Had not Roland despised Isobel for her wantonness? When Penruthin's gaze shifted to hold hers, it bored into her eyes, calculating her reaction.

Cold eyes, commanding obedience. Alaric's eyes...

All her confusions and suspicions about his true identity were resurrected. Foreboding speared her and she could not suppress a shiver. They had gone too far to turn back now. But what if she too had been duped and this man *was* Roland...?

She cut off the thought. Better that Roland had returned than that the prior kept his greedy hands on Penruthin land. Her troubled reasoning filled her with dread. She could not forget that the prior's spies were everywhere; watching, awaiting the slightest slip. Panic momentarily assailed her. If the man at her side were indeed Roland, the feelings he could arouse in her were doubly misplaced. For the sake of the honour of her family, she must never surrender to the seductive spell he could cast upon her. But, whichever son of Lord Edgar had returned, he was the only one who could save the people from the misery of the estate's neglect.

"Eloise—the dance." Penruthin's fingers tightened upon her elbow, reminding her of the part she must for the moment play. Her suspicions must be answered. At the first opportunity she would question him and insist on the truth.

Reluctantly, she permitted him to lead her on to the

floor where a space had been cleared for the dancing. The moment he took her hand and bowed to her, she knew the stately procession of steps would be torture as she was turned beneath his arm. Every eye in the room was upon them as they twisted and turned in time to the slow beat of the music.

"You dance with the grace of an angel, and rival them with your beauty." Penruthin had eyes for no one but her.

Treacherously her heartbeat quickened. She did not trust him when he was at his most charming. Glibly she turned his compliments aside, willing the dance to end. His nearness pervaded her senses. His deep coercing voice bathed her in compliments, and his wit roused her to merry laughter until she felt herself succumbing. A glare from Isobel filled her with triumph. She was furious at the attention Penruthin was showing to his wife.

As the dance continued, Eloise became aware of subtle changes in the mood within the hall. At first she thought that the growing tension she sensed stemmed from her own need to counteract Penruthin's charm. Her nerves were strained from playing the role of a devoted wife, but gradually she realised that her apprehension went deeper than that.

A party of strangers dressed like merchants sat at the middle table. That was not unusual, for Penruthin was known for its hospitality to travellers. But these men glanced furtively about them as they leaned over the table to address a villager. Several of the villagers themselves now seemed uneasy. Men-at-arms, earlier won over by Penruthin, now appeared belligerent as they downed cup after horn cup of ale.

From the alertness of his gaze, Eloise realised Alaric had also noticed the changing atmosphere. He stopped dancing and, still holding Eloise's hand, called out to the minstrels.

"Enough of such courtly grandeur. Strike up the country dances for all my people to enjoy."

His hand slid around Eloise's waist as he spun her round in a reel, the floor quickly filling with dancers. Most of the villagers and servants were relaxed and enjoying themselves, but occasionally Eloise's heart clenched as she noticed the merchants moving amongst the people. Too often for her comfort, watching eyes slid away from her gaze. Distrust was growing and with it danger.

Several times Penruthin squeezed her hand in the dance, reassuring her. It warned her of a greater threat which was becoming harder to ignore with every hour in his company. His touch made her acutely aware of herself as a woman. She needed her wits to remain clear so that she might combat any treachery from the prior or Sir Stephen. But now she suspected that the greater treachery lay within her own confused feelings. No matter how she counselled herself to guard against this man who claimed to be her husband, his touch was enough to set her blood on fire.

Throughout the dancing he continued to praise her accomplishments, grace and beauty. Eloise told herself they were the compliments of a practised womaniser with no purpose other than to charm her. Why, then, did her heart respond with frantic leaping, and her body burn to be held in an ardent embrace? Was this not the tender lover she had yearned for, who would one day claim her as his bride? Tonight she could not fault Penruthin's manner towards her. His smile was tender whenever he addressed her, showing all present the regard in which he held her. It was a far cry from the humiliation of the wedding banquet; but then, on that occasion, he did not have so much at stake.

Unused as she was to flirtation, she accepted his compliments with grace, knowing that outwardly they must appear a loving couple. They were players in an elaborate masque of deception.

The strain built to an intolerable level. The smile was nailed upon Eloise's face, and she was aware of the tension coiled like a snake about to strike within Penruthin's body.

"I had better dance with Isobel," he announced as their fourth dance together finished. "There is no point in antagonising her."

Eloise crushed a slither of jealousy. She knew he was right. "I will greet the merchants who have partaken of our hospitality. They seem to be upsetting the villagers with their talk."

"Take care," he whispered grimly. "They could be the prior's men hired to spread rumours."

His consideration prompted her to remark, unwittingly testing him, "Isobel could be your undoing. As your mistress, she knows more about you than I do. I always thought it strange how she hated Roland with a passion. That was until Githa told me he had resisted her seduction."

The skin was stretched taut across Penruthin's lean cheekbones. Was it guilt at perpetrating a deception? She saw dark smudges under his eyes. Remorse smote her. How could she have forgotten that it was his first day from his sick bed? He had not spared himself since early morning; no wonder he looked tired and strained.

His expression resumed the guardedness she distrusted. "Aye; Roland, had he survived, would have found no welcome homecoming at Penruthin," he answered gruffly. "Isobel's evil mischief would have ensured that. He was always the outcast."

"May his soul rest in peace," Eloise answered, still searching his face.

It revealed nothing.

She left him to find the merchants. "You look worried, Lady Eloise," Captain Maddock said, appearing at her side as she again scanned the hall for some sight of them.

"There were merchants at the feast. I no longer see them. I would have bidden them welcome to Penruthin."

"They arrived at dusk, my lady. They disdained to bed down with the men-at-arms in the hall, and declared they would prefer the peace of the priory. I've not heard the portcullis raised for them to cross the drawbridge to the priory. Would you have me summon them?''

''No.'' She studied the battle-scarred face and wondered how much she could trust him. She had to trust someone. ''They seemed to be speaking with the people and servants in a way which disturbed them. One must always guard against dissenters.'' She deliberately kept the subject upon general unrest, not specific to Penruthin. ''Wat Tyler's peasants' revolt last century is a lesson we should remember.''

''They were asking a lot of questions about his lordship's return,'' Maddock replied. ''It's bound to cause interest.''

Chill tentacles of alarm wrapped around Eloise's spine. Leaving the captain, she circled the hall, stopping to speak with those still sober enough to listen. From their comments she learned that Penruthin had spent most of the day inspecting the castle and had ordered work to begin on repairs tomorrow. He did not waste any time. Noting that one or two villagers melted into the crowd before she could speak with them, her unease grew.

Seeing that Penruthin and Isobel were not dancing, but that they stood talking close together, another stab of jealousy attacked her. Isobel's face was adoring as she gazed up at him. Her desire for him was blatant in the possessive touch of her hand on his arm, and the way she swayed against him, so that her breasts rubbed against his elbow or chest. Penruthin's back was to Eloise so she could not see his expression. From the inviting smile on Isobel's lips he was obviously not discouraging the woman's attentions.

Eloise stiffened, angry with herself that it should trouble her. But it *did*. The pain was like a spearthrust, cold steel tearing into her slashed flesh. Her knuckles showed white as she balled her fist over the ache ripping through her heart. It was her own fault; she should have known that he would not change.

The smell of sweating bodies, the vomit from drunken soldiers doubled over in the clean rushes, the cloying smoke from the torches and oil cressets, was oppressive. Eloise needed fresh air, a moment alone to assess the events of this night and its possible repercussions. She no longer felt in control. Having taken Penruthin's side, it was like a stone thrown into the still waters of a lake, the ripples spreading out in a widening circle. Nothing could stop its motion or the consequences.

Her hurried passage to the door was barred by the broad figure of the blacksmith.

"You wish to speak with me?" she gave him permission to address her.

"There's rumour being spread that 'tis not Sir Alaric who has returned." The blacksmith's brown eyes insolently held her gaze. "'Tis said he's Roland, the bastard. There's not a villager here who does not rejoice that the prior's hold over us will be curbed. But..." He paused, hesitating to continue, and his gaze slid to the scuffed toe of his boot. "The people are restless, my lady. Roland was always the most popular son of Sir Edgar. Bastard or not, he's still our lord's son. If Sir Alaric is…''

Eloise stopped him before he was indiscreet. ''Roland could never have inherited Penruthin. If Alaric is dead, then the title and property goes to Sir Stephen as the younger legitimate son. However, if Stephen were to die without an heir—and he has been six years wed without signs of one—it was agreed between my father and Lord Penruthin's father that I would inherit Penruthin so that the lands of Penruthin and Whytemead remained jointed.'' She studied him closely to ensure that he had understood her words, then added meaningfully, ''But, since *Sir Alaric* has returned, there is no question of Penruthin belonging to anyone but him.''

As she was speaking the blacksmith was shifting uncomfortably and looking over her shoulder. A faint smell of sandalwood reached her, warning her that Penruthin was close by. She turned and saw him standing directly behind her. How much had he heard? As usual his expression revealed nothing of his thoughts.

''My lady, the hour grows late.''

She saw the pallor in his face and nodded. Tonight she still had a role to play. Placing her hand over his, she allowed him to escort her from the hall. Isobel was nowhere in sight. Many of the servants and villagers had fallen asleep where they sat, either slumped on the floor, or with their heads on their arms where they rested on the table. Several couples were sauntering from the room with their arms linked. They would be lovers this night, if they were not already. It showed her the emptiness of her life, the hollowness of a virgin bride.

Penruthin halted outside her door. She tensed, not knowing what to expect.

"Goodnight, Eloise; pleasant dreams." So saying, he raised her fingers to his lips and with an enigmatic smile left her.

Before she turned into her own room, she saw Captain Maddock take his position on guard in the corridor. Three other men-at-arms were preparing to sleep rolled in their cloaks on the floor, each positioned within their captain's call should an alarm be raised.

Upon entering her room, the void, which she had felt watching the departing lovers in the hall, expanded. Her large bed looked lonely and unwelcoming. She pressed a finger to her throbbing temple and sat on her dressing-stool for Winifred to remove her hennin headdress. Her fingers massaged the indent the stiff fabric had made along her hairline and she sighed. She should be relieved that Penruthin had not attempted to force his attentions upon her. Why, then, did her eyes prickle with unshed tears and should she feel more lonely than she had done in her life?

The next morning Eloise was roused by the sound of harsh men's voices and the alarming ring of dozens of swords clashing in combat. Thrusting aside the bedcovers, she ran to the window, fearful at what scene of battle she might discover. The courtyard was filled with fighting men. Penruthin was amongst them, his sword flashing in the early morning sunlight as he pressed home his attack and beat back his opponent. The guards were fighting each other, with deadly intent. They had turned upon Penruthin and his few loyal supporters.

Frozen to the spot with horror, she could only stare helplessly. Then slowly it dawned on her that although the men were fighting with a ferocity which chilled her to the bone, any lethal strike was halted before it entered an opponent's body.

She exhaled with relief. She had forgotten that Penruthin had ordered the men-at-arms to begin their training this morning. With her hair loose about her shoulders, she stood at the window watching. Penruthin was pushing himself hard. His skill, even slowed by lack of practice, outmatched any guard who came up against him. Her attention was held spellbound by his tall, lithe figure, pride swelling within her as she recognised the dexterity and prowess of his swordplay. He was dressed in black hose and a tan leather jerkin, the full sleeves of his creamy white shirt rolled back past his elbows to reveal his sun-bronzed arms. Her throat dried as she watched him. Even dressed simply, he was the most imposing figure amongst the fighting men.

With a flick of his wrist he disarmed his opponent,

the sword arcing through the air to thud into the ground several feet away. Wiping his brow, he stood back, waiting for the man to retrieve his weapon. The breeze lifted her unbound hair and snaked tendrils of its ebony tresses across her cheek. She held it back with her hand and, as though sensing her presence, Alaric looked up at the window. He lifted his sword in salute and several of the men nearest to him turned to see who he was acknowledging.

"Our lord would have spared us aching limbs on the morrow, if he had stayed in the warmth of his wife's bed." The ribald comment carried to Eloise.

Penruthin grinned, but she did not catch his reply. With his gaze still upon her window, he put a hand over his heart and bowed to her. The gallant gesture made her catch her breath. With difficulty she forced herself to remember that before his men he was playing a role—that husband and wife were united upon his return. Then, with a sharp twist to one side, he rapped a chatting soldier across the buttocks with his sword. "I did not give you leave to rest. Any diversion which distracts you on the battlefield could cost you your life."

That he had allowed his own training to be diverted brought a warm glow to her body. It was impossible to stop his actions affecting her. The moments when he showed her tenderness and concern revealed a tantalising world of what her marriage to him might have been—or could be. She wrapped her arms around herself and savoured the thought. It was tempting to believe that his tenderness was sincere.

With a start she mentally shook herself, upbraiding herself out loud. "Heavens, Eloise, you are acting as lovesick as a moon-calf. Penruthin is a womaniser. He is charming you to gain his own ends. If you begin to trust him, to believe in him, you will be lost."

Belatedly aware that she was still wearing only her chemise, she rang a hand bell to summon Winifred. When her maid appeared half dressed and with her wimple all askew, Eloise tutted.

"It's unlike you to oversleep, Winifred."

"Oversleep, my lady? The morning Angelus bell has barely stilled its ringing. Few servants have stirred from their drunken slumbers. His lordship was up with the dawn and bellowing for the guards to assemble." She put a hand over her mouth to cover a yawn. "I hadn't expected you to rise for another hour, my lady."

Eloise was startled at the earliness of the hour. It must be years since Penruthin had wielded a sword in anger. He was eager to waste no time in improving the performances of both himself and his men. Or was it something more sinister? The fear that his sword-skills might soon be challenged? She shivered. She did not trust the ease with which the prior had accepted Alaric's return. The wily fox was playing for time.

Chapter Six

All morning Eloise occupied herself with overseeing the running of the household. With Stephen no longer controlling the accounts, she summoned Thomas Hampden, the steward, and demanded to know how much of her dowry was left.

He scratched his bald head and looked nervous. His fifty-four years sat ill upon him, his face heavily lined with worry and his eyes sunken. He had served Alaric's father for a score of years before they left for France. "I told his lordship yesterday, there is no money in the coffers. There has not been for over a year, my lady."

Staring at his short, wiry figure, Eloise felt nausea rising in her stomach. Without her dowry, she was penniless. If her marriage to Penruthin was annulled, no other landed knight would take her without a dowry. Her old home at Whytemead Castle was a ruin and needed a fortune spent upon it to make it habitable. If she demanded the return of her dowry, where would Penruthin get the money? He would insist they remained wed. That would ensure there was one less debtor hounding him to settle impossible debts.

The steward was still talking and her attention was suddenly caught. "Sir Stephen's last visit to Court was on money borrowed from the Lombards. The interest is due. We'll have to sell the grain to pay for it."

"We cannot sell the grain; the people will starve," Eloise asserted. The situation was far worse than she had envisaged. "I knew my dowry was being squandered, but I never realised there was no money left."

Thomas Hampden shifted uncomfortably, unable to meet her gaze. "There's always been debts, but never the like of this. Thank God that Lord Penruthin has returned. He has ordered that Sir Stephen and the Lady Isobel sell some of their jewels. He declared that the debt is not the responsibility of the estate since it was incurred for their self-aggrandisement." Thomas's eyes gleamed at the memory. "Sir Alaric was furious. For a moment, I thought he'd take a whip to his brother. His lordship always had the devil's own temper and was overfond of the whip. But he merely gave his brother that withering stare of his."

The steward's wide brow creased like a bloodhound's as he shook his head, his voice heavy with worry. "Sir Stephen turned nasty then. Things he said don't bear repeating, but he did keep going on about how Sir Alaric was a fine one to talk of the money being used for self-aggrandisement. Hadn't he been forced to wed to clear the debts he'd run up at the London tailors?'' Thomas Hampden blanched, too late recalling to whom he was speaking. ''No disrespect to you, my lady. It were what Sir Stephen said.''

Eloise took no offence. ''I am aware of the reasons why Sir Alaric married me. Thank you for your honesty.''

She felt her marriage had become a cage with its door slammed forever shut. Yet her fears for her future were outweighed by those of the present. There was no money to pay the guards. How long would Penruthin keep their loyalty if the prior again dangled a purse of silver before them? One week—two? The prior would not waste time. He dare not. Few people knew of Penruthin's return. If the guards turned against him again, he could be overpowered and killed. How safe would her own life be then?

Panic gripped her. The prior dare not let her live; she would have to be silenced. Ignatius would then concoct some story to satisfy the King and Court. In that moment she knew that whatever the outcome, her life was irretrievably bound to the man who professed to be Alaric of Penruthin. It did not lessen her guard against him; on the contrary, it strengthened it.

For the moment her resentment was turned upon the cause of her dilemma. She paced the tiny room high in the gatehouse. ''It is an outrage that the Penruthin coffers are empty and yet the priory is full of riches,'' Eloise raged. ''Riches bought with my father's gold.''

The steward twisted his age-freckled hands, his voice fragmented. "I was powerless to stop Sir Stephen using your money. The prior accused me of heresy when I explained it was not for the use of the Church."

"At least you tried. I do not blame you, Thomas."

He shook his head. "I should have done more. You were so young and defenceless. But it was the winter after the first heretics were burned. I was terrified. I'm a clerk, not a brave man or a warrior. I could not bear the thought of being burnt alive. I kept quiet after that."

"You were right to fear the prior," she comforted, knowing that he'd had no choice. "Your family would have been turned out and homeless if you were accused of heresy, or even dismissed out of spite. If you had not followed the prior's orders, he would have found someone who did."

The old man's eyes glistened and his throat worked furiously as he struggled to overcome his emotion. "You have a generous heart, my lady."

She waved a hand dismissing his compliment. "So what are we to do to make amends, Thomas?"

"At least his lordship has lost his spendthrift ways," he added more hopefully. "Yesterday he demanded that the priory accounts be shown to him. The prior refused. Prior Ignatius left the priory soon after that with just two guards. The prior will waste no time in gaining the ear of his cousin at Court."

Eloise felt her nausea returning at the news of the

prior's departure. Why had Penruthin not informed her? It was a ten-day ride to Court. If the King remained stricken with his madness, how many friends could Penruthin rely upon to support his cause? Seven years away from Court meant old ties could conveniently be forgotten. Many courtiers were too self-seeking for their own interests to worry about another's downfall.

Her temper simmered. Penruthin was treating her the same as Stephen, discounting her position. She would not be ignored. She had a right to be consulted. Wasn't it her life that was in danger as well?

"Damn Penruthin's arrogance," she muttered as she left the Master of Rolls' room and went to the courtyard to demand Penruthin speak with her. There had been no let up in the men-at-arms' training and it was now past noon. Some of the soldiers were leaning on their swords, their faces slick with sweat and their lungs labouring for breath. Penruthin was not in the courtyard and she was informed by a page that he was inspecting the horses in the stables. Without pausing Eloise crossed the uneven flagstones of the Inner Bailey to the stables.

"There's not a decent horse amongst the lot of them." Penruthin's strident tone was unleashed on the head groom. "My brother calls himself a knight, yet where are his destriers, his hunters? That pretty Arab gelding is a woman's horse, not a man's. Two destrier colts were ready for training when I left here. They'd be invaluable now. Where are they?"

"They were sold." The head groom answered. "As were the hunters. Sir Stephen don't care for the rigours of the hunt. Says he has gamekeepers to keep his larder stocked."

Penruthin swore roundly. "No wonder the estate is in such dire straits when its guardian is a milk-sop too self-indulgent even to hunt. Leave at once for the horse fairs. I need two decent destriers and a gelding that will not put the name of horseflesh to shame."

"How are we to pay?"

"Pay?" Penruthin snapped. "I'm not a peasant! The breeder will send me his account."

The head groom coughed. "There's not a merchant who will do business with us unless the goods are paid for on purchase. Sir Stephen owes everyone for miles."

"Devil take Stephen! I will not add to our debts," he ground out, his fury barely suppressed in his gruff tone. "Send a page to fetch my father's gold chain from my room. That should pay for the horses."

Eloise knew better than to question the expenditure on horses as the head groom scurried past to obey his lord's command. If the prior had gone to London, it was likely that Penruthin would be summoned and questioned. The prior wanted to prove that he was an impostor. Penruthin's main defence was his prowess as a knight. It was not unknown for a dispute to be settled on the tourney field as Penruthin had earlier threatened. For that he needed a trained destrier and they were even more expensive than a suit of the finest German armour.

Eloise stepped forward. Penruthin stood, hands on hips, staring unseeing at a damp patch on the stable wall. His tall frame was taut, his fury leashed and as tightly sprung as a war-catapault about to be fired. His hands flexed over his sword hilt, the tendons standing out in his sun-browned arms. He had survived the Moors' captivity only to return to England and face ruin. The tilt of his head was proud and Eloise was drawn to place a comforting hand on his shoulder. She resisted. He had shown by ignoring her position here that he did not need her counsel or her comfort.

Hearing the rustle of straw beneath her feet, he spun round to see who disturbed him. His expression scarcely softened upon recognising her. His mind was still far away on the thoughts which troubled him.

"My lord, there is much which needs your attention, but I must speak with you in private."

"Leave us," Penruthin ordered another groom, who was mucking out the dirty straw with a pitchfork, "and make sure no one enters the stable whilst the Lady Eloise is here."

She bristled. "I do not conduct conversations in stables."

He eyed her stonily. "We are alone here, Eloise. Outside or in the castle we are spied upon." He turned aside and checked the girth of a mare which had just been saddled. "I'm about to ride around the castle walls to assess the repairs needed. We can talk tonight before we dine; I'll come to your room.''

The curt dismissal roused her antagonism. ''I'm not here to discuss pleasantries. I've just come from the Master of Rolls. I've seen the accounts and I learned that the prior set out for London yesterday. That's why you're inspecting the battlements. Do you fear a siege? Why was I not told?'' So fierce was her anger that she began to shake.

Penruthin frowned. ''I wanted to spare you the worry. I doubt even our greedy prior will risk a siege. His methods are more underhand. There's no need for you to be concerned; everything is being dealt with.''

He was evading the issue. Her temper soared out of control. Without considering her actions, she struck out at him. ''As everything was dealt with before you arrived. Over my head. Haven't I been humiliated enough?'' Her fists slammed into his chest, the years of frustration and having her orders countermanded driving her beyond reason. ''My money was good enough to provide your family with lavish entertainments and jewels. I'm just an inconvenience who has to be tolerated. I will *not* be discounted in this way. I am Mistress of Penruthin. I deserve the respect of being consulted on matters which concern my own welfare.''

Her wrists were caught and held firmly against his chest. ''Eloise, I meant no insult. Truly, my intent was to spare you worry.''

She was breathing heavily, her eyes blazing with

condemnation. "When will you stop treating me like a child? I *hate* your arrogance. I'm fearful that the prior will carry out his threats. He's a vindictive, sly toad, who's just realised he could lose all the wealth he has amassed by being brought to account for his infamy." She punctuated each sentence by a struggle to be free from his hold. "But what of you? The enemy within…a stranger to me. A man who holds my life in his hands."

"Eloise, I am not your enemy." Exasperation hoarsened his voice.

"Are you not?" she continued, undeterred. "You've shown yourself to be no ally—just another tyrant." She paused in her struggles to glare up at him. "Clearly, I am now so unimportant to you that I can be discounted," she went on. "My family's wealth is all gone. Why trouble yourself with a pauper, even if your family made me one?"

She was wriggling and struggling like a wildcat in his hold. Incensed at being unable to strike him with her hands, she lashed out with her feet and felt a satisfying moment of triumph when her heel grazed down the length of his shin. He winced, but his hold did not loosen.

His grey eyes glittered with an icy light. "Cursed vixen," he growled. "Damn you, keep still."

In answer she kicked him a second time. All at once she was lifted off her feet. His arms circled her like steel clamps as she continued to writhe in his arms.

"Put me down. How dare you? Put me down!"

Her face was on a level with his and her furious glare matched the brittle glint in his eyes. "I'll not put you down until you stop fighting me. I'm not your enemy, Eloise. And I did not mean to offend you."

There was no contrition in his voice; she heard only the arrogance. It was like a torch to tinder. She fought harder. Every twist and turn crushed her body closer to his iron frame. Her breasts throbbed where they were pressed hard against his torso. But she was too angry to stop. Arching her back, she was determined to free her hand and slap the haughtiness from his face.

Anger gave her greater strength. When she reared back he was caught off balance. Relentlessly, she squirmed and kicked even as she became aware that they were falling. Moments before they crashed down onto the soft straw, he twisted so that his body cushioned her fall and his weight did not land on her slender form.

Before Eloise had time to draw breath and take advantage of a position which could make her escape easier, he rolled her beneath him. Her wrists were clamped down on to the straw above her head, and his thighs straddled her hips.

"By the rood, you're a hellcat!"

"Get off me!" she responded, her eyes blazing.

The touch of a woman pressed so intimately against his body brought the expected response from Penruthin. His loins ached to possess her. It was torture to hold back as he was struck afresh by her beauty. His gaze lingered appreciatively on the firm swell of her breasts, rising and falling in her anger. Today she wore a dress and matching low hennin headdress of palest primrose. It accentuated the creamy texture of her perfect skin, giving her an angelic beauty. Except there was nothing angelic about the fiery sparking in her sapphire eyes. They were those of a woman of passion.

His ache for her intensified and he gave a sharp gasp to control his breathing. She was also innocent. In the past he had mocked the code of chivalry, playing upon it to suit his whims, for women fell for gallantry. Those beautiful women had fired his blood, but never touched his heart. They had sensed his aloofness and had responded more ardently, seeking to entrap him into something he could not feel. He had wanted no emotional ties. That was before he had returned to Penruthin.

A hunger had risen in him, growing with each day to see the castle and lands restored to their former glory. The people's welcome had moved him deeply, but not so much as the moment he had set eyes upon Eloise. He had seen her doubts, the suspicions shading her lovely eyes and brow. Yet she had defended him. It had roused an unaccustomed protectiveness within him.

He had judged it nothing more than that, but now the heady scent of her fresh perfumed body wafted over him. The slender column of her neck, with a tantalising pulse throbbing at its sensitive hollow, was temptingly close. He resisted the impulse to kiss that beckoning pulse.

The strain of curbing his desire spurred him to taunt her, "Should not a wife obey her lord's will?"

"If she is indeed his wife."

She defied him with a stubbornness which roused his need to tame her. "You deny the inevitable, Eloise, which was proved when I kissed you the other morning."

A light flared in her eyes which was then deliberately doused. "You may tumble your whore in the stable straw, but not me."

The heat of her body contoured to his flesh was almost his undoing. He wanted her but she was proud, and pride was always dangerous when crossed. Any victory he won over her today would be a hollow one. The passionate side of her nature would resent his dominance and lead to hatred. To force his will upon her now would taint something that was becoming very precious to him, whereas to withhold, and to win by subtle seduction and persuasion, would be a triumph and joy to savour.

The throbbing in his loins and the ache to possess her made him deliberately provocative and he could not resist plaguing her. "Then you would be the loser, for you will never know the pleasure of unrestrained lovemaking where two people meet as equals."

He grinned at seeing the blush spread up from her neck to heat her cheeks. Then he rolled off her quickly before his restraint shattered, his features deliberately masked as he reached for her hand to assist her to rise. ''I've battles enough ahead, without making an enemy of you, Eloise. I had hoped for a truce.''

She was drawn up to stand close to him, her hand held fast. Suspicion showed in her eyes and he regretted his rough treatment.

''Our fate is bound together *for the moment*,'' she emphasised coolly.

''What fate binds it is often loath to part.'' There was a softer note to his voice she had not heard before.

She regarded him sideways, her breathing finally steadying. He was looking at her in that provoking and admiring way which made her knees have no strength to support her. It would be all too easy to yield to the promise in his eyes, but she was made of sterner fibre, and she kept her voice cold. ''I did not seek you out to parry words, sir. I expect you to honour your promise and not molest me.''

The woman provoked too far. He grinned wickedly. ''Is this molesting you?'' He stroked her cheek with the back of his hand, his fingers working along her neck, making lazy circles with his thumb. At her sharp intake of breath, he was relentless. ''Or this?''

He bent his head, his breath fanning her cheek as he lightly took her ear lobe into his mouth.

Her involuntary gasp of pleasure made him straighten, his gaze merciless as it pitted hers.

"Choose your words carefully when you challenge me, Eloise. I have never failed to pick up a gauntlet."

She veered backwards, her flushed cheeks and erratic breathing telling him that she was fighting her growing attraction to him and the emotions he aroused. "I want to know the truth of what has happened to you since you rode out of Penruthin seven years ago," she demanded. "There's enough lies and deception surrounding us. It is time we were honest with each other."

Dark lashes shielded his eyes as he plucked a piece of straw from her veil before he answered. "Honesty stems from within, Lady Eloise. You have been denying what is between us."

Voices outside told of Stephen approaching. He quickly brushed several pieces of straw from her clothing and felt the quivering in her body his touch evoked. "We will talk later. Though you may not like all that you hear."

"What is it you would know about my absence?" Penruthin slanted a look across at Eloise as he stood in the window embrasure, one leg lifted to rest on the cushioned seat.

Eloise was seated by her sewing-frame. She could not see his expression, as his face was in shadow. Putting aside her silks, she stood up and moved to the window. Now as she looked up into his handsome face she could see him clearly. She would know if he was telling the truth.

"I learned that after your father's death you went on pilgrimage with your brother. How were you captured by the Moors?"

"We were overrun on the road. A pilgrim's staff is little defence against forty scimitars. The only reason we were not killed was that they were looking for slaves to man their warships. What happened to us in those years is something I want to forget."

Having learned from her father something of the horrors the oarsmen suffered on those hell-ships, she was loath to pursue the subject, but she had to discover more about him. She had to allay the suspicions which were nagging at her mind. "After your capture, were you and your brother kept together?"

"Yes." His reluctance to speak was obvious from the heaviness of his tone. "They could see the antagonism between us. It was still strong then. They took delight in chaining us together, knowing it would be an added torture for us to endure. To cut a long story short, we eventually escaped when the ship was rammed during a battle. Usually in such cases the slaves drown as they remain manacled to their oars. It was always in our minds to find a means to escape. It was what began to unite us."

He paused, his face dark and forbidding as the memories carved bitter lines around his mouth and eyes.

"So how did you escape?" she prompted.

Before answering, he began to pace the chamber. "There'd never been favourable circumstances be-

fore. We were chained and guarded all the time. Roland found an iron nail on one of the few occasions
they allowed us on deck. The lock securing the
slaves' chains was behind his oar. It was not often
that our guards shirked their vigilance. If they did,
Roland would practise picking the lock.''

His pacing halted and he stared at the silver crucifix
on the wall, his voice grating with remembered pain.
''It took him months to learn the skill. Then we had
to await our chance. There were times I thought we'd
die before there was an opportunity to snatch our freedom.''

''It is a mark of your courage that you survived for
so long,'' Eloise responded, moved by the images
conjured of his ordeal.

He shrugged, discounting her praise as he resumed
his pacing. She noted that he was never still for long.
The restlessness and constant motion was a legacy
from his long confinement; freedom of movement
was as vital to him as breathing.

''Many slaves die within a few months,'' he said
bleakly. ''Strangely, it was our enmity which kept the
two of us alive. Even then we were rivals. We goaded
each other. We were both determined to prove ourselves the better man by surviving longer than the
other. Gradually, over the years, the rivalry changed.
Slavery is a great leveller. It forms bonds between the
most unlikely companions.''

''Your father will rest in peace knowing that you
had overcome your differences,'' Eloise observed,

hoping to give him comfort. Her tender heart ached to learn that the two brothers had suffered so much. "It was always a cause of great unhappiness for him."

He stared at her for a long moment in silence. Then he lifted his gaze to the window, taking in the activity within the Inner Bailey. "Talking about Penruthin kept us sane. Neither of us could stand Stephen and we knew that in his hands Penruthin would suffer. It was not until after the escape and my brother lay wounded, that I realised my hatred had turned to respect."

He paused, his eyes glazing. The tension in his figure told her he was remembering his captivity. Finally, he said, "I owe my brother my life. When the ship was rammed, we were fortunate to be on the far side of the gaping hole. It gave us a few precious extra seconds. Roland picked the lock. But, as we ran the end of the heavy chain out of the menacles about our ankles, a beam supporting the upper deck fell across my brother's leg. There is always confusion at such times. The guards are too intent upon saving their own lives. The slaves are abandoned. Even then we knew our chances were slim. A rammed ship can go down in seconds and we were weak from poor food and constant beatings."

Eloise shuddered at the pictures he painted. It made the humiliation she had endured at Penruthin seem petty in comparison. Only an exceptional man could have survived such adversity. His closeness had always affected her profoundly, but its effect on her now was stronger. His courage pulled at her heartstrings in a way that his handsome looks and masculinity never could.

He placed a foot on the window-seat and leaned forward, an elbow resting on his upraised knee. His fist clenched, the knuckles showing white through his browned skin. His voice was gruff, clearly finding it difficult to speak of such agonising memories as he continued: "Together we managed to haul the beam aside. The ship was fast filling with water. I could see he was in pain and unable to put any weight on his injured leg. I managed to drag him out of the bowels of the ship and over the side."

Abruptly he whirled away from the window. "We even managed to steal two swords from dead bodies and thrust them into our belts. The battle was still raging all around us. We'd engaged a Spanish galleon and they were bombarding the water with cannon shot."

Eloise inhaled sharply, her anguish showing on her face as she pictured the horrors they had endured. Without realising it, she had reached out to take his hand as his striding brought him close to her. No words seemed adequate to convey the compassion and admiration she felt for him. It overwhelmed her, shining in her tear-streaked eyes.

Alaric's expression softened as he stared down at her. He swallowed several times to control his painful emotions before continuing his story. "Fortunately we could both swim and there was a strong current which bore us away from the wreckage. There was land in the distance. Three hours later, exhausted, we collapsed on a beach. It was then I saw his injury. His leg was blackened and swollen like an inflated pig's bladder. It was broken in three places.''

He rubbed his free hand across his jaw and beneath her fingers clasping his other hand, Eloise felt his tension mounting.

"I fashioned a splint out of driftwood, though I knew it would be useless. One of the bones was sticking through the flesh. If his leg was not amputated, he'd die of gangrene. I've seen it happen so often after a battle.''

He turned away, but not before Eloise had glimpsed the anguished glitter in his eyes. "He would not hear of it. Perversely he argued that he'd rather go to his Maker whole and what use was a one-legged knight? He knew his injury was his death sentence.''

"I know it is not easy for you to speak of this," she said softly. "I appreciate that you are telling me.''

"It is important that you of all people understand," he ground out.

"Did he suffer for long?" she asked softly.

His eyes were tormented. He was a man looking into the deepest pits of hell. He drew a harsh breath and swallowed before continuing. "Even if he could have been treated, it would have been weeks before he'd have been strong enough to travel. We did not know if we were in enemy or friendly lands. We dared trust no one to help us. He ordered me to leave him. Said he'd not return to Penruthin to be a burden to anyone.''

Eloise felt her cheeks dampen with tears. He seemed to be dragging his voice up from his boots.

It cracked as he continued, ''We were still arguing when we saw a ship anchor offshore. When the long-boat approached the beach, their black robes and turbans showed us that they were Moors. Our ragged appearance declared us escaped slaves and they would kill us.''

The tendons in his bronzed neck corded and his fingers curled around hers, iron-hard with tension. ''He sacrificed his life so that I stood a chance of survival. They would question him before they killed him and he would say that he had escaped alone. He reminded me of Penruthin and the fate which would befall it under Stephen's weak rule if I did not return. He made me swear upon our father's memory that I would go and not attempt to try and save him.''

He blinked rapidly, his eyes overbright. ''I ran to the safety of headland rocks where I could hide until nightfall. Whilst I waited I heard his scream. He'd held out for an hour against their torture without a sound. Later as dusk was falling I saw them toss his body back into the sea. I knew then that, to honour his courage, I must return to Penruthin and restore it to its former glory.''

He was studying her intently as he finished speaking. His long dark lashes glistened with the moisture of the tears he held in check. Beneath the granite-hard exterior was a man capable of the greatness of spirit to forgive and to mourn. There was a sensitivity she had not expected. Perhaps she would have not been so surprised if it had come from Roland, but from Alaric? On the otherhand, what man could have survived such horrors and *not* become more humane in his feelings for others? It was the sensitivity which heartened her. It battered at her defences. Her arms ached to hold him close to help him forget his suffering.

"You are Penruthin's saviour." Her voice was husky with emotion. "It's not too late to save it from debt."

Gently, his thumb wiped away the wash of tears streaming down her cheeks. "Would that I had returned sooner. I had not reckoned upon the fever which kept me ill and weak for weeks at a time," he added, softly. "And you make me feel unworthy of your tears. Or were they for my brother?"

"They were for you both," she admitted. "He gave his life bravely. I will always think of him with affection. I am ashamed that I doubted you, my lord. It cannot have been easy for you to speak of your experiences. I am glad that you were honest with me. Though I can understand your thinking a woman would not want to hear such horrific tales of suffering."

He stood very still, not trusting himself to move or speak. Her compassion moved him. There was so

much he had not told her. So many dark motives
which could never be voiced. "I think you want to
hear, even less, that because your dowry is spent, you
now have no protector but myself. You have made a
powerful enemy in Prior Ignatius."

"I do not find the thought of your protectorship as
onerous as once I might." After his confession, she
could be no less truthful with him. "I appreciate your
honesty."

There was a stiffness again in his manner which
disquietened her. "I fear the steward only told you
part of the misappropriation of your dowry. Stephen
has sold all your tin and copper mines. The land alone
can never support an estate such as Whytemead."

Eloise became deathly pale. For a moment Penruthin thought she would swoon. Her eyes were round
with horror, beseeching him to deny his statement.
His fury at the way her fortune had been plundered
by his brother mounted. Couldn't they have left her
property alone? Were they so confident that the Lord
of Penruthin would never return to bring them to justice? Obviously, they did not care what happened to
the Lady Eloise.

He went cold at the thought of what would eventually have become of her. They could never let her
approach a court for annulment of her marriage. She
would have certainly ended her days enclosed in a
nunnery. Such an imprisonment for a woman of spirit
was as cruel as the captivity he had suffered. Damn
Stephen. May the prior rot in hell for his greed!

He was jolted from his thoughts by the sapphire ice of her eyes. "My father married me into a brigands' lair. With my wealth gone, I will not remain here to be tolerated upon suffrance, once your position is secure and the people safe from the prior."

"I have given my word to protect you," he announced gruffly, taking her arm.

Rebellion snaked through her. Her hatred returned in all its fury. She saw a life stretched before her devoid of affection, her title as Mistress of Penruthin empty and without substance.

"I don't want your pity," she stormed.

His fingers burned into her flesh. With the sunlight behind him, his figure was a menacing silhouette against the mullioned window.

"Has your hatred for me over the years clouded your reason?" he demanded hoarsely. "Has nothing I have said this afternoon proved that I have returned from my captivity a different man? You are a beautiful woman. Any knight would be proud to have you as his bride, even were you to go to him dowerless. And you did not. You brought wealth to Penruthin."

The heat of his fingers through the thin silk of her gown was rousing a physical awareness in her body. He had moved so that his figure was no longer shadowed. The scent of sandalwood and the musky fragrance of his maleness permeated her senses. The sunlight turned his complexion to pale amber, and the blue tinge of his beard beginning to show on his angular face was disturbingly masculine. That he seemed unaware of the effect his nearness was having upon her made it harder to withstand the way her senses played traitor with her emotions. It was galling that his presence could make her forget her resolution. How was it possible that a man, whom she told herself that she despised, could so bedevil her in his manner?

"Lady Eloise, you have a right to be angry with your position here. My family has failed you. I will not let you suffer. Let me make amends—for everything."

"You can be charming enough when it suits you," she flared. "Have I any choice for the moment?"

Her scorn rubbed the raw edges of his fierce pride. Coldly, he regarded the woman now bristling with anger. Her words struck at his own guilt. All the security her father had sought by her marriage had been stripped from her. She was making his task here harder. Yet as he stared down at her proud beauty, his animosity faded. Like him she had forgotten how to trust. Would that he could spare her the further pain that now seemed inevitable.

As her eyes continued to flash their rebellion, a demon rose within him, tempting him to teach her once and for all that he was her master. The fresh perfume of her skin wove a seductive spell around him. The temptation to make her his was overwhelming. But, as he gazed into her lovely face, he knew he could never force her against her will. With an iron will, he controlled the burning desire raging through him to crush her in his arms, and kiss her until she yielded in breathless submission. Even then, the demon would not be silenced.

Isn't that what she would expect of the arrogant, selfish man she had wed? And it would only earn him her deeper hatred. The attraction was there, but the minx was too stubborn to acknowledge it. Absurdly, it was important to him that she submitted to the man he was now, and not to the man who had ridden out of Penruthin.

To counter the temptation he stepped away from her. "You have a right to be angry," he conceded. "But you will always have a choice. I want to see Stephen and the prior brought to justice. I shall insist the Church returns your dowry. And somehow the copper and tin mines will be restored to provide you with an income."

Eloise clasped her fingers together. Her emotions cavorted in confusion. She had seen the desire which darkened his eyes and had despised him for it. Then a shutter had come down over his expression. He was again a man of stone. He could force her to honour her marriage vows, after which there would be no question of an annulment. Right was, after all, on his side for him to demand his marriage rights. Or did he not want to burden himself with a penniless bride? Once free of her, he could seek out another rich heiress to restore Penruthin to its glory.

Unaccountably, the fact that he did not deem her worth the trouble of attempting to make her truly his wife pricked her pride.

Chapter Seven

"My lady, since you have expressed your desire to be involved with the welfare of the estate and its people, perhaps you would accompany me. I am about to inspect the villages." Penruthin was halfway to the door, clearly unworried whether she accepted his offer or not.

She hurried after him. "I would welcome that. It is a long time since I have been permitted to leave the castle precincts. And then always with an armed guard to ensure that I did not escape your brother's clutches."

Beneath his breath she thought she heard Penruthin curse. When he turned to her his expression was softer, and her heart twisted as again he reminded her of the kindly Roland. "I fear it will be unsafe for you to ride abroad without an escort, my lady. I would not put it past the prior to hire men to abduct you and keep you hostage. I hope you will not take my company as a sign that I regard you as a prisoner."

An hour later they were riding through the second village. An escort of a score of armed men, all born on Penruthin land, rode behind them. They were the only guards he was prepared to trust. A shout from a cowherd heralded their approach and the people came out of their dilapidated thatched huts, or stopped their outdoor work, tools still poised in their hands. Several faces were wreathed in smiles as they recognised their lord and lady; others reluctantly tugged their fore-locks, their expressions servile, although their eyes remained wary.

Penruthin halted before the long pole of the car-penter's lathe in the centre of the clearing. The car-penter, William, was the head man of the village, his once tall figure now round-shouldered from forty years spent stooped over his bench and lathe. He put aside his chisel as his youngest son stopped working the pedal that turned the lathe. As he regarded Pen-ruthin in silence, his three tall sons came to stand behind him.

The huts here had fared better than those in the last village which had neither carpenter nor thatcher in residence. The cattle pens showed recent repairs, the new wood lighter than the original aged grey staves. There were only two milk cows in the pen where Eloise had expected to see at least ten. A hasty survey of the nine huts showed two of them in ruins and uninhabited. Between the vegetable plots only a hand-ful of scrawny hens scratched for food. By the fast flowing stream was a blackened shell of a building.

"What happened to your mill?" Penruthin demanded.

"Burned last spring," William grunted. "We now have to take our grain to the priory to be ground, and they take one sack in three as payment."

Penruthin's eyes narrowed with anger. Eloise leaned towards him and lowered her voice. "The miller was hanged, my lord. He was accused of evading his taxes. The man had no money. You can see how poor the villagers are. He milled their corn in exchange for food for his family of eight. The prior turned the family out of the village. I was not told until it was too late to save them. I only learned of it through a servant."

"What happened to the millers' family?" Penruthin rapped out.

"They went into the forest. Where else could they go?" William hawked and spat on to the ground. "There's families enough sought refuge there to escape the prior's vengeance."

Anger tightened the muscles in Penruthin's throat. "The forest has always been the haunt of outlaws. Those living there can be arrested and hanged." He controlled the rage grinding through him. He could not believe how badly the people had fared under the tyranny of a man of God. "If you know of those villagers' whereabouts, send word to them that their homes will be restored and repaired. The mill must be rebuilt. I give you permission to cut the necessary wood for its work, and to repair your houses. If I remember the miller's family correctly, he has two sons who should now be old enough to work the mill. Can word be sent to them?''

The carpenter nodded assent, the wariness in his eyes fading.

Penruthin studied the ravage of the land. ''What happened to the livestock?''

''Run off last month by the mercenaries from the castle.'' William's tone was surly. ''They sell them in the market.''

Anger burned in Eloise at such injustice and she saw a vein throbbing in Penruthin's temple as he rapped out, ''And I take it these men were not punished?''

''The mercenaries can rape and plunder all they will,'' William declared, tersely. ''They were brought to the castle to instill terror into the people. It's how the prior ensures that the high taxes are paid.''

''It will continue no longer,'' Penruthin said as he urged his horse into a canter.

Fury lashed him. There was so much injustice, so much suffering. He rode hard, aware that Eloise kept pace a horse's length behind him. Absently he noted her skill; riding perched on the side-saddle with both feet on its wooden platform was precarious. She had superb balance, woman and palfrey moving in graceful unison.

When the trees lining the path cleared and an open moor lay before him, he urged his horse to a gallop. Eloise ensured her mare matched his angry pace.

They rode in silence for three miles before he finally slowed his gelding, turning it back towards Penruthin Castle. He was deep in thought and Eloise did not break his silence. She had known something of what the prior had been up to but, kept as she had been, a virtual prisoner in the castle for the past year, she had never been allowed to visit the villages and she was appalled by what had happened.

A half mile from the castle, they entered a large coppice. Penruthin dismounted and signalled for his men to stay back. Tethering his mount to an overhanging branch, he came to Eloise's side.

"Walk with me, my lady."

At her assent, he placed his hands about her waist and lifted her to the ground. She was released immediately. Pinched white lines ran either side of his flaring nostrils and his eyes were as dark as storm clouds.

"I want to talk away from prying ears," he explained as he marched deeper into the hazel trees. "So many crimes have been committed against the people, the prior will never allow them to come to light. There is more danger than I first believed."

He struck a tree trunk with his gloved fist, giving vent to the anger which ground through him. "The mercenaries cannot be trusted. I've no money to pay them. They have no loyalty but to the highest paymaster. With the coffers empty, I can't even hire other men. The only men-at-arms I trust are the score now with us. What match are they against the small army the prior will raise?''

''Did you not demand Stephen's and Isobel's jewels from them?'' Eloise responded. ''Sell them, and you can have your own army.''

Penruthin hooked his thumbs into his sword-belt and glowered at a hare that crouched in frozen fear a dozen paces away. His tension showed in the rigidity of his stance, the hollows and angles of his face chiselled with suppressed rage. ''My brother refuses to part with his plundered riches. He's still determined to prove that I am Roland. He wants Penruthin for himself.''

Eloise shivered. He had kept his voice neutral, reminding Eloise how adept he was at concealing his emotions. ''Once you return to Court, your old friends will know that you are Alaric. There must be many memories only he and they had shared.''

He regarded her darkly, his hands gripping his sword hilt. Shards of grey steel flecked his eyes. ''I do not need to prove who I am. Why should I face such an inquisition?'' Arrogance poured from every line of his tall figure, his head tilted back in the way Alaric had always held himself when at his most contemptuous and scathing.

Eloise sighed. With an effort she quashed her rising anger at the hauteur she despised. ''Then send word to Lord Kilgarron to supply you with men. He recognised you at Glastonbury. He will not ignore such a demand from an old friend.''

"I did not meet with Kilgarron." He fired back at her as he paced. The rapid steps trampled violets and jack-in-the-pulpit plants. "I told Stephen and the prior that to gain time. I was careful to avoid anyone once I returned to England. You saw the state of me. Do you honestly believe that the Peacock of Penruthin would allow acquaintances to see him thus?"

He had not looked at her during his outburst. If he had told one lie to save himself, how many others had he spoken? Had he tricked her?

Years of distrust could not be easily put aside, despite the growing attraction she felt for him. Had he played upon her finer emotions when he spoke of his captivity, to ensure she was pliant to his wishes? How easily his charm could manipulate those around him. It had always been so with Alaric. Yet why should he have lied about meeting Lord Kilgarron, unless he had some darker secret to hide...

She looked through the cropped trees, the coppiced hazel branches spanning out like the petals of a water lily from their base. None had been cut this year. Daniel and Sam, the two woodsmen, had been the last of a long line of villagers abandoning their homes to live as outlaws in the forest. Through the branches she could just make out a burial ground. It was a place she had visited often before the prior had ended her morning rides from the castle.

She began to move in the direction of the graves. She wanted to trust him, to believe everything he said. Yet the nagging doubt would not be laid to rest. To ensure that Penruthin followed her, she addressed him over her shoulder. "Without a trained band of men to support you, how do you propose to keep Penruthin? If you think that the prior is capable of abducting me, then he would not hesitate to ambush you on your way to Court. Your death, contrived as an accident, would make Stephen the undisputed Lord of Penruthin. Though little use it will do him since he's flooded it with debts."

"It will give him greater power at Court. And he has always wanted to triumph over me. That's why he married Isobel. He thought I cared for the woman."

The derision in his tone made her look at him sharply. "She was your mistress; you must have had some regard for her."

He did not answer and she turned to him. His expression was bland; empty of any emotion. For a moment she thought he was not going to answer, and her temper soared.

"If you cared nothing for her, then the way you treated me upon our marriage was even more despicable and unforgiveable."

Her anger provoked a flicker deep in his eyes, but it was gone before she could assess it.

"She was a diversion from your repugnant marriage?" The words were out before she could stop them. And she hated herself for allowing him to see how deeply he had hurt her. She tweaked the folds of her gown angrily as she strode purposefully towards the burial ground.

Her arm was grabbed and she was pulled round to face him. "What must I do to prove to you that I am not that same callous man? I cannot turn back time. Marriage to you would not be repugnant to me now."

"Because you need me as an ally?" she accused.

Where his fingers touched, her flesh was bathed in a spreading radiance. He stood so close she could feel the tangible threat of his male strength. The knowledge that he needed her caused her emotions to spar with themselves. It was impossible to deny her attraction to him when he was near, when he was deliberately setting out to charm her.

She whipped up her anger, refusing to succumb to his coercion. What wizardry did this man weave? One moment he was capable of casting her spirits to their darkest depths. Then simply—with a smile, a kind word, a look which foretold of hidden delights within her reach—he rendered her breathless, expectant and elated. Every particle of her body ached to submit, yet at the same time all her senses warned her to resist him.

"I need you, Eloise." The words were so softly spoken, their inflection pure seduction and enticement. The innuendo in their depths had nothing to do with the trials which faced them. His gaze was unwavering upon her face, seeming to pierce to her soul. Her heart clamoured against her breastbone and her breath stilled with expectancy. He remained a hand's breadth away, drawing her like a lodestone to submit to his will.

She could feel herself weakening, and searched his tanned face for tenderness, for some sign that he cared. She needed to know this was not some trick to exert his mastery over her. His grey eyes smouldered, beckoning, promising... Indolently he lifted a hand to brush aside the silk of her veil from the side of her cheek. His finger wound the delicate fabric into a spiral, moving slowly down its length to rest on the bare skin above her low-necked bodice.

"Can you not accept that I have changed? That I regret the barriers erected by the past?" he cajoled, as he rubbed the backs of his fingers across her creamy flesh.

Beneath his touch her skin tingled and her breathing quickened, her breasts swelling and aching, her body aroused with an indefinable yearning that was both a torture and a foretaste of paradise.

"Even after all I have told you, do you still have your doubts as to who I am, Eloise?"

"You must be aware that I do." Her voice was husky, betraying the turmoil within her.

He stood so close his feet were lost amongst the heavy folds of her skirts. Inexorably their bodies were drawn together until hips, thighs and chests rested against each other. The light contact sent a shaft of heat through Eloise's clothes. Her breathing became painful, and she swallowed, running the tip of her tongue nervously across her parted lips.

Penruthin smiled enigmatically. "But you don't doubt me enough to denounce me to the sheriff."

"Whether Alaric or Roland, you are the saviour of Penruthin. You are the people's choice."

His eyes were flecked now with enticing golden lights as his gaze caressed her features and his mouth lifted at the corners. "But am I *your* choice?"

He was enjoying taunting her. And, damn him, he was too aware of the effect his nearness had on her. She cursed her inexperience. It was impossible not to be affected by his charm. He was manipulating her and, when he looked at her as he was doing now, she found she did not care. And that could be fatal.

The conscious effort to drag her gaze from his bedevilling stare was harder than she could have believed possible. It wasn't whether or not he was her choice that was now so important to her. Was she *his* choice? If she taunted him in like vein he was bound to answer yes, because he needed her goodwill and support.

His eyes hooded as if he had guessed her thoughts. He tilted back his head in the arrogant pose Alaric had used so often in the early days of their marriage. It goaded her defiance.

"You know my choice. To be free of this marriage."

"Still so stubborn," he laughed softly with the old assurance that roused her festering resentment.

His breath fanned the top of her head, light and warm as a midsummer's breeze. Did she sense it or had his lips touched her hair? The sensation was gone before she could be certain, but the notion had been so powerful that a cascade of shivers travelled the length of her spine. The scent of him was all around her, a heady mixture of the sandalwood he favoured and of woodsmoke and horse-leather, subtly overlaid with his masculine musk, which was becoming so enticingly familiar.

His hand remained on the sensitive skin of her collarbone and now his thumb traced lazy circles. It set up an expanding ripple flowing out from its centre to spread with seductive heat throughout her body. Annoyed that she could respond so wantonly to his touch, she jerked her head away.

His eyes were guarded. He caught her about the waist. "You must trust me, Eloise." His hold was gentle, but firm enough to alert her that he would not permit her to escape. She held her breath, anticipating he would kiss her. When he did not, an infuriating ache of disappointment lanced her breast. She swallowed against the bittersweet pain of irrational longing. Then with a slow smile he took her hand, raising it to his cheek before pressing his lips against her fingers. Her breath fluttered as an exquisite thrill sped through her. His gaze never left hers, now warm and intimate, cajoling. When he turned her palm to his lips and his tongue ran along its hollow, she gasped, startled that so light a touch could have such effect. It bathed her nerve-endings in a delicious tingling warmth.

The glint in his eyes teased, but within their pewter depths were poignant fires, the tempting, dancing lights reflecting something more profound, a sensual, dangerous allure, beyond reason, beyond rational thought.

"Eloise, you have no idea how you tempt a man." His voice was so low she had to strain to hear.

Her brow raised in question, but his lashes had lowered to shield his emotions from her. Only a rapid pulse in his throat showed he was not entirely in control of his feelings. Did he then care for her? If only that were the case, but the Alaric of old could not be trusted especially in matters of the heart. Even so, caught in the snare of his masculine allure, her palms moistened with nervous expectancy.

At the touch of his lips skimming hers, she swayed unresistingly towards him. His mouth savoured hers, his tongue circling the outline of her lips, tenderly parting them to explore the velvet softness of their inner heat. Her young woman's innocence was breached by age-old instincts. Her mouth opened like a blossoming flower beneath his expert kiss. She was gathered closer in his demanding embrace and, of their own volition, her arms spread around his shoulders, her body subjugated by the hard strength of his lithe form.

A sigh, soft as a butterfly alighting on a petal, escaped her throat. As his kiss deepened, his hands moving to first bind her closer, then to explore the contour of her hip and caress her ribs, every one of her senses was tuned to the pleasure he evoked. The scent of wild jasmine floated seductively around them, the mellifluous notes of a blackbird accompanied the rapid pounding of her heart. The taste of his breath was like ambrosia on her tongue, and every particle of her simmered with new and exultant sensations. She willed the kiss to go on, never to end. She had never dreamt that a kiss could be so profound, provoke so much feeling of bliss. When his mouth left her lips to travel to the hollow of her neck, her head rolled back and she gasped, softly, "Alaric. Oh, Alaric."

Without warning she was brusquely released. Her eyes flew open. For a moment her vision was filled with his ruggedly handsome countenance, the desire in his eyes, causing her heart to snatch. He withdrew a step, hauteur replacing the tenderness of only moments earlier. There was a brittle gleam in his eyes which she found impossible to interpret, so she fell back on her old resentment. He had kissed her to teach her a lesson, the arrogant lord unable to countenance any rebellion against his will.

Feeling a blush heating her cheeks, she turned away. How could she have allowed her guard to slip so easily? Her anger became a liferaft.

"You haven't changed. You're just as callous and unfeeling as ever. I'll not be just another woman to be tricked by your charm. It's Penruthin you want, not me. I'm just a means to an end."

"Eloise, you are not..."

She closed her ears to his words. She knew the power of them too well to risk falling again into the trap he would set for her. Through the trees she saw the graves and was reminded of her original intention.

Stoking her rage, she stepped past the last of the concealing trees into the clearing. The graves ranged before her. There were ten of them, forlorn mounds, unmarked and covered in grass. Yet the grass had been kept short and no debris littered the graves. One of them had been more assiduously cared for. A bunch of pink and blue wildflowers were stuck into a pottery jug.

Penruthin was staring at them in puzzlement. ''There was no village here, so why so many graves?'' he queried. ''And why were these people not buried in the nearest churchyard?''

Eloise leaned back against a tree trunk, watching Penruthin. ''They are the heretic's graves and denied the benefit of holy ground.''

A muscle twitched along his jaw and was quickly suppressed. ''They have been tended. One more than the others.''

''Githa sees to that,'' she remarked, her gaze assessing his face for any sign of emotion.

A pallor spread across his cheeks as he stared at the grave with the flowers. ''Is that then Clothilde's grave? Githa was some relation to her, I seem to remember my father mentioning?''

''It is.''

He turned away from her but she noticed that his

fists were clenched as he strode back to the horses. Was it anger or grief which smote him? He had certainly been affected by seeing the heretics' graves. Yet he had given Clothilde's no more than a cursory glance. Roland had been devoted to his mother; only Alaric would be indifferent to her fate. Whatever truth Eloise had hoped to discover from Penruthin's reaction at the graves, continued to elude her.

When she returned to the horses, Penruthin was deep in conversation with the servant-at-arms, Hal Benson. Hal at five-and-twenty was the oldest of the village men who rode with him.

"How many of the people from the eight villages on Penruthin and Whytemead land now live with the outlaws?" Penruthin continued to fire his questions.

"Mayhap upwards of fifty."

"How many of those are of fighting age?"

"No more'n two dozen. And that would be stretching it some."

Penruthin weighed this and regarded the mounted soldiers. "There's but a score of you. What about the men in the villages? How wide is the dissent spread by Prior Ignatius? The priory holds land further afield, encompassing a dozen or more villages."

The sergeant drew his thin lips back over decaying teeth in a conspiratorial grin. "There's men a-plenty willing to fight to see that evil priest meet his Maker in hell."

Eloise's heart clutched with fear. "My lord, do you mean to raise an army from the villagers? They are untrained. The Church will never countenance insurrection! Whilst any shadow remains over your right to your father's title and lands, any man who rides with you could be hanged for his loyalty.''

Penruthin studied her, his expression serious. ''I understand your concern, my lady. I need to know what followers I have; I am desperate for men.'' He smiled, but her heart twisted further as she saw that it did not reach his eyes. They were chill splinters of resolution.

''There's men enough who will fight,'' Hal Benson stated. ''Too many of their women have been dishonoured by the mercenaries not to want revenge.''

Penruthin nodded. ''Soldiers who fight to right injustices and to avenge family honour, are always a force to be reckoned with.''

As he spoke, his hands spanned Eloise's waist and he lifted her effortlessly into the saddle. His touch caused a shiver to skim along her spine and bury itself deep in the pit of her stomach. It wasn't misbegotten passion that now made her heart thud. It was naked fear.

She reached for his hand, which rested on her saddle pommel, her voice low and vibrant as she sought to reason with him. So far no blows had been struck in conflict. She wanted the prior to pay for his crimes, but thought of the deaths a feud could bring alarmed her. ''My lord, you can only triumph over the prior if you meet him in a court of law. Too many men will die if you try to fight him.''

"There will be no fight, unless the prior provokes it. I despatched a messenger to Court this morning requesting audience with the King."

Eloise's fear deepened. "The King is said to have lost his wits. And Ignatius' cousin has a voice which is heeded at the privy council."

"Then we must pray for a speedy recovery for our sovereign," Penruthin answered crisply. "In the meantime, I must use whatever means in my power to protect these estates from further plundering."

He leapt nimbly into the saddle and without another word wheeled his horse and set off at a fast canter towards the castle.

As they rode under the portcullis, Eloise felt the hairs at the nape of her neck begin to prickle. Something was wrong. She scanned the battlements. The men-at-arms stood stiffly to attention. Did they hold their halberds and crossbows just a little too much at the ready, as though expecting a command for action? She glanced at Penruthin and saw that he too was surveying the Outer Bailey. He gave a barely perceptible nod to Hal Benson and the sergeant fell back, as though inspecting the rear of the guard. Her unease mounted. Where were the usual servants, busy about their work? When a guard's gaze slid away from hers, she knew some trap awaited them.

A shadow fell over their party as they rode beneath the gatehouse arch leading to the Inner Bailay. It was then Eloise saw Stephen and Isobel waiting at the top of the keep steps. They were dressed in their finest attire. Their figures were glittering from the array of jewels which sparkled in the sunlight. The cost of the gems alone would have rescued Penruthin from its debts. Beside them Captain Maddock was bound in chains.

Eloise smothered a cry. Her body drenched in a cold sweat. They were betrayed. There was a slithering and clatter of hooves behind them. Eloise turned to see Hal Benson lying low as he galloped through the portcullis and over the drawbridge. A shout went up from the sentry. Two guards on the battlements lifted their crossbows and fired their bolts.

She cried out, "Sweet Jesu, spare him! Spare us all!"

The sergeant had ridden out of sight. Had he been hit, or had he escaped to alert someone of their danger?

"After him!" someone yelled from the battlements. "None is to escape."

Two guards mounted saddled horses and galloped after the fleeing rider. The tableaux in the courtyard seemed to be played out in slow motion. Eloise's heart pounded as she cast about for some means of escape. They were surrounded by guards, the men's faces impassive and without mercy.

Stephen laughed. The harsh sound startled a lone magpie where it had been scavenging on a pile of household rubbish. A bad omen. Single magpies were supposed to herald sorrow.

"This time, brother, there is no escape!" Stephen bellowed.

Armed guards were running out of the doors at the base of the turrets, merging with those already surrounding the riders.

"Arrest the Lady Eloise and her paramour," Stephen commanded. "The impostor will moulder in our dungeon until the sheriff arrives to conduct his trial. The men who ride with him will be hanged as an example to others who would turn traitor."

"Curse you, Stephen," Penruthin raged as he drew his sword. "This is infamous."

He struck at the mercenaries who ran forward to tear him from the saddle. The other guards fought bravely, but they were outnumbered at least seven to one. Eloise's bridle was snatched by two soldiers. She kicked out at them as they attempted to pull her from the horse.

"The treachery is all on your part, not ours!" Eloise shouted to be heard above the clash of steel. "Lord Penruthin is the true heir to these lands. Sir Stephen is the usurper."

"Silence her!" Stephen yelled, his face mottled with anger.

A glance showed Eloise that Isobel was gloating. She had urged Stephen to this because Penruthin had refused her favours. Perhaps it had even been planned before the prior rode out, to lull them into a sense of false security.

The rough treatment she was receiving at the hands

of the guards attempting to drag her out of the saddle warned her that they could expect no mercy. She lashed at a scarred face with her riding-whip, the only weapon at her disposal. He grunted with pain and temporarily released his hold on her leg. When two soldiers grabbed her feet, she was jerked off-balance. She clutched at the saddle pommel in vain and, with a cry, her body was pulled to the ground. She landed on the flagstones, grazing her knees; her veil was torn as she was hauled unceremoniously to her feet.

"How dare you put your hands on me," she fumed to cover her mounting fear. She would never let Isobel see that she was frightened. "I am Lady Eloise."

"Yer ain't such a lady if yer've bedded yer husband's bastard brother," a bearded guard snarled. His breath reeked of soured curds as he thrust his face close to hers and cruelly wrenched her arm behind her back. Her other arm was taken by another ruffian, bruising her flesh.

"Take your hands off the Lady Eloise," Penruthin shouted whilst still engaged in fighting with three guards. He was breathing heavily as he ran one through the gut. Freeing his sword he pushed the dying man into the path of his two other assailants. "Lady Eloise has done nothing wrong. The lady is pure and I will not have her…"

"You're in no position to demand anything, my bastard brother!" Stephen cut in.

Four guards were now pressing Penruthin into a hard fight for survival. His sword wove like quicksilver, parrying each blow. The swift reactions of his lithe body as he ducked and leapt aside saved him time and again from the lethal steel flashing across his body.

Isobel grew more incensed by the moment. "Damn your useless hides. Arrest him, guards. To the dungeon with him."

One by one the loyal escort of local men were being overpowered and marched away until only Penruthin remained fighting.

Isobel laughed shrilly. "Impostor, your whore will be our prisoner. Prior Ignatius knows how to deal with her kind. It will be the whipping post first, then the stake for her. And you'll live long enough to see her fry before I have you boiled in oil for daring to impersonate Alaric."

"He is no impostor," Eloise cried out, desperate to save Penruthin. Isobel's spite proved that he had rejected her and, despite the danger to them, that knowledge brought a rush of warmth to Eloise's breast. Wide-eyed with terror for Penruthin, she searched the white faces of the remaining guards and villagers. The villagers and servants were being held back by a line of men-at-arms.

The two guards who had ridden out returned with Hal Benson's body thrown over his mount. Two crossbow bolts were embedded in his back.

Eloise screamed. "Will no one stop them?" She knew she expected too much. The guards would have been bribed and the people were unarmed and no match against trained soldiers. Her gaze was riveted upon Penruthin as he fought on. His back was against a high wall and he was keeping the four men at bay. His sword struck like lightning, but it was obvious that he was tiring. He was too hard pressed to fight and answer for himself.

Eloise held herself erect although the arm twisted behind her back felt as though it were being wrenched from its socket. She was propelled towards the keep steps until she stood directly below the sneering figures of Stephen and Isobel. In desperation she tried a last plea to win the support of the guards and people. She would not be dragged away unheard.

"You wrong your lord. He is no impostor. He is a man of honour. Lord Penruthin has treated me with the respect due to my rank," she proclaimed. "I am a maid."

Stephen sniggered. "What more proof do we need that it is Roland who has returned? Though Alaric had no love for his bride, I doubt he would have missed the opportunity to deflower a virgin! He was diligent enough in populating the villages. There's at least six of his bastards that I know of. But Roland would likely not deflower a noblewoman under false pretences. That you remain a maid proves his guilt."

Eloise felt as though she had been punched in the stomach. She had not known of Alaric's bastards. She rode the blow, keeping her head high and defiant. "Perhaps you judge your elder brothers by your own low standards of morality. My husband is a man of honour and has respected my sensibilities.''

Stephen guffawed with insulting derision. Eloise was torn between defending her virtue and watching Penruthin who was still fighting for his life. His hair was streaked dark with sweat and it was obvious that he was almost exhausted.

''You cannot take justice into your own hands, Sir Stephen,'' she flared. ''It is for the King to decide whether Lord Penruthin is an imposter or not.''

For an instant Eloise saw behind the anger on Stephen's face to the fear which drove him. They would never face trial. Here in the isolation of Penruthin Castle their deaths would be arranged to look like an accident.

Fear engulfed her. She screamed again as she saw Penruthin stumble. A guard seized the opening presented and ran him through the arm. The amount of blood seeping through his velvet doublet meant he must be weakening fast.

Hatred burned in her as she regarded Stephen with brimming eyes. She was so proud of Penruthin's courage—a true knight. ''You, who are too cowardly to face your brother on the tourney field, take vengeance like a woman. But you cannot silence our cause, even if you have us killed. You forget Lord Kilgarron knows of my husband's return. Questions will be asked at Court,'' she bluffed.

''Kilgarron never saw the impostor. That was a lie. Did you think I would not send word to him? Kilgarron was not at his castle. He has been at Court all summer. That lie proves he is Roland.''

''It proves he knew that you could not be trusted. You proved that by ordering him arrested on his arrival when you could not possibly have known which brother he was. And you cannot judge Alaric now, by the actions of the man who rode from here seven years ago. Captivity has changed him.'' Eloise eyed him with all the disdain she could muster through the agony in her shoulder socket.

As she finished speaking there was a groan from several of the villagers who were watching Penruthin fight.

Thomas Hampden shouted a warning, ''Behind you, my lord.''

Eloise's heart clenched with fear. Penruthin had been forced to turn to face two assailants on his right and his back was no longer protected by the wall. The steward's warning was too late. A third opponent held his arm aloft and the side of his sword hilt crashed down onto Penruthin's bare head. Eloise screamed as she saw him go down and seconds later his senseless form was dragged towards the dungeon. Three of the guards who had escorted them lay dead on the flagstones. Eloise had no way of knowing how many of the others had been wounded before they too were overpowered and taken to the dungeon.

Her stare was focused on the still unconscious figure of Penruthin as he was dragged from sight. A vicious pull on her arm made her bite her lips to stifle a cry of pain. She was propelled up the steps, her glare contemptuous as she was marched past Stephen and the smirking Isobel.

"Lock her in her room and keep a guard on her door," Stephen ordered.

"You won't get away with this!" Eloise forced out, through a red haze of pain as her arm was threatened with dislocation. "Lord Penruthin sent a messenger to Court this morning."

Stephen grinned evilly and pointed to a man's figure swinging from a makeshift gibbet behind the bailey gate. "He was ambushed at the first crossroads. So die all traitors who turn against their rightful lord. Say your prayers, Lady Eloise. There are precious few days left for you in this world."

Chapter Eight

An owl hooted on the thatched stable roof of the castle. Its call was barely audible over the revelry, which had overspilled from the great hall into the courtyard. Sir Stephen and the Lady Isobel were celebrating their victory.

It was a warm night and Eloise stood with her head pressed against the wall of her window embrasure. She had not moved since dusk, finally worn out from hours of angry pacing. Her glazed eyes had been unappreciative of the spectacular purple and crimson sunset, and later of the pale silver moon shining in a black velvet, star-speckled sky.

This was the second night of her captivity. All day her nerves had been shredded by the sound of hammering as the carpenter erected three-sided gallows. The men-at-arms would be hanged at dawn. Her heart wept for the brave men who had supported them. They did not deserve to die.

She pressed a hand to her mouth, her tears spilling

hotly over her fingers. She had had the means to save those men. But at what cost! At midday Sir Stephen had come to interrogate her. She had ignored him.

"I have nothing to say to you," she finally said to get rid of his loathsome presence. "Anything I have to say will be said before the King and his Court. They are the only people who can judge my husband."

"He is not your husband." Stephen had screamed in impotent rage. He had slapped her twice and she had tasted blood in her mouth where his ring had torn her lip. "He is an impostor."

"You cannot bully me into speaking against him." She glared her disgust at him.

He had changed tactics and become wheedling. "You are not to blame. Anyone could make a mistake. Roland and Alaric were impossible to tell apart from a distance. It was only Alaric's short hair and peacock's finery which showed the difference between them. No one can blame you for mistaking the man, by being taken in by the impostor. But we can do nothing to save you if you remain so stubborn."

Eloise clamped her lips closed and turned away. She would never betray Penruthin to save herself. But what if it was Roland who had returned and not Alaric? her conscience questioned. She knew that could never change how she now felt for him. However, if he was Roland, Stephen was indisputably his father's heir. The thoughts sped like flying arrows through her mind. Stephen would not hesitate to shut her away in a convent and ensure that her own inheritance was lost to her—which was why she refused to acknowledge that the man claiming to be her husband might not be Alaric.

At whatever cost, she would fight Stephen. She was not her father's daughter for nothing. She would not meekly give up her inheritance. Family honour would not permit it. She had to defy Stephen. There was only one course open to her and she would not shirk her duty. Had not everything Penruthin told her confirmed her belief that he was her husband?

Or had she chosen to hear only that which she wished to hear? She frowned, remembering that not once had he actually told her that he was Alaric. Ruthlessly, she smothered the nagging doubt.

At her silence Stephen grabbed her shoulders and shook her. The expression on his face was demonic. "If you won't save yourself, what about the guards? They are innocent men tricked into believing that Roland is their lord. A word from you can save them."

She stared at him, her fleshing chilling. His lips had drawn back into an evil smile. "I thought that would get your attention. Just say you were duped, that the men-at-arms were tricked by the impostor's charm. Why should so many men die because of Roland's treachery?"

"Why should innocent men die for taking orders from the man they believe to be their lord?" She hurled back at him. "Is that how you reward loyalty?"

His thin lips drew back over yellowing teeth. "The men-at-arms hang at dawn." Spittle splayed from his mouth, and his eyes were narrowed slits of venom. "You will be forced to watch it, my lady. It's not a pretty sight to witness a man choking to death. It can take one-third of an hour for some of them to die. They kick and squirm, bladders and bowels emptying, their eyes rolling in their sockets and their faces turning blue, their tongues lolling from gaping lips like maggots crawling engorged from their putrid nests."

Eloise gagged on the brutal picture he had painted. Swallowing hard, she controlled her nausea. To send so many men to such a terrible death would be burned into her conscience, giving her no peace until the day she died. But to save them would have far wider consequences. It would give the prior back his power. How many other lives would eventually be sacrificed? The prior would resume his tyranny, burning as a heretic anyone who crossed him. More people would be driven from the villages. Life in the forest was harsh. Few outlaws escaped the purges periodically sent to flush them out. Scores of them would be hanged as outlaws. She could not condemn the people to that fate.

"I will not betray my husband. He is the rightful Lord of Penruthin," she answered emphatically. "If you hang the guards for their loyalty, then you are a murderer and will burn in eternal hellfire."

"Not I. I shall have the prior's Absolution. And

you will burn in this world. For heresy and open rebellion. Prepare yourself for the flames, my lady.''

He stormed out of her chamber, leaving her trembling. Terror washed over her at the horrific death he
had threatened. She drew several shaky breaths and
conquered her fear. Instead she concentrated on the
anger she felt for the injustice and the evil being perpetrated within Penruthin's noble walls. An image
haunted her of the men who tomorrow would be
swinging from the gallows. And what of Lord Penruthin himself?

With a sigh she stared down into the courtyard. It
was illuminated by a large fire over which an ox had
been roasted. Flambeaux were stuck into wall brack-
ets at intervals around the Inner Bailey, turning the
lime-washed stonework to orange. Figures crossed
and recrossed in the firelight. Their grotesque shadows were deformed into gargoyles as they were
thrown up by the torchlight onto the surrounding
walls. As the night lengthened, it was obvious that
the mercenaries had been drinking heavily.

A high-pitched scream drew Eloise's attention and
she saw a naked serving-maid, clutching a thin strip
of cloth to her half-formed breasts. It was all that
remained of her ripped dress. She was pursued by two
burly men. One dived at her fleeing legs and brought
her tumbling down on the ground. Then both men
were upon her. Her screams were pitiable. No one
came to her rescue and Eloise turned away, unwilling
to watch the violation of one of the castle servants.

The girl could not be more than fourteen. Stephen had condemned her and Penruthin to rot in hell, but the castle itself was like Satan's lair this night.

She closed her eyes to shut out the horrific images. They were supplanted by the last sight she had had of Penruthin being dragged to the dungeon. She had received no word of how he fared, or how he had been treated. No servant had been allowed to tend her. She had been given no food since being locked in her room yesterday— Not that she could have eaten—she was too worried about Lord Penruthin and the fate of the guards. If Stephen would risk hanging the guards without a trial in the country court, then he must believe himself unassailable.

Her hand trembled as she lifted it to massage her aching temple. If only Penruthin Castle were not so isolated. Any atrocities could be committed and covered up, the people terrorised into silence. She pulled her thoughts up short. She must not start thinking that way. It would destroy her. She had been brought up to believe in English justice. Her father had been a powerful man and a respected adviser to the King. Henry VI would never allow any harm to come to his daughter. Especially as she was innocent.

Angry shouts dragged her attention back to the courtyard. Four drunken guards were fighting over the winnings from a dice game. One was knocked to the ground, the blow sobering him slightly. "Take yer winnings," he slurred. "There's plenty more where that came from. Didn't Sir Stephen tell us we'll all be rich?''

Eloise's heart plummeted. Her voice crackled as she spoke her thoughts aloud. ''You delude yourself, Eloise, if you think King Henry will ever learn of your fate. He'll be told only of your death and the death of Lord Penruthin, a tale contrived and convincingly concocted by Prior Ignatius.''

She turned to lean her brow upon the cool stones of the wall and gaze down in to the courtyard. It was generally growing quieter. A glance at the moon showed by its position it was not even midnight. The drunken guards had celebrated too well and were falling asleep where they slumped on steps or flagstones. She had not slept last night and she felt her eyes begin to droop with exhaustion.

Her last thoughts were of Penruthin and how magnificently he had fought the guards. His face enlarged in her mind, those grey enigmatic eyes, glowing with assurance and seductive promise. Her lips inexplicably burned as she recalled the intensity of his kiss. And as sleep overcame her she could not help wondering what it would be like to be loved by such a man.

In the dungeon, lying upon mildewed, rat-infested straw, Penruthin was wide awake. His arms ached where they were shackled high above his head, his body contorted by the manacles about his ankles which prevented him from rising to his feet. The shackles chafed, already rubbing against the old scars from the slave-ship fetters. He was alone in a separate cell and he could hear the loyal guards praying in the cell opposite. At dawn they would die and he was responsible for their deaths. It filled him with remorse. He'd seen too many good men die as slaves to the Moors. He cursed himself for not expecting Stephen to act so swiftly. No doubt it had been planned by the prior. He should have realised that the prior would leave him no time to gather loyal supporters.

Rage gnawed at Penruthin's gut at the way he had fallen into their trap. The prior was probably now pleading his case to the sheriff. He probably had not even gone to Court, which was why Stephen had acted so quickly.

There was no light within his cell and when Penruthin glimpsed a growing yellow orb through the bars of the door, he was alerted to danger.

He sat up with a jangling of chains. The movement brought a grimace of pain to his face as the blood began to flow through his cramped limbs. By the time the lantern hovered outside his cell, his expression was composed. The agony that assaulted his body was blocked by a will which had conquered pain throughout his years as a galley-slave.

When the door opened he showed no surprise as the silk skirts of his visitor rustled across the filthy floor. Isobel wrinkled her nose in disgust as she eyed his tattered doublet and shirt which had been ripped as he fought to escape capture.

"Not so fine now, are we, my proud peacock?" she sniggered, holding the lantern high to take in the extent of his degradation. The words were slurred, revealing that the woman was intoxicated. Sober, Isobel was vindictive; drunk she was vicious and malicious. "I warned you I would not be spurned. I always wanted Penruthin Castle as my home and finally it will be mine."

He did not answer. But a mocking smile lifted his lips as he held her gloating stare. It was always easy to rouse this woman's temper and when angered she rarely considered her speech. He could learn far more from her by silent goading than by coercion.

"You still think you're so damned superior." Her voice rose an octave as she responded to his baiting. "You thought you could cast me aside as you did other women. You chose that mewling child-bride over me. And now you will both die."

Isobel swayed and the lantern tilted precariously.

"Take care with that lantern or we will both fry," he derided.

"Bastard!" she spat. The rose-pink veil, which matched her low-necked gown, quivered with her rage. "You always were so self-righteous. But you'll die in ignominy. Bastard by name. Bastard by nature. That's how you'll be remembered."

"Bastard by nature perhaps," he taunted. "I would

have to be, to have chosen you as the means to humiliate an unwanted child-wife.''

Her eyes glinted evilly. "At last you betray your true self. You are Roland, the bastard. You always despised me. Alaric loved me. He would never have scorned me on his return."

The chains rattled as he drew up a knee while regarding her sardonically, "Why should I revere a woman who has brought corruption and ruin to my home? I never said I loved you." The arrogance in his tone brought her head up. "I have never told any woman that I loved her."

"It was a common enough boast of Alaric's. You merely ape your brother's words, Roland."

"Do I?" He outstared her, his grey eyes aloof.

Beneath his piercing gaze, her eyes widened. Her guard dropped. The drink befuddling her wits allowed her hurt to show. She shook her head. "Oh, Alaric, why didn't you love me? I loved you. You are the only man I ever wanted."

"Isobel, this does no good." He didn't want to hear her confession.

She shuddered. "You always walked out of any scene. You never listened to anyone. Well, you will listen to me." The nastiness had returned to her voice. "Penruthin Castle and its land was the only thing you ever cared for. That's why you wed the simpering ninny Eloise. Penruthin was something you and Roland had in common. He hated you because you were his father's heir. He was the eldest. He could never forget that. But for being baseborn, he would have been Lord of Penruthin, not you.''

She tottered tipsily and put a hand to the slimey wall to steady her swaying person. ''I was certain that you were Roland when you returned. There was no welcome in your eyes for me and I saw how you looked at Eloise. I hated you for that. And of course I could not allow you to steal Penruthin from my husband.'' Her lips curled back into a sneer. ''It no longer matters which brother you are, legal heir or bastard. I've had my revenge on you both for spurning me. Did you know I tried to seduce Roland and failed?''

The drunken ramblings were rousing his temper. He had underestimated Isobel's spite. He feigned nonchalance as she prattled on, but his body was tense. Any information he learned could be invaluable. As she spoke her face had hardened. All trace of her once outstanding beauty was stripped from it as it turned into an ugly mask distorted by her need for revenge.

''A pity Roland never learned how I paid him back.'' Her voice cackled, malicious as an old crone's. ''I used to taunt the whore Clothilde, tell her that her precious bastard son was dead. She went mad in the end. It was easy to convince the prior that she was a heretic. The lecher had been spurned by her. He, like me, never forgets or forgives.''

Feeling his rage about to explode, Penruthin clenched his jaw. Years of iron control over his emo-

'tions were tested to their limit as he sat unmoving and expressionless.

She laughed again at his lack of reaction. "Could it truly be that you are Alaric? I hope so. It will make my revenge the more triumphant. It is the haughty Alaric I want to see broken, his arrogant pride smashed by my hand. I want you to die knowing I am Mistress of Penruthin and that I will be the cause of your precious estate's ruin."

Her flesh quivered as she silently laughed, her tongue running salaciously over her lips. Revenge was an aphrodisiac to her perverted mind. A hand slid over her full breasts to her rounded stomach and she sighed lasciviously before adding, "There will be no heir to continue the Penruthin line. The name of Penruthin will be forgotten. If it is recalled at all, it will be linked with infamy."

"Why do you want to destroy Penruthin, if it is the home you coveted?" He needed to know the depths of her hatred, to be armed against any eventuality should a chance of escape present itself.

Her eyes narrowed. "Don't tell me you forget our last conversation before you rode out? I told you I carried your child. That if you abandoned me and left Penruthin you would regret it. But then, of course, Roland would not know of such a conversation."

In response to her taunt, he lifted a dark mocking brow. "You told so many lies and used so many threats to try to keep me in England." Penruthin's derision held all the hauteur for which he was renowned. ''My place at that time was at my father's side. Did you expect me to stay in England, whilst my bastard brother won glory and fame on the battlefield?''

''How glibly you answer,'' she spat. ''But then I suppose even enemies confide in each other, when thrown together in slavery.''

He did not rise to her baiting. It goaded her further. She leaned closer, her heavy, musky perfume sweetening the air, until he caught the stench of sour wine and vomit on her breath.

''I wasn't lying. I carried your child. Whether you are Alaric or not, you will still suffer knowing how I have succeeded in ruining your family. I have vowed to destroy the only thing both Roland and Alaric cared for—Penruthin Castle and its lands.'' She straightened and almost overbalanced before steadying herself. ''I knew you'd never marry me, so I decided to take Stephen as my husband. He may be weak, but he was not prepared to have your child inherit Penruthin in place of one of his own. He insisted I visit the old woman in the forest to get rid of the brat. The old crone almost got rid of me as well. I was ill for months.''

Isobel paused, her hatred blazing in her slitting eyes. ''At every pain which ended the life of my child and twisted my body in agony, I cursed you and Stephen. I vowed then that the ruin of Penruthin would be the price of my suffering. The old crone was amongst the first of the heretics to be burned. She left me barren, but I did not tell Stephen that. It suited me that all the men of Penruthin would suffer, as I had been made to suffer the torture of the old crone's bloodied bodkin.''

"Then why is the Lady Eloise your enemy?'' He reasoned. "She has done you no harm.''

"No harm? You would have wed me if it hadn't been for her riches. You'd have had to, since I was pregnant. Your father would not have allowed a woman of my station to be so dishonoured.''

He regarded her coldly. "You delude yourself, Isobel. You were sent here by your widowed mother after the scandal you created by seducing the young Earl of St Austyn. My father took you in because he loved his elder sister and she was ailing. She hoped that once the scandal blew over some elderly knight might marry you, cherishing your beauty, for you had no dowry. There was never any question that I would marry a pauper cousin. Especially one with a ruined reputation. I suppose you seduced Stephen and he, weakling that he is, was besotted by you.''

"At least he's capable of emotion. Unlike you,'' she screeched. There were tears forming in her eyes. Penruthin, sensing that she was about to become maudlin, changed the subject. He needed her to be angry if he was to learn anything of use from her.

"So your need for vengeance extends to Eloise.'' he said. "I heard how she demanded her rightful place on the dais and in the running of the household. That's why you hate her. You thought you could manipulate a child-bride, but the courage of the grown woman was no match for you.'' He hid his revulsion as he added more softly, ''You were a beautiful woman, Isobel. But you were always flawed by your spite. That will one day destroy you.''

''Not before I have destroyed you and all you ever cared for.''

He shook his head, deliberately taunting her, ''You will reap what you sow.''

She snorted her disgust. ''Dear God, your pilgrimage has turned you into a saint. Or has it unmanned you?'' she taunted with malicious joy. ''Is that why you did not touch your bride? Because you are no longer a proper man?''

Putting down the lantern, she knelt in the straw. ''Is that why you've been so cruel to me?'' She reached for him, her hands caressing his shoulders and chest as she leaned closer. She was breathing heavily, desire slackening the muscles of her face. ''I always wanted you in my power, my love. You are tied and cannot escape me now. We were always so good together. We can be so again.''

He tensed. ''Your games do not interest me. You'd be better served taking your perverted pleasures where they will be appreciated.''

With a triumphant cackle, she reeled back from him. ''Those are the very words Roland said to me. You are Roland.''

He grinned enigmatically. ''Apparently my brother and myself were more alike than I had realised.''

As the cell door slammed behind her Penruthin sighed. He had always known Isobel was vindictive, but not so completely evil. The thought of Eloise a prisoner at the mercy of Isobel and Prior Ignatius filled him with rage. The intensity of it startled him.

He pictured the way Eloise had looked whenever she defied him. The wench could be provocative and beguiling, without even being aware of how easily she could tempt a man to forget honour. The way her blue eyes flashed when her temper was roused, was as provocative as it was challenging. Courage was something he respected in men. To find it so strong in a woman roused his admiration. There was a dignity in her graceful carriage which made all other women appear insipid in comparison. And the passionate nature he had glimpsed, together with the radiance of her noble spirit, were rare qualities. Beautiful, desirable and spirited, she was all a man could desire in a wife.

He pulled a visor down over such thoughts. He needed to concentrate all his attention on any means of getting out of this dungeon. Frustration made him jerk angrily on the chains. They were embedded deep into the stone walls and would not budge. Ever since his capture by the Moors the odds had been stacked against his survival. But he had survived. With each hour he had been at Penruthin he had come to believe that he had been spared to save its people. He could not believe he had endured so much only to be killed by Stephen's spite and greed.

* * *

Bony fingers shaking Eloise's shoulder brought her awake with a gasp. A stooped figure stood over her and she put up a hand to protect her eyes from the glare of a candle.

"My lady," Githa whispered. "Don't make a sound. The guard outside your door has had his wine drugged. I've brought you some food."

Eloise stood up quickly. Too quickly. Lack of food made her head swim. She put a hand to her temple, sweeping back her unbound hair which fell to her hips. As the room steadied she bit hungrily into a capon leg and regarded the faithful servant.

Her mind raced, filled with exciting possibilities. "If you drugged one guard's wine, you could drug others. This could be a chance for Lord Penruthin to escape and also the guards who are to be hanged tomorrow."

Githa paled. "'Tis too risky, my lady."

Eloise was fired by her idea. "No, it isn't. Besides, what have I to lose? Stephen will not allow my husband and me to live. The men-at-arms have been drinking heavily all evening. Most of them will be in a drunken stupor by now. All it needs is for you to prepare some drugged wine for the guards on duty in the dungeon. I'll steal their keys. And also the key to the postern gate—raising the portcullis would make enough noise to rouse the dead, so I daren't risk that. It couldn't be simpler."

"God-a-mercy, my lady." Githa shook her head in

astonishment. "It could be done. But you cannot risk it alone. I will help you release our men."

"No. If I fail Sir Stephen will…"

Githa cut her short, refusing to be put off. "Sir Stephen is too drunk to do anything until morning. It is the only chance there is."

Eloise hugged the old woman close. "Your loyalty will be rewarded. Thank you."

She was halfway to the door when she looked down at her primrose silk gown. She did not want it betraying her before she reached the dungeon. Snatching a green woollen cloak from its peg and with her mind still racing with all that must be done, she ran to a coffer. She lifted out her father's sword. Stephen had gloated as he displayed her brother's sword taken from Penruthin when he was unconscious. Fortunately, he had forgotten this second sword. She had no reservations now about Penruthin using it. On the point of leaving her room, she asked. "Are the servants all asleep?"

"Even if they were not, no one would raise the alarm that you had escaped." Githa no longer looked so worried and had caught Eloise's enthusiasm for the escape. "They are sullen and angry at what has happened. There's not one who hasn't got family in the village and who is not indebted to you and the ways in which you helped them when you could."

"Have you enough herbs to drug more wine?" Eloise said with sudden alarm. Her plans depended on the prison guards being incapacitated.

"Yes, but I shall need more help. Winifred will be furious if she learns what has happened and she has had no part of it. She has a special fondness for the guard, Gilbert, who is amongst those who are to die tomorrow. If you are to escape she will want to be with you."

Eloise smiled. "I would welcome Winifred joining us. But do warn her of the dangers. So far she has not been implicated in the crimes of which Penruthin and myself are accused. If she comes with us and we are caught…"

Githa waved her hands in denial. "God willing, we shall succeed. They will not expect women to attempt a rescue. It's a clever plan, my lady."

Eloise's mind was now set on the task ahead. She would not turn from it even if it cost her life. "Rouse Winifred. Then prepare the wine and have her bring it to the dungeon. The guards will not be so suspicious if I am accompanied by my maid."

"But what if they raise the alarm at seeing you free, my lady?"

"I have a plan to fool them."

With thudding heart, Eloise crept silently through the castle. Each time she came close to a sleeping guard her breathing stilled. Every nerve in her body screamed that he would awaken and discover her. Stealthily, she stepped over the sprawled figures. Several times whilst her foot was poised over a slumbering form, the man would snort and grunt in his sleep. Her flesh chilled with fear and she froze, too petrified to move. With another snort the guard would turn on to his side. Once the hem of her skirt was caught beneath an outflung leg. Her strained nerves twanged like a bowstring as she gently tugged it free.

Then she was at the head of the stairs leading down to the Great Hall. There was no other exit from the upper apartments. Fortunately most of the candles and torches had guttered out and there was little light.

Wrapping her cloak tight around her body, she glided like a ghost, seeking the darkest shadows. Every step was fraught with danger and her legs trembled. At each sound her heart leapt to her mouth. The hall, filled with sleeping men, had never seemed so vast, the door so far away. It was traversed without incident and at the outer steps to the courtyard she parted from Githa.

"God be with you, Githa," she whispered.

"With you too, my lady."

At the outside doorway, Eloise hesitated and drew back into the shadows. Hastily she scanned the courtyard. It was unfortunate that here the flambeaux were still alight, although their flames had burnt down to produce only a pale flicker of their former brightness. Even so, they could betray her presence. Fortunately, there was no signs of movement from the guards. She lifted her gaze to the battlements. Against the moon-bright sky, she saw that the crenellated walls were deserted. At any other time she would have been furious that Stephen's pleasure-seeking had instilled such laxity in the guards.

It was all going so smoothly, she felt a moment's elation as she ran silently down the steps and across the flagstones. Halfway across the courtyard, she heard a man's laugh from the direction of the stables.

Her heart pounding wildly, she ducked behind an empty wagon and peered through its wheel-spokes. The sound of her heartbeat was like thunder in her ears. Surely she would be discovered? A groom and a young serving-girl, who were clearly lovers, sauntered arm-in-arm out of a storeroom clutching a large jug. The girl staggered and giggled.

"Watch the wine," the groom warned as he held the jug carefully. Then pressing a kiss to her cheek, he guided the giggling woman towards the stables.

Not daring to breathe, Eloise watched their progress as they disappeared from sight. She lifted her eyes heavenwards and mouthed a silent prayer of gratitude.

It was then she heard the low growl close by. The castle dogs were vigilant alarm-raisers. If one began to bark, all her plans would be in ruins.

The wolfhound continued to growl menacingly. It had been scavenging around the dying embers of the courtyard fire for discarded oxbones. Eloise froze. She strained to glimpse its shadowy form in the darkness, and seeing its pale grey coat with a black patch over one ear and eye, she relaxed. He was one of her favourites, but almost blind with age and she was upwind from him.

"Athel," she called his name softly. With a whimper he ambled towards her on legs stiff with the evil joint which claimed so many dogs and people in old age. His wet nose was thrust into her palm and his long wiry tail wagged. She gave him an affectionate hug, his friendly presence a good omen amongst so much hostility in the castle.

Giving Athel a last pat she silently covered the short distance to the dungeon steps. Her head lifted proudly. She must appear confident or her ruse would fail. The stairway was poorly lit and she had not gone far when the musty, mildewed stench of the dungeon assaulted her nostrils. At the end of the steps was a narrow passageway with two thick iron-studded doors at the far end. Before them was a low table and two stools. Both guards were slumped over their arms and snoring loudly.

With her gaze fixed anxiously upon them, Eloise did not falter. The one nearest to her had a large bunch of keys hooked on to his belt. For a moment she was tempted to risk lifting it and trying to free the men on her own. She discarded the idea immediately as being too dangerous. Better to outwit the guards, than for them to be disturbed halfway through an escape attempt.

Standing by the guard's elbow, she cleared her throat. "Sleeping at your post is a whipping offence," she said sharply.

Both guards started awake and jumped to their feet. "My lady, we…but…" the one with the keys began to apologise.

"'Ere, ain't yer supposed to be Sir Stephen's prisoner?'' the other more nimble-witted man challenged.

Eloise eyed him haughtily. "A misunderstanding. Sir Stephen has convinced me that everyone was tricked by the impostor. I will be testifying against him at his trial."

Hearing light footsteps approaching from behind her, she paused until Winifred joined her. "Everyone has been celebrating that the impostor has been found out. Did your companions remember you on duty down here? I suspect not. You have been diligent in your duties and I always believe in rewarding those who prove themselves loyal."

She nodded for Winifred to put the wine-jug on the table between the two men. The one with the keys licked his lips in anticipation.

"While you are enjoying your wine I would speak with the impostor. I want to tell him what I think of a man who would trick a woman in the despicable way in which he did."

"Happen you can say that any time. Why is it so important at this ungodly hour?" the second guard remained surly.

"You dare question me?" Eloise reprimanded, then softened her tone. "I am so angry at the way I was deceived I am unable to sleep."

"There ain't no 'arm in the Lady Eloise seeing him," the first guard unhooked the keys from his waist. "And she did bring us the wine. Which was more than the other one did. All we got from her was a tongue-lashing." He chuckled darkly. "Not that the Lady Isobel got any pleasure from visiting the impostor's cell. She came out of there like an avenging fury."

Eloise held her breath, her stare remaining imperious as she regarded the second guard, who seemed hesitant.

"Never did understand the ways of noblefolk." With a grunt he sank down on his stool and poured himself a large measure of the wine into a chipped horn cup.

Eloise gestured for Winifred to light a lantern from one of the flambeaux. She did not speak as the guard opened the cell door. Across the narrow passage she could hear a lone voice murmuring the Lord's Prayer as the man struggled to come to terms with the last night of his life.

"Wait at the door," Eloise commanded Winifred. "Just hold the lantern high enough so that I can see into the cell."

She was not prepared for the spasm which gripped her chest on seeing Penruthin chained to the wall.

"Were such brutal manacles necessary?" she questioned the guard.

"Sir Stephen's orders. We ain't ter take no chances, 'e killed three guards and wounded four others before they overpowered 'im. Take my advice, my lady, and don't get near 'im. Perhaps I should stay wiv yer."

"Did you stay with the Lady Isobel?" She gambled that he had not.

"No, my lady."

"Then go and enjoy your wine," she said, forcing a tight smile. "You've earned it."

All the time she was speaking she was aware of Penruthin's glittering grey stare. His form was little more than a pale outline against the stone wall.

She stepped into the cell and, for the benefit of the guard, said scathingly, "They have chained you like the cur that you are. You played me for a fool. You had no care for the dishonour you brought to my name." She paced back and fro as she spoke, clenching her fists and striking them against her side as she whipped herself to a greater fury.

Penruthin's initial delight upon recognising her faded immediately. It was humiliating that she should see him chained. When she began to speak, accusing him with such venom, he was unprepared for the pain her contempt caused him. Then to his astonishment as she passed back and forth in front of him, her voice rising in gathering fury, she winked at him, a ghost of a smile touching her lips.

For several minutes she continued to berate him. A voice from the second cell rose in his defence. "My lady, you wrong our lord; he meant you no disrespect."

Penruthin remained silent as Eloise played the part of an outraged woman to perfection. How had she escaped her own guards? Had she then some scheme for an escape? She was a resourceful and courageous woman. The lantern showed the pallor of her lovely face and he could see the lines of tension in the stiffness of her shoulders. There was a fierce light in her eyes which caused his pulse to race with expectation.

At his fellow prisoner's protest, Eloise spun around to glare in the direction of the other cell, her voice rising in fury. "No disrespect, you say! This man has taken my good name and cast it into the dust in his greed to cheat the rightful Lord of Penruthin of his inheritance."

Eloise did not pause in her tirade while she glanced frequently at Winifred keeping watch by the door. When the maid gave a brief nod, her body flooded with relief that the guards were finally succumbing to the effects of the drugged wine. She had been in the cell but a few minutes, but the strain and danger she was in made each second drag like an hour.

The next time she crossed in front of Penruthin's prone figure, she drew her father's sword which was hidden beneath her cloak. She laid it in the straw at his side. When her sharp ears detected the soft thump of an inert body striking the ground, she glanced at Winifred. The maid held up her hand cautioning her that one guard still remained alert.

"You do not answer me," she continued to berate Penruthin. "You have shamed your knightly code. You have shamed the memory of your father."

A muscle pumping along his jaw warned her that she was going too far. But she could not let up until the guard was unconscious. With every moment which passed she feared the sergeant-at-arms might come to inspect his men. Hourly patrols by the sergeant on duty would be routine in any efficiently run garrison. But Stephen's constant drunkenness had made the guards lazy and she did not expect such vigilance tonight. Still, she must be alert to cope with any eventuality.

Then the sound of the wine jug being knocked to the floor and smashing told her it was time.

Winifred disappeared from the door and returned almost at once with the keys held triumphantly in her hands.

"Thank God," Eloise said, startled that her hands shook so violently as she took the keys from her maid. "We must work quickly."

She knelt before Penruthin explaining, "The guards here are drugged and the rest of the garrison are drunk from Stephen's misplaced celebrating." As she spoke she inserted one key after another into the fetters on Penruthin's wrist. She had to lean across him as she worked and found his piercing appraisal disconcerting. With the two days' growth of beard and his fine velvet doublet torn, he looked as predatory as a brigand and just as dangerous. No wonder they had chained him!

When the eighth key was inserted unsuccessfully into the lock, she mouthed an unladylike oath. At Penruthin's chuckle she glared at him.

"I'm glad you find this amusing. I'm terrified we will be discovered."

"You've achieved too much for us to be thwarted now." The admiration in his voice brought a rush of heat to her cheeks.

"I wish I were not shaking so much," she admitted. "Why does there have to be so many keys?"

"You are remarkable, Eloise," Penruthin praised. "What a brilliant performance of an outraged woman! For a moment, I believed you."

The key turned in the lock at last and she sighed as the iron manacle fell away. As he rubbed life back into his numbed arms, she tackled the leg fetters. They parted and clattered to the floor with the second attempt. She tossed the keys to Winifred to unlock the other cell and free the men. Knowing that Penruthin's limbs would be stiff and weak from being cramped for so long, Eloise held out a hand to assist him to rise.

She braced herself as he momentarily swayed against her. The pressure of his fingers on her arm and shoulder was enough to send a spark of sensuality thrilling through her. When she lifted her gaze to meet his, the expression in those grey depths was so compelling that her lips parted and her throat became dry.

Immediately his arms closed around her, her body crushed against his and his mouth claimed hers. The hard pressure of that brief, but wholly encompassing kiss, spoke more eloquently than any words he could have uttered. It branded her his possession.

"You have my undying devotion for this deed."

The words spoken, she saw the look of surprise on his face that he had voiced them. Then his expression cleared and with a shrug, he stooped to pick up the sword. Recognising it, he spared a few precious seconds to regard her with a penetrating but unfathomable stare. Finally he said, "I will be worthy of your father's sword and the honour you do me this day."

Without another word he was out the door and the freed men were tumbling out of the second cell. Several had made improvised bandages to cover their wounds. He put up a hand for silence, his own voice low. "Not all the guards are drugged so take care. I want them bound and gagged and locked in these cells. If any resist then knock them out, but avoid unnecessary killing."

"Githa is waiting outside with the keys to the postern gate," Eloise informed him. "Why bother with locking up the guards? It will delay us. We must make our escape on foot. I thought we would take refuge in the forest until word can be sent to someone you trust to give us horses so we can travel to London."

"No." His tone was emphatic. "I will not run from my home. That would pronounce me guilty. The guards must be locked up. They cannot be trusted not to turn against me again. Penruthin Castle can be held with a dozen men."

Eloise's mind reeled. "'Tis madness. The danger..."

"It is the only way." He faced her, his expression softening at her obvious concern. "I will not skulk in the forest and be branded an outlaw. But you have risked enough. I fear I can spare but one man to escort you and your maid to safety."

"And thus deprive you of three supporters," Eloise returned, lifting her jaw a notch to an obstinate tilt, which warned that she would not be swayed. "Winifred and I can use a bow. I taught her myself, to wile away unfulfilled hours. Captain Maddock kindly improved my skills at the archery butts whenever he could spare the time. You would be better served sending a trusted messenger to a lord who will aid your cause."

Whilst they were speaking, Captain Maddock had ordered the two drugged guards locked in a cell, and had sent the men outside to bind and gag the rest of the garrison. Winifred had gone with them.

Penruthin was eager to follow, but paused to insist, "Dear lady, what better trusted messenger could I have than you?" His dark brows drew together and his voice deepened to a respectful timbre which set her pulses galloping. "I would be happier knowing that you were safe."

Her heart leapt at his concern. But she shook her head. "If I leave, our enemies will imply that I deserted you. I am Mistress of Penruthin; my place is at its lord's side. Besides, have I not burned my boats this night? The world will now see me irrefutably as Lord Penruthin's wife. Better to die with courage de-

fending one's belief's than with dishonour. For me
there can be no turning back.''

"May God spare you and keep you safe, dear
lady.'' His hand touched her cheek with a reverence
which filled her with elation. "You are a courageous
woman.''

His eyes blazed with such fierce admiration, it
brought a return of the fire to her cheeks, its flame
searing through her body to her soul.

Chapter Nine

Half an hour later all the guards were locked in the dungeon. Penruthin sent four trusted men to ride to the villages and summon all males of fighting age to the castle.

"You are preparing for a siege?" Eloise questioned as she joined him in the Great Hall where she listened to him giving precise orders to the small troop of guards and the gathered servants. "How long can we hold out? And what will holding Penruthin prove? You must still appear at Court to answer questions about your captivity. It is the only way your claim to Penruthin can be verified."

"The siege may have to hold for as long as the King remains ill. Too many of the privy council governing in his stead will have been bribed by Prior Ignatius and his family. The King is a just man. I pray that the shock and grief of losing his lands in France, which brought on his madness, soon pass. Until then we must stand firm. Now I have to deal with my brother and his wife. They will be kept under guard in separate chambers so that they cannot plot together, but they will not be harmed.''

Eloise was moved by his compassion. Many men, after such treatment as they had received at Stephen's hand, would have wrought a bitter vengeance upon them. The atmosphere in the castle was strange. The assembled men were edgy with suppressed excitement, but this was also tinged with fear for what the future might hold. Eloise did not doubt their loyalty to her and Penruthin. They knew the high cost involved if the prior should ever regain his control over Penruthin land. They would be ruthlessly persecuted and crippled by taxes.

All at once, Eloise felt weariness seep into her bones and she looked up at a window set high in the hall walls. The first glimmer of dawn was lightening the sky. No wonder her limbs seemed to have no strength; she'd had no more than a couple of hours' sleep in two nights. The roof-beams began to dip and sway crazily around her and the whitewashed walls with their heavy tapestries undulated back and forth. She shook her head to try and clear her wits and heard Winifred cry out,

''My lady, you are exhausted.''

Faces swirled around Eloise as her knees buckled and she felt herself slipping into unconsciousness.

Strong arms caught her up before she crumpled to the floor. She was vaguely aware of being clasped tightly against a man's hard chest and of the swaying motion as she was carried up a flight of stairs.

She struggled to remain conscious, despising any show of weakness. "So foolish of me," she managed to whisper as her bedchamber door was kicked open and she was carried within. The mattress was cool and blissfully welcoming to her back as she was laid upon it. Her eyelids fluttered, but she had no strength to keep them open. Her last conscious memory was of firm lips tenderly brushing her mouth.

During the next two days Eloise saw little of her husband. When she did so, he was often at a distance. He would be riding out with an escort of men to hunt for game, or in the tilt-yard supervising the training of the villagers in the use of arms. Sometimes she would glimpse him on the battlements talking to the masons who had arrived to strengthen the walls. Even at meal times he was absent, often closeted with the steward or another castle officer. On the third evening she saw him closing the door of the Master of Rolls' room having just gone inside. The brief glimpse she caught of his face showed her it was haggard with fatigue. He was pushing himself too hard and he had barely recovered from his fever.

It was not just concern for him which made her anxious. After the tender exchanges during their escape, he had not sought her company. Had she imagined them? She had thought a bond had begun to form between them. Obviously not. She became suspicious that Penruthin was deliberately avoiding her. Having won her to his side, did he now discount her as unimportant? The old resentments rose. She saw the questioning eyes of the servants and retainers watching her as she dined alone on the dais. Stephen and Isobel were still prisoners in their rooms. She felt more isolated than ever before.

Dejectedly, her gaze moved around the hall. It alighted on Ian, a blond curly-haired page who stood at the end of the dais waiting to do her bidding. A shy boy of nine years, he had joined their household six months ago and was the youngest of the pages. He seemed to have difficulty in standing still and a grin flitted across his face every few moments. A suspicious-looking bulge beneath his short tunic moved.

"Ian, what have you there?" Eloise asked.

The boy stopped grinning and looked worried. "Nothing, my lady."

She regarded him sternly. "I regard honesty as one of the greatest of all the virtues. Tell me what you have inside your tunic, Ian."

He fidgeted, unable to look into her face. She had noticed that on many mornings his eyes were often red from weeping and he was teased by the older pages. He was missing his family and, remembering her own unhappiness and homesickness during her first months at Penruthin, she smiled and beckoned to him. "I'm not scolding you, Ian. But you must be truthful with me when I ask you a question."

With head bowed he came reluctantly forward. The bulge in his tunic moved restlessly.

She held out her hand. "Show me."

"I didn't mean no harm, my lady." His lips quivered as he opened his tunic and held out a black and white kitten.

Eloise smiled. "It's too young to leave its mother, Ian. Look: its eyes are barely open. It needs its mother's milk to live. Why don't you put it back with the rest of the litter?"

"Then it will grow wild like the other castle cats, my lady. I can give it milk."

It mewed piteously. "You must take it back to its mother," Eloise reasoned. "Or it will die. If you want one of the kittens when it is old enough to leave the mother, I do not see why you should not make a pet of it."

The boy's face lit up. "Thank you, my lady. But it's Tiny I want. She's the smallest of the litter in the armoury tower."

Eloise dismissed the page and rose to leave the Great Hall, her meal half-eaten. Her appetite had deserted her in recent days. The window of her room was shuttered against a heavy downfall of rain but, even so, from the adjoining tower where Isobel and Stephen were imprisoned she could hear the sound of Isobel's shrill voice raised in drunken anger. Most days Isobel was drunk by early afternoon and continued to shout abuse at her husband, or proclaim her miserable fate, until she fell into a stupor in the evening.

In no mood to suffer Isobel's rantings, Eloise sighed and, picking up a lute, she began to strum upon it. As her body relaxed she sang softly, a ballad of a knight parted from his lady by an evil brigand who held him to ransom. Eloise's voice was filled with yearning as she sang of the lady's vain endeavours to raise the extortionate ransom. Winifred entered the chamber and Eloise cut the song short.

"My lady, you sing so beautifully," Winifred encouraged. "Lord Penruthin has paused by his door to listen. Will you not continue?"

Eloise put aside the lute. The song echoed her own frustration. She felt irritated that it was Winifred who had entered her chamber and not her husband. She sighed. Penruthin was her husband in name only. It was foolish to feel piqued that he did not seek her out. Yet his absence galled her.

"Am I ugly, Winifred? Or so lacking in charm that my husband despises me?"

"My lady, you know that you are not."

"Then why am I ignored, discounted as unimportant?"

It was so rare for her to voice a weakness that Winifred looked at her with a knowing smile. "It never worried you when Sir Stephen ignored you, except if he crossed your will. It is not your will which is pricked by Lord Penruthin's seeming neglect, is it my lady?"

Eloise cast her a baleful glare, but did not reprimand her impertinence.

Winifred added, "Have you considered that Lord Penruthin is but obeying your wishes? Did you not make it clear to him that this marriage is repugnant to you?"

Eloise regarded her maid for several moments, her expression carefully guarded.

"Have you changed your mind, my lady?" Winifred pursued. "Lord Penruthin is a handsome man. You have to admit that he has changed from the arrogant knight you married."

"I don't know what I feel, Winifred," Eloise answered. "I can't stop thinking about him. How can I get to know him if he denies me his company?"

Winifred smiled. "Aye, they do say absence makes the heart grow fonder. But your hatred for him festered over seven years. That will not disperse overnight. We women can be perverse creatures and Lord Penruthin is a man experienced in our ways. He was attentive enough at first and you spurned him. Perhaps now he seeks to win your interest by not pressing his attentions upon you. From the looks of it, it's worked."

Eloise's eyes sparked with a dangerous blue fire. "You may unlace the back of my gown; then leave me, Winifred. I find your insolence wearying this evening."

Far from chastened, Winifred hummed softly as she did her mistress's bidding and she was smiling broadly as she curtsied. "I bid you goodnight, my lady. Lord Penruthin was very taken with your singing. The song of a siren has lured many a man to—"

"Goodnight, Winifred," Eloise cut in sharply.

Alone, she removed the veil and fillet from her hair and began to brush the hip-length tresses until they shone like polished ebony. She removed her outer gown and her chemise and, taking up a thin cream silk nightrobe, belted it about her slender waist. Outside it was no longer raining and, opening one of the shutters, she saw the full moon shining through the thinning clouds. Too restless to settle, her glance returned to the lute and this time she began to play a plaintive love-song. Four candles in an iron sconce illuminated the room with a soft intimate light. She kept her head bent over the strings of the instrument, her long hair flowing to the floor as she sat in the window embrasure.

When she heard a tap on the door, she ignored it and continued her song. At the sound of the latch lifting she closed her eyes, each note carrying with it a seductive promise and resonance of tender yearning.

She knew it was Penruthin who had entered; she could smell the pleasant scent of sandalwood he favoured. Still she played on, refusing to acknowledge his presence. Every pore of her body was aware that he was watching her, the tingling along her spine telling her that he had silently moved closer. As she sang the last verse, the huskiness in her voice almost be-

trayed her; her heart was beating so fast it was difficult to maintain the rhythm of the song.

Her fingers caressed the last chords and she slowly
opened her eyes. Penruthin stood partly in shadow.
His dark-green doublet was open to the waist, the
white of his shirt, which was unlaced at the collar,
accentuated the swarthiness of his skin. His dark hair
had fallen over his brow, softening the rugged lines
of his face.

"You have the voice of an angel, Eloise," he
praised her in a thick voice. "It chases away the cares
of the day and makes the problems ahead seem in-
substantial. It is the first peace I have known since
my return."

Laying aside the lute, she stood up but did not approach him. "Is it not a wife's duty to ease the cares
of her husband's day?"

He folded his arms across his chest and she sensed
the tension within him. "I fear that the peace of this
night will be short lived. A scout has ridden in to say
he spotted Prior Ignatius returning with the High
Sheriff. They must have been caught in the rain and
taken shelter for the night elsewhere, but I expect
them tomorrow."

"And how will you receive the High Sheriff? With
honour, or will you refuse him entry?"

"I had hoped first to have convinced Stephen to
act honourably. His actions towards me have shown
I cannot trust him. I welcome the chance to speak
with the sheriff. And we have the advantage that Ig-

natius will not be expecting me to be in control here with Stephen the prisoner.''

''Then we cannot fail. The sheriff is a just man.'' She moved closer to him. The tenderness she encountered in his gaze made her body burn with yearning to be held in his arms, to feel again the magic his kisses could evoke. Had Winifred been right? Was Penruthin waiting for her to make her feelings known? She no longer viewed him as an enemy, and she was startled to realise how much she had missed his company in the last days. ''My lord, isn't it time we...''

She broke off, embarrassed, her hand placed lightly on his chest where she could feel the powerful beat of his heart. Inadvertently her fingers slid inside the tunic to rest upon the hard-muscled flesh. The touch of his skin seared like a flame. The hairs on his chest were silken, the flesh beneath vibrant and alive. The steady rhythm of his heartbeat resounded through her fingers, up her arm, and into her body where her own heart echoed the wild primeval beat.

Her lips parted in a tremulous smile. ''United, we cannot fail to convince him of the prior's evil.''

He did not respond but stood looking at her, his expression shielded by the shadows. His nearness was causing her body to glow with an languorous heat. She wanted to feel the strength of his arms around her, to chase away the demons of doubt, to be assured that Prior Ignatius no longer would have the power to destroy them.

"Did you not say that 'our fate is bound together and that what fate binds it is loath to part'? I am no longer certain that I wish for an annulment, my lord. Penruthin has long been my home and the people have a special place in my heart."

He had not moved and suddenly her courage deserted her. She felt as gauche as a milkmaid, aware that she was unversed in the rituals of love. She turned away, fearing that he was laughing at her. Her head tilted higher as she added, self-consciously, "I will remain your wife, unless you wish it otherwise."

She heard the sharp expulsion of his breath. Then his hands spanned her ribs, drawing her back against the hardness of his chest. When his lips touched the side of her neck, spirals of delicious heat eddied through her veins. Sensuously her head rolled back and she luxuriated in the pleasure his lips evoked.

"Dearest Eloise. Penruthin's coffers may be empty, but you are its greatest treasure." He planted tender kisses in her hair, along her ear and the pulse at her throat. "It is what I wish more than anything."

There was a husky catch to his voice and she realised that the aching void in her heart during the last days had been the dread of unrequited desire. Her love for him burned through her now like a blazing comet and her hands covered his. They were wider than her own slender ones, the skin darker, tougher. His whole body had the greater strength to force her to yield to his will. But now, she was willing.

Penruthin tasted the freshness of her skin as he

pushed the neckline of her silk robe lower. Her perfume filled his senses. Her skin was softer than silk as he pressed kisses upon her neck and bare shoulders. He was aware that she was naked beneath the robe. Ever since he had awoken from his fever in her chamber, he had wanted her. She had tempted him like no other woman.

Gently he turned her to face him and began to kiss her. His lips were reverent, conscious of her inexperience, but his hunger was too intense to be denied and his passion became fierce. He felt her body quiver, not from anger, but from the sensuality he was awakening in her. Her hips moved against his, unaware of the torture she created. He cupped her breasts through the thin material, feeling her nipples harden with desire. A tug on the sash at her waist parted the robe. The perfection of high full breasts and slim waist were pliant beneath his experienced hands. She writhed in pleasure at his skilful caresses, moulding herself against him so that he was lost in wonder at the ardour of her response. The robe slid to the floor and there was no longer any barrier to his possessing her.

He carried her to the large bed, impatient now that his own clothing kept the touch of her flesh from his. She moaned softly as he lay down beside her, his leg pinioning her as his kisses whispered across her breasts and stomach. She was so lovely, so passionate and yielding; yet he knew instinctively that no other man had been permitted these intimacies. He would be her first lover. The only man to claim this beautiful and fiery-spirited woman as his own. More awesome still was the glow of love he saw in her half-closed eyes.

Instead of elation, this knowledge cast him into despair.

He rolled aside and, leaving the bed, backed away from her. With a cry, she clasped the coverlet across her body, her eyes wide with hurt at his rejection. Then an outraged fire lit her eyes. With a scream of rage she reared up and threw a pillow at him.

"Damn you! This is the final insult. I will bear no more."

A second pillow landed against his chest. "Get out! Never come near me again. I hate you. *I hate you!* I'm leaving Penruthin Castle tomorrow, never to return."

"Eloise, don't be a fool." He no longer dissembled. His expression showed his naked anguish. "Can't you see that I wish only to spare you a deeper shame?"

A third pillow thudded against the side of his head and he did not even attempt to duck from it.

"There is no shame in my bedding with my husband," she raged.

As the words formed and hung like a pall between them, she gasped and sat back on her heels, the cover clasped high to her chin. "Dear God, you *are* Roland, aren't you? You *are* an impostor."

When he did not answer, Eloise recoiled as the

truth dawned on her. "You are Roland! You tricked us all. You lied to me!"

"I never lied to you, Eloise," he rapped out, his body tense, his hands hanging loose at his sides.

Her stare was fixed on his bleak features. The steely glitter in his eyes speared her to the heart. Her own face was bleached of colour, her eyes wide, blue pools of pain.

The disappointment lashed her so acutely that she became defensive against her pain. "Then you deliberately misled me. You allowed me to believe that you were my husband. Why do you think I permitted you such liberties tonight?"

She flung the accusation at him. She did not stop to consider that she had wanted him to make love to her, and that he had not dishonoured her. She was too angry to acknowledge that he need not have confessed to her now. She was bristling with outrage. "Making love to me when you lived a lie was the ultimate betrayal."

His fists clenched as he placed them on his hips, his legs planted apart in an arrogant pose. "If that is how you wish to see it, you delude yourself," he answered stiffly. "I repeat, I never lied to you, Eloise. I told the story of Alaric's death, in a way which you interpreted as though Roland had died. It was what you wanted to believe. You knew that only if I were Alaric could I free the people from the prior's rule. You chose to believe I was Alaric."

Had she been so transparent? Feeling foolish and

ashamed of the self-deception she had deliberately woven to justify her deeds, she glared at him. "And how well it suited your ends. You have dishonoured Penruthin with your lies, as you would have dishonoured me this night." She was trembling with the force of her anger, an anger directed at herself for having been taken in by him, for allowing herself to dream that there could be happiness in her marriage. In her heart she knew that Alaric could not have changed so drastically and that she could never have fallen in love with the arrogant man she had married. Deep inside she was aching, torn by unseen talons. Her voice broke. "I trusted you."

Roland watched her. She was bristling like a wildcat at bay, and she was as unpredictable. She was beautiful and magnificent in her defiance. "I did not dishonour you, Eloise," he made a last attempt to reason with her. "I revere you too much for that. Had I not denied myself the joy of making you mine this night, you would never have guessed the truth."

He closed the gap between them and held her arms, forcing her to hold his piercing gaze. "I love you. I love you too much to shame you."

Every word he spoke smote her like a stone. Her eyes widened with pain, her throat closing with the force of the love she now saw blazing in his eyes. He did love her. And she had wanted that love as much as she craved life itself. But he was Roland, and she could no longer delude herself otherwise.

She slumped down, unable to meet that piercing,

all-encompassing grey gaze. His fingers were light upon her skin, but even so they scorched her flesh. Silently he commanded her to look up at him; she could feel the intensity of his stare penetrating deeply to the heart of her. Resistance was impossible. With trembling breath she lifted her lashes, and her eyes, translucent with love, reflected his yearning. Her husky voice was dragged from the depths of her soul. "Yes, I wanted to believe that you were my husband. Damn you for being so honourable. Damn you for showing me a glimpse of paradise in your arms, only to snatch it from me."

"Rather that, than have you hate me for deceiving you."

"I could never hate you, my love." Tears welled in her eyes. "What is so hard to bear is that Stephen has won. The people of Penruthin are his vassals and I can do nothing now to stop him."

Hands which wielded a sword with lethal mastery drew her to him with a touch as soft and gentle as thistledown. "My darling, I would rather face a hundred infidels than witness your tears. I never meant to cause you pain."

She took his beloved face in her hands and forced a tremulous smile. "You have given me the only happiness I have known for many years. You gave the people back their self-respect and they adore you. There is no man more worthy than yourself to be Lord of Penruthin."

"For that I thank you," he said with unfeigned

humility. He had braced himself against her hatred, not daring to hope that she cared for him. How could the proud Lady Eloise return the love of a bastard, even one who had won his spurs of knighthood? In France he had seen the interest of noblewomen towards him turn to disgust, if not pity, when they learned he was a bastard. It was a taint he would carry to the grave, and he had accepted it long ago.

Her face, white as a marble angel, prompted him to plunge on. "But I am an impostor. I never intended all this to happen. When I saw the changes which had taken place in my absence, and the plight of the people, I wanted to help them. When they claimed I was Alaric and the fever overcame me, fate took its own hand. I saw your influence in many things, but you could never fight Stephen and the prior by yourself."

He paused and drew a heavy breath before continuing, his hands gently stroking her hair. "As Roland, the bastard, I had no power. Only by pretending to be Alaric could I hope to stay alive long enough to bring the injustices perpetrated on my father's land to the attention of the sheriff. I also wanted to avenge my mother's death."

He smiled ruefully. "I was playing for time. But time will not be played with. Penruthin and the plight of its people held me captive, and its lovely mistress stole my heart."

"Oh Roland." Her heart swelled with the force of her love, wanting to hold him close but not trusting herself to do so, knowing the maelstrom of passion she would unleash. For the moment it was enough to talk, to clear the misunderstandings between them. "But you risked exposure as an impostor and a gruesome death on the gallows." Her hands closed over his, fear stark in her eyes. "You still risk that. If only Stephen had taken up your challenge to fight on the tourney field, you might have stood a chance, although as a squire you were not entitled to challenge your brother, who is a knight."

His expression hardened that she should questioned his integrity. "I was knighted in France before I left with Alaric on pilgrimage. The Penruthin arms on my shield may carry the bar sinister, but they give me the right to uphold the honour of my father's name." His lips curled back into a sneer. "As soon as I saw Stephen, I knew it would be no contest. Had he met me on the tourney field, I would have become his murderer. I challenged him only to goad him, to prove his cowardice to myself. He plundered Penruthin's wealth with the carelessness of a marauding Viking. I had hoped to save Penruthin without bloodshed."

"If you were knighted, why did you accompany Alaric on the pilgrimage? We heard he ordered you to be his squire."

"I had the same right as he to pray for our father's soul. We were united in grief."

He was begging her to understand—Roland of Penruthin, who had never pleaded for anything in his life. He should have stayed away from her, as he vowed he would do on the night she had rescued him from the dungeon. He had known then that she was a dangerous temptation. He had fought against going to her, until he had heard her singing. Her voice had been filled with longing. The siren had beckoned and he had been vanquished.

When she did not speak, he misinterpreted her silence. "It would have been better for everyone if I had died and Alaric had been the one to return."

"No. Do not say that." Eloise's mind was in turmoil at his revelations. "You are the one who could have saved Penruthin. You are the moral heir as the eldest son and the only one who truly cares for the people. Alaric would have resumed his old spendthrift ways once he returned. In that he was no different from Stephen. I do not believe imprisonment could have changed him." She put her hand against his cheek. "It was always you I prayed for. It is you I have always loved."

A groan was torn from him as he crushed her to him. His lips were warm and passionate, stealing her breath in an amorous kiss and setting her blood aflame. His kiss deepened, his supple mouth ravaging, fiercely possessive, evoking sensations so exquisite that she clung to him in wanton abandon. Fiery wings of pleasure sped through her veins as his ardent kisses roamed with tantalising slowness over her feverish flesh. Her breath escaped with an ecstatic sigh as his hands slid down her spine, moulding the contours of their bodies so that she could feel the vibrant pounding of his heart pulsating against her breast. Her

senses spiralling, she was transported to dizzy, breathless ecstasy, each kiss and caress instilling a magical,
encompassing fervour which craved fulfilment.

Eloise gloried in Roland's love, knowing that time
was against them. Once it was known that he was the
impostor, he must face the consequences of his mas-
querade. Fear for him made her respond with still
greater ardour.

In all his amorous encounters Roland had never
experienced such rapturous soul-consuming passion,
which was now destroying his control as her tongue
stroked the soft flesh of his neck. The silky caress of
her perfumed skin against his lips was an exotic lure,
a dangerous, forbidden, alchemy. The exquisite torture of the need to possess her, aroused by the sultry
heat of her body moving sensuously against his hard
body, was almost beyond endurance. Desire drove
him to the edge of reason; temptation beckoned, ca-
jolled, demanded. His powerful frame shuddered and
it needed every particle of his willpower to release
her.

"I love you too much to shame you, Eloise." His
breathing was laboured and his hand trembled as he
raised her palm to his lips. "My darling, you know
there is no chance that we will be allowed to marry."

Wrenching away from the torment mirrored in her
eyes, he strode to the window and slammed his ballad
fist against the stone mullion. The pain went unno-
ticed as chivalry and honour battled against the demons of desire which could destroy them both.

Wrapping the sheet around her, Eloise went to him, unable to bear his suffering which echoed her own thwarted longing. When she placed her hand on his arm, she felt his tension in the anvil-hard muscles. "I will always love you, Roland, but we are trapped by circumstances and honour. Once Stephen learns you are Roland, he will not allow you to live. There is too much danger here. Go from Penruthin. Save yourself."

He whirled around. "I will not abandon you or Penruthin's people whilst there is still a chance. I will speak with the sheriff tomorrow." His gaze caressed her. "I have never envied my brothers their lands until now. Without lands, I am nothing. I am unworthy of you. You have a duty to marry well and safeguard the people of Whytemead."

"But once the sheriff hears our story, surely my dowry will be returned to me? I will have plenty for us both."

He shook his head and, as she felt him stiffen, her heart sank. He was too proud to marry her and live upon her bounty at Whytemead.

"It's you I want, Roland," Eloise pleaded, unable to bear the thought of never again feeling the joy of his arms around her.

He smiled and she placed her hand to his cheek, her eyes troubled as she held his forthright gaze. "Until the sheriff arrives you must, of course, continue in your ruse as Alaric. It is too dangerous otherwise."

Roland nodded. "But I will go to Stephen now," he said. "He must be made to see reason. As Lord of Penruthin his duty is to his people. Prior Ignatius must be brought to justice and, for that to happen, Stephen must be persuaded to speak out against him."

Eloise shivered, her fingers threading through his hair. He kissed her brow and his arms held her close against his chest. "I fear for you once it is known you are Roland. You have risked so much already. If anything should happen to you…"

He stopped her words with a long, lingering kiss. When he drew back he cupped her face lovingly in his hands. "I've always known I was in danger by impersonating Alaric, but my motives were honourable in wishing to save the people. Nothing has changed."

She swallowed, fighting her growing fear for his safety. "I know what you say is right, but kiss me again." Eloise rose on tiptoe and linked her arms around his neck. Her impassioned lips would not be denied and, as his mouth claimed hers, he lifted her into his arms and walked with her to the bed. Laying her tenderly on the mattress he straightened. "Goodnight, sweet temptress, dearest love."

As he strode purposefully through the castle he cursed his brother's weak character which had destroyed Penruthin. Stephen had not ruined his home out of malice or greed; he had been no match for

Isobel's spite or the prior's avarice. They were the true culprits.

The events which had happened since his return had moved too fast for him to consider the future in great detail, but whatever happened, he must now make Stephen see reason; he must remind him of his duty and somehow make him overcome his weakness of will.

From the window opposite the Lord's chambers, Isobel had watched in drunken horror the tender way in which Alaric had kissed Eloise beside the unshuttered window. The soft candlelight had spared her none of the details. Her eyes had slitted with fury on seeing Eloise come into view dressed only in a sheet. Obviously, her husband had just made love to her; Alaric had held her so lovingly. Every movement, the way they seemed unable to keep their hands off each other, revealed a tenderness Alaric had never shown towards her when she had been his mistress. Jealousy gnawed savagely in Isobel's breast. Alaric loved Eloise. How dare he scorn herself so callously?

Isobel smashed the goblet she was holding against the wall. She deserved better from Alaric. She would not be spurned and discarded like his other women. She had earned her place as Mistress of Penruthin and she would not surrender it.

Her face twisted with ugly fury, her eyes viper-bright and malicious. Alaric would not have Eloise. Neither would he have Penruthin. She had planned the ruin of Penruthin for too long be thwarted of it now. Her heart raced with contemplation of her revenge. It would be the sweeter now that Alaric would see its destruction by her own hand.

To concentrate his thoughts, Roland had climbed onto the castle battlements. The night breeze whipped his hair back from his face as he gazed over the wall at the dark outline of the village, a few of its cottages lit by the dim glow of burning rushlights.

His gaze travelled over the familiar towers and crenellated walls of the castle. As though to carve the image into his mind, he surveyed it. Torches illuminated the high stone walls. He could see his guards patrolling the battlements, vigilant in their duty. An unexpected pain gripped his chest and his knuckles whitened as he gripped the rough parapet. A rare sigh escaped him. A bastard was not supposed to have feelings of pride, or wish to uphold the heritage of his home; his tainted noble blood was not expected to clamour for justice when he saw his father's honour destroyed. A bastard had no rights under English law, was considered a nonentity. But pride in his family heritage could not be stifled just because he had been baseborn. As his father's son, he had the right to do everything in his power to safeguard Penruthin's interests and protect the family honour. With this thought, he turned to approach his brother's apartment. As he drew near he could hear Isobel raging across the landing.

"There must be some means by which we can get out of here." Her words were slurred by drink. "Alaric escaped from the dungeon. You can't even get out of your own room."

"Rest your shrew's tongue, woman!" Stephen shouted. "Alaric had the quick wits of Eloise to help him. If you stopped your drunken ravings long enough to give me some peace, I might think of something."

"I doubt it," Isobel sneered. "You always were weak and useless."

Roland nodded to the guard to open the door. The room revealed to him in the candlelight had been wrecked. The bed-hangings had been ripped from their posts. A tapestry lay torn and crumpled on the floor where it had been wrenched from the wall. All over the rushes were broken shards of pottery and dented silver cups and flagons. Isobel in her ungovernable rages over the three days of her imprisonment had smashed and torn everything she could get her hands upon.

Isobel's nightrobe gaped open and the loose kirtle she slept in had fallen down over one arm, revealing a heavy blue-veined breast. She made no attempt to cover herself as she swayed drunkenly and lifted her goblet in derisive salute to Roland.

"Our gaoler condescends to visit us."

Roland regarded her in disgust. Her fair hair was matted and hung in straggles to her waist. A village bawd had more dignity. He gestured for the guard to open the door to Stephen's room, and Isobel stumbled in ahead of him.

His brother was sprawled in a X-shaped chair, his shoulders slumped in defeat. Unlike the swaying figure of his wife, Stephen was sober, his eyes bleak with fear at his anticipated fate.

"So what is to be our punishment?" Stephen could not keep the tremor from his voice.

"That is up to you," Roland began, finding it difficult to control his resentment that this weak and effectual man was his father's heir. "You have allowed too many evil influences to bring shame and dishonour to our name."

Isobel sniggered maliciously. "Saint Alaric has returned to lord it virtuously over us all. You cared for nothing but your own self-gratification all the years you were at Penruthin; Stephen but followed your example."

"Or yours," Roland said, his temper beginning to slip. "If a man cannot govern his wife, he cannot govern his lands." He breathed deeply to overcome his anger and turned back to Stephen. "I have not sought you out at this late hour to argue."

Stephen straightened in his chair, his expression sly. "I told Isobel you would not harm us. Not your own brother."

"As you would not have harmed me, Stephen?" Roland snapped and saw the fear return to his brother's eyes and his face turn corpse-white.

Roland took a reliquary from the pouch at his waist. "Do you recognise this?" he asked Stephen.

"It belonged to our mother, the Lady Matilda," Stephen replied guardedly.

"She was a pious woman and placed great faith in it," Roland pursued. "I demand that you swear on this piece of the True Cross that you will oppose Prior Ignatius and that, when he is brought to account for the burning of the villagers as heretics, you will testify that he has abused his position. A messenger has been dispatched to the Abbot of Shergrove, Prior Ignatius' superior. He has been given a full report of the atrocities the prior has committed in the Church's name."

"He is a powerful man," Stephen hedged. "He has influential cousins at Court." He glanced at Isobel, seeking her support.

"Don't listen to him!" Isobel screeched. "He'd have you imperil your soul. Ignatius will excommunicate you. Do you want to burn in hell?"

"Once disgraced, Ignatius will have no power," Roland said sharply. "Swear on this holy relic, Stephen."

Stephen's gaze was drawn by Roland's stronger will and commanding tone. Nervously moistening his lips, he put a shaking hand on the reliquary. "I swear."

"Also," Roland continued, "I want your word that the Lady Eloise's dowry shall be restored to her. If the Church will not repay that which Ignatius has spent on the priory, then Isobel's jewels can be sold to repay the dowry which was misappropriated."

"You will *not* have my jewels!" Isobel's face contorted with rage.

Stephen hesitated. But Roland ignored her outburst, his expression formidable and uncompromising as he regarded his brother.

"It will be done," Stephen agreed, quietly.

Roland nodded.

"Fool!" Isobel snarled at her husband, replenishing a large goblet with wine. She drank it down. Her eyes were malicious slits as she regarded Roland over the rim of the goblet.

To his surprise, Roland pitied Stephen. It was obvious that he loved Isobel. She continued to glare at Roland and tossed back another goblet of wine.

"Don't listen to Alaric," she berated. "He's trying to trick you into something. Already he has demanded my jewels. He'll be throwing us out of the castle next." Her voice rose with growing hysteria. "I am Mistress of Penruthin. Not her. Not that sly bitch you married. I should have been your wife, not Eloise. You loved me. She has bewitched you. I've seen the way you look at her. I *won't* be cast aside."

Stephen rounded on his wife, his voice taut with pain. "You swore you never loved Alaric."

Isobel laughed cruelly, her words slurred and wild with hatred. "You always were a weak fool, Stephen. But you had your uses. By marrying me you gave me the power to destroy that which Alaric cherished most—his home.''

''No. It is me you love. Not him.'' Stephen lunged at Isobel, his hands outstretched to circle her throat. As his grip on her neck tightened, Isobel screamed.

''For God's sake, man!'' Roland hauled Stephen away. ''She's evil, but don't stain your hands with her death.''

Stephen staggered back. The three days' growth of beard shadowed his fleshy jowls and his eyes were wild and reddened from lack of sleep. He reeled back into the shadows cast up by the candles and stared incredulously at his hands. ''I love her. I never meant to hurt her. But she drives me mad with her taunting.''

Roland turned away, unable to face the tears which were spilling down his brothers' cheeks. There was a scraping sound which alerted him, then the glint of a yellow flame reflected on steel. His own sword was freed from its scabbard in a single movement, and he parried his brother's lethal lunge.

''It's your death I want, not hers,'' Stephen seethed. ''I wish you'd never returned. You defiled Isobel's innocence. I'll kill you for that.''

Besotted with his wife, Stephen had believed her lies that Alaric had seduced her. Stephen's frenzy brought a strength to his attack which Roland had not expected.

''Put down your sword,'' Roland countered, deflecting the point which was aimed at his heart. "You are no match for me. I don't want to hurt you."

For some moments he was hard pressed to parry the blows away from his body. Unwilling to wound Stephen, he was forced into defence.

Isobel screamed and ran to the door. "Guards! Guards! Lord Penruthin and Sir Stephen are trying to kill each other. Stop them!"

"Stay back!" Roland shouted as he heard the guard step into the room. In the distance he heard the rapid tread of unsteady footsteps. Isobel had escaped. What mischief did she plan? Mischief it must be for her not to stay and watch the outcome of the fight.

Roland moved from defence to attack. His sword became living steel, its movements almost invisible to the eye. The metal sliced through the flesh of Stephen's arm and his brother cried out and dropped his sword. Stephen fell to his knees holding his wound, blood trickling through his fingers.

"Mercy! Have mercy, brother. Don't kill me."

Breathing heavily, Roland stepped back. "I never meant it to come to this, Stephen. I want your word you will denounce the prior."

"Yes. But you will not punish Isobel for her outburst? Despite all that she has done, I love her."

Roland was already at the door, fear closing around his heart. He was impatient to catch up with Isobel. "Then deal with your wife now. She cannot be trusted."

Chapter Ten

Roland ran out of the room and heard his brother call out, "Wait! You misjudge her."

Stephen's footsteps were behind him. Instinct and fear made Roland retrace his steps to Eloise's room. He bounded up the steps of the tower and, as he ran into the corridor, he saw a light flickering behind Eloise's open door.

As he reached the doorway he was unprepared for the evil vengeance Isobel had wrought. She was laughing and muttering as she touched a burning flambeaux to another tapestry. Already the bedhangings were alight and the room was filling with thick smoke. The dry hangings lit like tinder, the flames snaking over the bed canopy. Behind the growing wall of flames Roland saw Eloise's still figure.

"Eloise!" he shouted.

She did not stir.

Several paces took him across the room. Isobel threw herself at him to stop his rescue. Her hair was wild and her face was twisted with hatred.

"She will die, as is fitting, by the flames. She's a witch. She's bewitched you. You were mine. Only mine."

"Put down your torch," he commanded, snatching at it. She danced away, but her drunken step was unsteady and she fell against the wall. His fears were all for Eloise, not Isobel. "Stephen, get her out of here," he shouted as his brother entered the room.

"Dear God! No!" Stephen gasped. "What have you done, Isobel?"

Roland ran to the bed, shouting. "Guards! Help put out these fires!" His attention was now focused upon Eloise. Why did she not awaken? The flames were all around her. Isobel had been thorough, setting the torch in several places to the hangings. Behind him he heard Isobel chanting.

"I'll not be cast aside. You will all die. Penruthin will be a ruin. And by my hand. I told him it would be so. So will it be!"

Roland was driven by his need to save Eloise. He heard her groan softly and then start to choke as the smoke swirled about her. He was not aware that his skin blackened and was scorched as he ripped down the burning hangings and threw them aside. He was coughing and half blinded by the thickening black smoke. Behind him, above the roar and crackle of the flames, he could hear Isobel laughing and Stephen scuffling with her.

"You won't have to sell your jewels," Stephen reasoned. "I'll find another way to repay Alaric."

Roland ignored them. Only Eloise was important. He had to save her.

His arms tightened around Eloise's unconscious figure and, as he lifted her from the mattress, he saw the large lump which was forming on her brow. Isobel had knocked her out as she slept so that she might not escape the flames.

The smoke was choking him, the raging heat of the fire coating him in sweat. The bed was now surrounded by a wall of flame and orange tongues were licking across the rushes. Shouts of ''Fire!'' were rousing more guards to fight the blaze. Clutching his precious burden close to his chest, Roland staggered towards the door. Before him was a tunnel of fire from the brightly burning tapestries and rushes. Above the roar of the flames Isobel's demonic laughter filled his ears. Then the laughter turned to screams.

Eloise was choking, her throat was raw and her lungs were bursting. There was a vicious throbbing in her head and, as she struggled to open her eyes, she found herself pitched into hell. Flames leapt up all around her. She was floating and it took a moment to realise that Roland was carrying her, his body crouched low as he ran towards the door.

More flames sprung up before them and her glazed and smoke-tearful eyes recognised Isobel holding a torch. She was wrestling with Stephen, their figures macabre silhouettes against the orange flames. Then the fire flared brighter. Isobel had been laughing wildly and tossing her head. Her tangled loose hair had caught alight.

Within the speed of several of Roland's long strides Eloise saw Isobel become a living beacon. Her screams of agony and terror echoed the screams of the heretics Isobel had callously watched burn to death.

The figure engulfed in fire was running ahead of them towards the door. It was pursued by a sobbing Stephen. "Stop, Isobel."

But she was beyond hearing, driven to demented flight by terror and agony. The guards, who had started to form a human water-chain fell back in shock at seeing Isobel, their faces masks of horror. As he ran, Stephen stripped off his robe and dived at his wife to bring her to the ground. With a sob, he threw himself on top of her, wrestling to smother the flames of her kirtle. His own long gown caught light and for several moments they were both engulfed, until the first bucket of water to arrive from the well was thrown over the two writhing figures on the floor. Stephen was dragged off his wife; his flesh was blackened but he was still breathing. Isobel was just a charred heap.

"Do what you can for my brother," Roland rasped, coughing in the thick smoke.

Saved from the burning room, Eloise clung to Roland as he slumped against the wall, his chest heaving. He held Eloise tighter and, burying his lips in her hair, croaked, "Thank God you are safe."

When a bucket of water was thrown over them both, she realised that their clothes had begun to smoulder.

There was a scream of agony from Stephen as he was lifted on to a makeshift stretcher made from a door torn off its bracket. "Don't look, my love," said Roland, as he turned her face into his chest and walked slowly away.

She was trembling, her flimsy night-clothes moulded revealingly to her body by the water. Roland pressed her body closer to his, shielding her from any glances from the guards. The strength of his arms was a haven after the horrors she had just witnessed. Her mind grappled to work out what had happened. She was shocked to acknowledge that Isobel must have set fire to her room; that Isobel hated her so much she wanted her dead. And Roland had saved her.

Her tremors became more violent, not merely from shock. She was more aware of his masculinity and power than ever before. Her entire being pulsated from his nearness and she clung to him, relishing the pleasure and haven of his embrace. Her heart ached as she studied his handsome face, streaked with smoke stains. She loved him so much. How could she bear life without him at her side?

Eloise struggled awake through a haze of pain. The room she was in was dark and smelt strange—earthy and of cooking smells. Blearily, she pushed herself onto her elbow.

"Where am I?" Her voice was hoarse and her throat ached from the effort of speaking as she addressed a figure bent over the cauldron over the central hearth.

"My lady," Githa straightened and turned to face her. "You're in my hut. It was thought to be best for your safety. The fire at the castle is out of control and still raging." She held out a horn cup which emitted a sweet-smelling aroma of herbs. "Drink this, my lady. The posset will ease your throat and the pain in your head. That's a vicious bruise you have on your temple."

She screwed her eyes shut and massaged her throat before sipping the hot liquid. "Shouldn't you be tending Sir Stephen? His needs are greater than mine."

"I've not been allowed near him today. Prior Ignatius ordered that he be removed to the priory to be tended by Brother Bernard while I was out of the room. It was too late to alert Roland to countermand the order. The move could have cost Sir Stephen his life, but he survived it. The prior fears that, if Stephen regains consciousness, he will speak of things Ignatius would prefer to remain secret. Brother Bernard is competent enough in the ways of healing—for a man."

Eloise shuddered, seeing again the two burning figures. Stephen had risked his life to save the wife he loved. That had taken courage. A pity he had not shown more of it to defy the prior. "Will Stephen live?"

Githa shrugged. "It is in God's hands."

Eloise pushed back a tress of hair and found it sticky with smoke, the ends singed by the fire. Her hands and body had been bathed whilst she slept, but her hair was filthy. There was no time to wash it now.

It must be hidden under a veil. What veil? If the castle had burned, so had her clothes and possessions.

She finished the posset and already the pain in her head had lessened, allowing her to think more clearly. She threw back the bedcovers and rose unsteadily. Through the open shutter of the small paneless window she saw dark clouds in the sky. No, not clouds, she realised with a sinking sensation, but smoke.

She moved to the window and was appalled to see the blackened shell of the keep and the flames still leaping high as they devoured the thatches on stables and storehouses. The fire, fanned by the breeze, had spread alarmingly in the night. Several of the villagers' houses had also lost their thatched roofs, but mercifully the wind must have changed and most of the village had been saved.

"There is so much destruction," she said, hollowly. "What time is it? And where is Roland?"

Githa looked taken aback. "So *that's* why he looks so bleak. You found out that he was not Sir Alaric."

"But you are not surprised that I called him Roland." Eloise studied the woman and felt a sense of betrayal. "You knew. But, of course, your loyalty to his mother would have stopped you from betraying him."

Githa smiled knowingly. "At first that was so. Until I saw how he meant to bring the prior to justice and help the people. It was also obvious you were falling in love with him. What better way to resolve…"

"It resolves nothing. Stephen is Lord Penruthin,"

Eloise wrenched out. "I must go to Roland. The Sheriff is on his way. I must speak for him or his life may be in danger."

Githa sighed. "The fire has raged all night and he has not rested. Yet, despite needing every possible man to fight the fire, he has sent a messenger hourly to enquire as to your recovery." Her face was creased with concern. "And the sheriff is already here and lodged within the priory. Roland insisted that you be allowed to sleep to recover from your ordeal, telling the sheriff that the meeting must wait until the fire is out."

Eloise smothered an oath at Roland's stubbornness and bravery. "It is time Roland thought of himself, not others," she cried in exasperation, her fear for his safety chilling her to the core.

"Do you really think he would desert his people or, especially, the woman he loves?" snapped Githa.

"Of course not. It is that very quality of honour which made me fall in love with him." Eloise cast about for something to wear. "Roland will never speak in defence of himself. I must talk with the Sheriff first. But I shall need something to cover my hair."

Githa helped her into a plain homespun russet gown which belonged to Winifred. Before seeking out the sheriff, Eloise needed to inspect the damage to the castle. As she walked beneath the open portcullis, the devastation which greeted her wrenched at her heart. She had not realised how much it had come to mean to her until she saw it destroyed.

The courtyard was filled with pieces of furniture,

and the huge tapestries ripped down and saved from the main hall were piled on a cart. The stench of smoke and charred wood cloyed in her nostrils. Not a single pane of glass remained in any of the windows of the tall keep. The floor of the Great Hall smouldered. Its oak-beamed roof and all the floors above it were useless cinders. The heart of the castle was now open to the sky.

In the time it had taken her to dress, the stables had burnt to the ground and the horses had been taken out into the fields. As she walked she scanned the ruins. Men with blackened faces and red-rimmed eyes still fought to save the grainstore. Sparks from the stable had ignited the wooden structure of the laundry and the entire west side of the courtyard with its dozen outhouses was in danger of going up, spreading the fire still further towards the infirmary.

Eloise ran to six men beating out the last of the flames from the rubble which had been the coach-house and harness store. "Leave that! Get the injured out of the infirmary," she ordered. "It could go up at any moment."

There was a roar like cannon-fire as another ceiling crashed inwards and Eloise turned to see the Armoury Tower ablaze. A file of men were staggering out of the tower, carrying armfuls of weapons and armour. Many of these were the men they had earlier locked in the dungeon. Roland had freed them. But then he would not have allowed them to burn to death. Somehow he had won their loyalty, for they all looked to be at the point of exhaustion, yet continued to follow his orders.

She marvelled at Roland's capacity to win men to his side. The mercenaries were aware there was no money to pay for their services. It was respect which made them follow him. And respect from such hardened men was only won by an exceptional leader.

Several men emerged from the tower and Eloise saw Roland amongst them. Her heart leapt with concern. His hands were bandaged and his fine velvet clothing was scorched in several places. A piece of cloth had been tied around his lower face to stop him breathing in smoke and he shouted at the villagers who had gathered close. "Get back! The masonry is unsafe. The tower could collapse."

Although she yearned to run into his arms, she resisted the impulse. She must speak with the Sheriff and inform him of all the good Roland had done out of love for the people, before he had announced his true identity.

From behind her there was a faint frightened shout. "Help! Help me!"

Eloise turned and looking up saw a young page waving frantically from the roof of the burning armoury tower. Rods of flames were shooting out of all the windows on the lower floors. The boy was trapped, and at any moment the roof could give way.

She saw Roland glance up at the boy's shout. Then, to her alarm, he ran back into the burning tower. Two other guards who followed him were ordered back.

She cried out, "No, Roland! It's too dangerous."

Her words were lost amongst the roaring of the flames.

"His lordship will be killed," a nearby guard voiced Eloise's fears. "The flames are funnelling up the stairs. Even if he gets to the boy, there will be no way out."

"Sweet Jesu, don't let him die!" Eloise fervently prayed. Her gaze was riveted upon the roof of the tower where Roland would appear. From the amount of smoke pouring out of the windows, it was obvious that inside the tower was an inferno.

"Are there no ladders to reach the top of the tower?" she demanded of Captain Maddock, who had come to stand at her side.

"The last was burned in the night when the stables caught fire," he answered gruffly.

Above the roar of the flames Eloise heard the page crying out with fear. What had the boy been doing in the tower? As she strained to recognise him she saw that it was Ian, and remembered his showing her Tiny the kitten. Now, as she stared, she saw that he appeared to be clutching something inside his doublet. The young fool had risked is life to save the kittens born in the armoury tower.

A black spiral of smoke momentarily obscured the top of the tower. Eloise pressed her hands together, her lips moving in silent prayer. Where was Roland? "Dear God, let him be safe. He is so brave, so reckless. He has endured so much. He cannot die now."

There was a sickening rumble within the tower. Eloise's heart lurched. Another wooden ceiling had crashed inwards. Sparks flew out of the third-storey window, followed by spears of flames which reached up to the top of the crenellated tower.

The sound of her frantic heartbeat reverberated through her body as she strained to see through the smoke and flames. The breeze parted them enough to show her that two figures now stood on the roof. Thank God! Roland had reached the page safely. But how could they possibly escape from the flames and smoke now pouring from the windows? And why were they hesitating? She wished she could see clearly, but the two figures were indistinct. Then she saw Roland lift up the young page and throw him over the far side of the tower where the murky waters of the moat would break his fall. Through the thick smoke, she saw Roland poised on the tower's parapet. She gasped as he vanished, diving into the moat.

Panic washed over her in sickening waves as she sped towards the drawbridge. Was the moat deep enough to save their lives after plunging from such a height? At least Roland could swim; that was how he had escaped the slave-ship. But the moat would be dangerously low after a dry summer, and much water had been taken from it to fight the fire.

Her lungs were bursting as she leaned over the drawbridge to scour the water for sign of Roland and the page. The sides of the moat were steep and covered in green slime, indicating that several feet of water had been taken from it during the night. There was no sign of Roland or the page.

Gasping with fear, she lifted her skirts and ran to-

wards the burning tower at the far corner of the moat.
Behind her she heard the heavier tread of Captain
Maddock and several men. On reaching the ground
opposite the armoury tower, she still could not see
Roland or the page. No! He could not be dead. Not
now. Not after all he had suffered and survived.

Dimly she became aware of several figures approaching from the priory towards them. She ignored
them. Her mind was locked in fear for Roland. Panic
threatened to choke her. She loved him so much. It
could not end—not like this.

In her distress it took several moments for her to
notice that the green algae covering the top of the
moat had been disturbed around the far side of the
tower, where they had plunged into the water.

''Roland!'' she screamed, unaware in her fear for
him that she had betrayed him. ''Roland! Ian!''

A movement to her right caught her eye and she
saw Roland clinging precariously with one arm to the
slippery slope of the moat. At any second he could
slide back into the water and one or both of them
could drown. The page was unconscious. Roland
must be drawing on the last reserves of his strength
to hold on and keep the page's head above the water.
His fingers were frantically clawing for a hold, but he
kept slipping back.

''Over there. Make haste!''

She ran forward and watched with thudding heart
as Captain Maddock threw himself onto the ground
and reached out a hand to haul Roland to safety. Another guard jumped into the moat and momentarily

disappeared from sight beneath the water. He emerged spluttering and helped to push the two figures higher onto the slope. He in turn was hauled to safety by two companions.

Roland was breathing heavily as he fought to regain his breath. The page was deathly still but, as Captain Maddock flipped the boy on to his stomach, he coughed and vomited some water.

Eloise knelt at Roland's side. Tears blurred her vision and her throat was uncomfortably tight. "You could have been killed," she murmured, fighting to control the need to hold him in her arms and reassure herself that he was safe.

He hung his head and reached inside his doublet to pull out two wet and unhappy kittens. One was the black-and-white Tiny. "Someone had better ensure these live after all the trouble I've been to," he said by way of answer. "How is the boy?"

"Alive—thanks to you," Eloise answered. "As I am, also."

The catch in her voice made him look up and for a timeless moment she was transfixed by his grey, all-consuming stare. Even with his clothes sodden and his dark hair plastered to his skull, he was an imposing figure. Her heart clenched and she was inwardly shaking to realise that he had come so close to death. Her love was bright and unguarded in her eyes and she saw his own gaze soften in a way which made her entire being quiver with longing.

"So the truth is out," Prior Ignatius bellowed, destroying the intimacy of the moment. "The Lady Eloise called you Roland."

Until now she had been too concerned that Roland be rescued to have noticed the prior. Her careless cry had given him the weapon he needed to bring about Roland's destruction.

"I said all along that he was an impostor," Ignatius continued to rant. "You have your proof from the woman's lips, Sheriff!"

Eloise glanced at the tall, slim man who accompanied the prior. Beneath a jewelled cap, his greying blond hair curled to his shoulders and, although his face was lean and austere, his expression was not unkindly. It gave her hope.

Turning to Roland, she whispered, "I did not mean to betray you."

Again his gaze tenderly held hers. "You didn't. Last night I informed the garrison as to who I am."

"Arrest him!" Prior Ignatius demanded.

Roland shot him a glaring look of disdain. "I'm not going anywhere until I have answered the sheriff's questions." Ignoring the incensed prior, he addressed the sheriff, "Have I your leave to change and appear before you in a more fitting manner? All your questions will be answered."

"For the brave way in which you saved this boy's life, you deserve that much."

As Roland walked away, the sheriff made to return to the priory.

Eloise stood up. "My lord sheriff, I am the Lady Eloise Penruthin. Will you not accept the hospitality of Penruthin? The Great Hall is burned to a shell, but the guest quarters within the Outer Bailey have been spared. The castle is the seat of justice here; not the priory."

"My lady, you and Sir Roland are accused of treachery and deceit, which make a mockery of the laws of justice which once governed Penruthin."

The coldness in his tone shocked her. The prior had spoken his poisonous lies to lethal effect. She returned the sheriff's stare with all the hauteur she could muster. "The treachery and deceit was not on my part. I have not forced my people to work extra days on my land to fill my coffers. Neither did I burn them at the stake if they questioned my orders. Prior Ignatius is the enemy of the people of Penruthin. I ask that you listen to what myself, Sir Roland and the people have to say before you condemn us."

His expression darkened. "It is not for me to pass judgement upon a member of a religious order," he informed her, coldly. "As for the bastard Roland, it is a different matter."

Eloise's fears for Roland mounted. "Sir Roland is a knight. He has the right to be tried by his peers. Prior Ignatius evidently has not informed you of his knighthood."

"Then you admit that there is a case for trial?" the sheriff countered, his lips grim and compressed.

"No," she replied firmly. "Sir Roland did not impersonate Sir Alaric in order to steal Penruthin from its rightful owner. He did it to gain time, until the injustices committed here would be brought to the attention of yourself and the abbot.''

Seeing the antagonism fade from the sheriff's hazel eyes, she pursued her point. ''A messenger was sent to the Abbott of Shergrove. The old Abbot, who was an uncle of Prior Ignatius, died two months ago. I trust that the new one will be less biased when hearing of the atrocities the prior has committed in God's name.''

The sheriff's lips compressed. ''If you and Sir Roland are so innocent, Lady Eloise, why was I not informed of Sir Roland's return? I learned of it only through Prior Ignatius.''

''A messenger was sent to you.'' She eyed him levelly. ''He was killed by Sir Stephen's men.''

''Don't listen to her!'' Prior Ignatius shouted as he thrust his immense bulk between them.

His unwashed body and the garlic and wine sauce which stained his habit offended her sensibilities. She controlled the urge to turn her face away from the stench of the man. Instead, she held his malevolent glare, her expression serene.

The prior thrust a greasy finger against her shoulder. ''She and her paramour have planned between them what to say.''

The sheriff hooked his thumbs into his sword-belt, his stare bleak with censure. Eloise felt a dart of alarm, then sensed that his anger was aimed, not at herself, but at the attitude of the prior. His gaze moved over her slim figure, which was stiff with defiance. When his eyes returned to hold her stare, Eloise felt as though her thoughts were being picked clean as a hawk shreds meat from a bone.

He rapped out gruffly, "That does not explain why I was not informed of the injustices you say the prior and Sir Stephen have perpetrated in recent years."

Eloise sighed. He was no one's fool and she must trust that he was honest and unbiased in his judgements. "I had no power. Prior Ignatius ruled here. Sir Stephen was too weak to defy him. Any messenger I sent was always intercepted. The one who did get through—when I demanded an investigation into the number of heretics Prior Ignatius ordered burned—did so at a time when you were at Court. The matter was dealt with by one of your officers. He was apparently in the prior's pay."

"Lies! All lies!" spat Prior Ignatius. "She'd say anything to save her lover. Whore! Fornicator!" He waved his arms wildly, his eyes rolling and saliva spraying from his mouth. "Hear how she questions the will of the Church. She's a heretic. She has no regard for the law. Jezebel!"

"That's enough, prior." The sheriff rounded on him. "I will speak with the Lady Eloise alone."

Eloise let out a relieved breath. Forcing a smile, she graciously offered the sheriff her hand. "I make no excuses for our conduct. As a man of discernment, you will judge wisely when you hear what has passed here. I will answer any questions you have whilst Sir Roland changes his clothes."

"It is a ruse to allow the impostor to escape," Prior Ignatius screeched. "The whore is the impostor's paramour. They have lived as man and wife since he returned.''

Eloise paled, her eyes glittering with contempt as she regarded the gross figure. ''How dare you malign my honour? Sir Roland is a man of impeccable honour. He has risked is life to save his father's castle. He has no cause to flee.''

Eloise stood back from the sheriff, her eyes flashing sapphire fire. ''If those are examples of the lies he's been telling you, then I am not surprised that you are hostile in regarding us. I would never dishonour my father's name. Were I a man, I would demand that the prior answer to my sword for such an insult.''

For a long moment the sheriff regarded her. ''I knew Sir John Lejeune of Whytemead well. I was his squire for a year before I earned my spurs. He was one of the most honourable men I knew. I will listen to you, Lady Eloise, before I make any judgement. But the prior's claims are serious if they are true.''

Chapter Eleven

A half hour later, just as Eloise finished telling the sheriff her account of the events since Roland's return, a page announced that Roland was waiting below.

"And you say that Roland never deceived you?" the sheriff probed.

Eloise shook her head. "He never lied to me. I assumed that he was my husband. It was what I needed to believe."

"And he treated you as his wife?"

For the first time during the interview, Eloise was unable to hold his penetrating stare. "Not in the full sense," she answered, softly. "I am a still a maid. During his time at Penruthin, Sir Roland treated me with respect and honour."

The sheriff continued to regard her with piercing intensity. "Do you think that it was Sir Roland's intention to maintain his role of impostor until Penruthin was his?"

Her gaze returned to hold his and was unwavering

as she answered firmly, "Most definitely not. Sir Roland was angry that shame had been brought upon his father's name by the tyranny of recent years. And that my dowry had been squandered. He also wanted the prior brought to justice, as do I, for the burning of the heretics. One of the heretics falsely accused was his mother."

Silence stretched between them for several moments. He was watching her closely and she became uneasy. "It is obvious that you care for Sir Roland. Is that why you are defending him so strongly?"

In his question lay the trap she dreaded. If he was corrupt, he could twist her words to condemn them both. "I do love Sir Roland. But I swear on my father's memory that I defend him because he is innocent of seeking to usurp his brother's place."

Eloise stood tall and unflinching under the sheriff's sharp stare. She knew that the prior would have spent the last two days blackening her character as well as that of Roland.

There was a knock at the door and a page entered. "My Lord Sheriff, the Abbot of Shergrove has arrived and has requested that he be allowed to attend this questioning."

The sheriff looked at Eloise. "Was it you or Sir Roland who sent for the abbot?"

"Sir Roland. He wanted the abbot to hear from the people of the prior's persecution."

He turned to the page. "Ask the abbot to join us. I will speak to him first, before Sir Roland is admitted."

The sheriff again regarded Eloise. "Will you wait outside, my lady? I would speak with the abbot and Sir Roland alone."

As she descended the steps to the courtyard, she curtsied to the abbot who was waiting to ascend. His flinty eyes sent a shiver of foreboding through her.

"Welcome to Penruthin," she greeted him. "It was good of you to journey so far."

"I am displeased with the rumours which have reached me concerning Prior Ignatius." His thin voice had no warmth. "They are serious allegations against a devout man of God." He swept past her, giving her no time to speak.

The abbots's antagonism increased Eloise's alarm. It boded ill for Roland. The Church closed ranks to protect its own and many of its members were corrupt. She knew nothing about this abbot. Would he put the Church's interest first and disregard the truth?

"Spare me men of pomp and circumstance," she muttered.

"I agree, but he is a fair man." Surrounded by four of the sheriff's guards, Roland addressed her with a wry grin. He wore a tunic and leggings of plain homespun and, for a moment, she wished she was a humble peasant who could run away with her lover.

Aware of Roland's scrutiny, she blushed. He looked tired and there were dark shadows under his eyes from fighting the fire all night. Yet to her he had never looked more handsome. Throughout her interview with the sheriff, her mind had wandered back to the night he had almost made love to her, and how her body had so eagerly responded. She could not blot out the fierce emotions his kisses had aroused as he held her so passionately. There was so much she needed to say to him, but could not do so with the guards present.

His eyes sparkled with open adoration as he regarded her but, before he could speak, a page called out from above them.

"Sir Roland! The sheriff will receive you now."

Roland made no excuses for his conduct as he answered the sheriff's and abbot's questions. But when he spoke of the persecution of the people, his anger was evident.

He was standing, whilst the sheriff and abbot sat in the only two chairs rescued from the fire. Since his years of being shackled in the slave-ship, he found it difficult to remain still and now he slowly paced the small room, his manner relaxed. "I had accepted since Alaric's death that Stephen was now Lord of Penruthin. I never intended to steal his inheritance. But, encouraged by his wife and Prior Ignatius, Stephen had misspent the Lady Eloise's dowry. The honour of my family demanded that that wrong be put right. The other events speak for themselves. That I was arrested and thrown into prison without being given a chance to prove my identity, proved that Stephen and Prior Ignatius were in league and had much to hide."

The abbot eyed him haughtily. "What proof have

you that Prior Ignatius is guilty of the crimes you state?''

''Question the villagers,'' Roland answered unhesitatingly. ''Look around you at their poverty and the wealth within the priory. Seven years ago, the monks at the priory lived austerely, as befitted their vows.''

The abbot leaned forward to whisper in the sheriff's ear. Roland could feel the abbot's hostility, but the sheriff seemed less antagonistic than he had been on his arrival.

When the abbot finished speaking the sheriff's expression was uncompromising as he dismissed Roland.

Emerging from the gatehouse, Roland saw again the smouldering ruin of his home. His anger rekindled. Greed and vengeance had caused this destruction. Isobel had paid with her life, but it seemed that it was she who triumphed.

The priory infirmary was deathly quiet after the noise of the castle where men had begun to clear the charred timbers and cart them away. Eloise faced Brother Bernard, who looked distressed at having to deny her entrance. He was short and slight of build and the most mild-mannered of men.

''It is the prior's orders, my lady,'' he said humbly. ''No one is to visit Sir Stephen and he is to be tended only by myself.''

Eloise stood firm. Behind her was Captain Maddock, another guard and Githa, who clutched a freshly-made unguent which would help Stephen's burns. Having already blustered her way into the priory, Eloise was not about to be stopped now. A major confrontation had been avoided as the prior himself was now answering the sheriff's and abbot's questions.

"The prior had no right to bring Sir Stephen here. He has abused his powers. It is little short of abduction."

He spread his hands helplessly. "Even so, my lady, I have my orders."

"Do you countenance abduction, Brother Bernard?"

The monk looked shocked.

"Then stand aside," she persisted. "Githa is more experienced with burns than yourself. She is cousin to the blacksmith. I wish her to attend Sir Stephen."

With an imperious toss of her head, she stepped around his slender figure and entered the infirmary. The stench of charred flesh stung her nostrils but, undeterred, she steeled herself to look down at the figure swathed in light bandages.

It was obvious that Stephen was unconscious. His face had escaped the fire, but his hands, arms and legs had been badly burned. Deep lines of pain were etched across his brow and around his nostrils and mouth.

"Has he regained consciousness, Brother Bernard?" she asked as she knelt beside the bed.

"No, my lady. And he is growing weaker."

Tears scalded Eloise's eyes as she knelt by the pallet. His bravery in trying to save Isobel had touched

Eloise. Clearly he was not all bad. He had been led
astray by a wife bent upon avenging the insult Alaric
had shown her by leaving for France.

There was nothing she could do and, leaving Githa
to tend Stephen, she went into the priory chapel to
pray. So much had happened, so quickly, that her
mind was numbed. How long she stayed there she did
not know, but the light filtering in from the stained
glass window had lost its brilliance when she heard
a footfall behind her. She was kneeling by the figure
of the Madonna in the side-chapel which was used by
the people of Penruthin, which had no church of its
own. Her figure was in shadow and she did not speak
as she saw Roland kneel before the altar. There was
weariness in every line of his body and, as he bowed
his head, she saw the overbright glitter behind his
lashes.

She rose stiffly and he came to his feet swiftly as
she approached him.

"Stephen is dead," he said hollowly. "He died a
true knight and with honour, trying to save the woman
he loved. He was conscious at the end and in intense
pain. I swore fealty to him as Lord of Penruthin after
telling him who I was." He swallowed. "He bore his
pain bravely. And though it must have caused him
agony to speak, he asked my forgiveness for bringing
Penruthin to the point of ruin."

Eloise hung her head. "He could not be all bad if
he was your half-brother. He did not deserve to die
so horribly."

The deep, mournful tone of the tocsin rang out proclaiming to all the death of Stephen, Lord of Penruthin. Aware that Roland wanted time alone in order to come to terms with his brother's death, she left the chapel. The brothers may not have been close, but she had heard the note of respect in Roland's voice as he spoke of Stephen's death.

Horses were saddled in the priory courtyard and, as she approached them, Prior Ignatius, accompanied by four guards, was led to the mounting-block. With a withering glare in Eloise's direction, he heaved himself into the saddle and was escorted away.

The fury on his face told her that he had been dismissed, but she would not learn his fate until she met the abbot and, as yet, no summons had come from him.

An hour later Roland came to her in Githa's cottage. He was carrying her father's sword—its sheath blackened by smoke but otherwise undamaged—and a silver casket containing Isobel's jewels.

"You are Mistress of Penruthin now. But I fear the living quarters of the castle are uninhabitable. It is a far worse ruin than your old home at Whytemead, and will cost all your fortune to rebuild."

"And I shall need a strong man at my side with knowledge of fortifications."

He gripped his hands together, as though fighting some inner torment, before he spoke. "You will need a *wealthy* husband. It is your duty now to marry well and safeguard the people of Penruthin."

Her gaze lifted to meet his and she was engulfed

by the bittersweet agony of her love. An impossible
love. With the castle ruined and so many people de-
pendent upon its rising again to prosperity, she had a
duty to marry as Roland said.

"Is there no hope for us?"

He planted his legs apart and folded his arms, a
fortress of closed emotion. "I am baseborn and you
are an heiress from one of England's oldest families.
I have no inclination to follow the path of the ancient
courts of love. I do not worship a woman from afar,
to be her slave, her knight errant. I want you as an
equal, Eloise."

"How can I convince you that you are that and
more?" Desperate to convince him, she flung her
arms around his neck. "Don't let your pride ruin our
chance of happiness."

A wry smile tilted the corners of his lips. "You
forget that the sheriff has not yet given us his verdict.
I could be a condemned man."

He had meant to taunt her, but his words filled her
with dread. "Don't speak that way."

With a sob, she held him tight and drew his head
down towards her. All her yearning and passion was
in her kiss. A tremor passed through him, but he did
not pull away. His body smelled of soap from bathing
to rid it of the stench of smoke; it also smelled tantalisingly of his own unique masculine scent. She
could feel his heat and strength causing ripples of
desire to spread through her limbs. When her tongue
explored the soft seam of his lips, he moaned softly,
his arms closing around her.

Roland groaned, knowing her kiss was intended to seduce him. He fought his response, restrained his hunger. But she had learned too well the wiles which could ensnare a man. She was luring him deeper into the paradise she would create for them, beyond reason, beyond sanity.

A discreet cough behind them startled them to break apart.

Captain Maddock remained at a discreet distance as Eloise straightened her veil. "My lady, the sheriff and abbot are asking that you attend upon them with Sir Roland."

Recovering her composure, she walked briskly from the cottage. To her surprise the villagers were crowded together. At the sight of Roland by her side they began to chant his name with loud acclaim. Clearly, they had forgiven Roland his necessary deception, in the light of what it had attained.

"We're with you, Sir Roland!" the blacksmith shouted. "If the sheriff's men try to take you, then they'll have to answer to us."

A chorus of agreement rose from the villagers. "There ain't but one way to right the wrongs here," one chirpy voice added. "That's for Sir Roland to wed the Lady Eloise."

Eloise felt her colour rising. The villagers' sentiments echoed her own, but few noblewomen could control their own destinies. Now hers was in the hands of the High Sheriff.

As she entered the gatehouse room, the sheriff and abbot rose to their feet. There was a cold formality in the abbot's manner which reeked of disapproval. Coldness spread through her veins as she waited for their verdict. Roland was at her side and the back of his bandaged hand brushed hers. She wished she could hold it, for her courage was ebbing as the silence dragged on. She was aware that, although Roland appeared relaxed, a tension coiled within him. The next words the sheriff spoke could mean the end of his freedom.

Outside, the chanting of the villagers continued, linking Eloise's and Roland's names. Would their loyalty move the sheriff to compassion?

The abbot folded his arms within the wide sleeves of his grey habit. ''The wealth in the prior's apartments, together with the empty coffers of the castle and the poverty apparent in the village, uphold the Lady Eloise's claims that her dowry was misappropriated by the Church,'' he declared heavily. ''Prior Ignatius informed us that they were gifts of atonement from Sir Stephen. But our order is one of poverty; and wealth has no place within it. Also, the money was not Sir Stephen's to give.''

Eloise slowly let out her breath, but the abbot's expression remained disapproving, alarming her that less welcome news was yet to come.

''Prior Ignatius has been ordered to return to the father house of our order in Normandy,'' he continued. ''The full amount of the Lady Eloise's dowry will be returned to her.''

''I thank you for the justice of that,'' Eloise began,

but was halted by a dismissive wave from the sheriff's hand.

"You are a young woman, inexperienced in the devious ways of the world. As a widow, you are now vulnerable and without a protector."

The sheriff then fixed his stare upon Roland, who did not move a muscle as he awaited the verdict on his own future.

"Sir Roland is guilty of impersonating his brother. But we have taken his reasons into consideration. Since he has refuted any claim to Penruthin, we consider that he was not guilty of the intent to steal his brother's, or the Lady Eloise's, inheritances."

Relieved, Eloise stared up at Roland. She marvelled at his calmness and the lack of emotion he showed. He merely nodded a brief acknowledgement to the decree.

The sheriff added, "From the strong-box saved from the fire, the marriage settlement between Lady Eloise and Sir Alaric shows that under its terms she is now Mistress of Penruthin. But there is the matter of the slur upon her honour. She was closeted several times alone with Sir Roland. To avoid any scandal it would be better for all concerned if Sir Roland and Lady Eloise were to marry."

Joy sped through Eloise and she struggled to concentrate on the rest of the sheriff's pronouncement.

"The abbot has agreed to perform the ceremony. Lady Isobel and Sir Stephen are to be buried this evening. The abbot deemed it expedient in the circumstances that we should waive the customary year of mourning. If Penruthin is to rise from the ashes, the work must begin without delay. Do you agree to our conditions, Sir Roland?''

Unable to contain her pleasure, Eloise smiled at Roland. To her surprise, his eyes remained troubled as he replied, ''I am deeply honoured.''

''Then prepare for your wedding, which will be a simple affair tomorrow.''

Until she joined Roland before the abbot in the priory chapel for their wedding, Eloise had seen little of Roland. When he was not closeted with the sheriff—who had demanded to know his plans for rebuilding Penruthin as a stronghold—he was organising the clearing and salvaging work at the castle. The previous evening, they had been lodged within the priory: she in the small women's guest-quarters and Roland on the far side in a room next to the sheriff. Even after the funeral there had been little time to talk, and Roland had appeared abstracted when they had found time for a moment unobserved.

Yet now, as he slid the marriage ring over her finger, there was such love in his gaze that it banished the unease caused by the earlier shadows in his eyes.

Finally, the ceremony and the simple wedding feast over, they were alone in the gatehouse rooms, the only suitable accommodation remaining within the ruined castle. The women had been working all morning to prepare their quarters. The plain wooden bed was adorned with garlands of wild flowers, the bedding scattered with rose petals, lavender and rosemary. The rescued tapestries had been hung to cover the bare walls to create an intimate atmosphere. Outside, the people were still celebrating around the open fire over which an ox had been roasted. A fiddler and piper were playing, serenading the married couple.

"God bless Lord and Lady Penruthin!" The cry which had been chanted all day was now slurred by the free-flowing festive wine.

Yet, even as the door closed behind them and Roland pulled Eloise into his arms, she sensed a tension within him, which she needed to question. "I know you love me, Roland, but does our marriage not please you?"

In answer he took her hands between his bandaged fingers and lifted them tenderly to his lips. "To have won you, my darling, is to have achieved my wildest dream. How could I not be happy?"

"But something is troubling you?" she persisted.

He kissed her brow. "I am churlish, forgive me. But it sits ill with me that so much has come to me though you, yet I have nothing except my love to offer you in return."

"How can you think that? You bring me your courage, your strength and protection. No man has greater love for these people and they adore you. You are the lord they wanted—Lord Penruthin's eldest son and the most worthy. And you won that right by risking your life to save the people from the prior, and the tireless way in which you fought the fire and then saved the page Ian's life."

He smiled tenderly. "Your love is the greatest trea-

sure I could ever win, but, to be truly worthy of both
you and Penruthin, I will not live on your fortune.
Once the building work is started I must seek my own
fortune. What I have, I need to have won by my own
hand. It is the only way I can keep my respect and
yours.''

She understood his motives, but her heart was sad-
dened by his stubbornness. But then, had he been the
type of knight who married a wealthy wife to win his
lands and fortune, she knew she would never have
lost her heart to him so unreservedly.

Her answering smile was enticing. ''Talk not of
leaving Penruthin on our wedding night.''

She looked pointedly at her wedding ring. The gold
was wrought into a lover's knot with a large emerald
at its centre. It was a ring she had seen Clothilde wear,
given to her by Roland's father as a token of his love.
Githa must have kept it safe as a legacy for Roland.
''My husband, there is one duty, even more important
than rebuilding the castle, which is also expected of
you.'' Her voice was low and throaty and, as she
spoke, she ran a finger along his shaven cheek. She
could not have enough of the touch of him, needed
to reassure herself that this was not a dream, but blissful reality.

The love and adoration in his eyes seared her to
her soul. He turned his head, his mouth seeking her
palm and his tongue flicking over the sensitive skin.
At her gasp of pleasure, he chuckled wickedly. ''Accuse me of neglecting my duty, would you?''

She was crushed against his hard body, his kiss

hungry and demanding as it ravaged her senses. Her response was immediate. With a sigh of surrender, she clung to him, her fingers entwining in his thick dark hair which lapped against his shoulders. The touch of his tongue teasing hers, exploring the soft silkiness of her mouth, roused a feverish desire. She sighed ecstatically as her head rolled back and his lips caressed the sensitive flesh at the hollow of her throat. Her body throbbed—tingling, pulsating with a myriad of rapturous sensations that made her hips undulate against the pressure of his arousal.

A soft groan tore from him and she felt a tremor pass through his powerful frame as he drew back and kept her at arm's length. His laugh was husky and quivered with the force of his desire.

"You are a temptress. My dearest love."

Every word was a caress. He reverently removed her veil and fillet and, with a provocative shake of her head, her hair tumbled loose from its pins, the glow of the candlelight glinting in the blue-black tresses as they cascaded to her hips. Her cheeks were flushed with the radiance of her love. His fingers were deft and sure upon the lacing of her gown. Her own were more impatient as she removed his clothing. When her hand slid across the finely honed muscles of his virile body, its perfection rendered her breathless. The candlelight had turned his skin to warm amber. Her fingertips moved slowly across his broad shoulders, discovering the power and play of his firm muscles and flesh. At his indrawn breath, she revelled in the pleasure her touch evoked in him. Her naked breasts lifted and fell with each rapid breath as she saw the dawning urgency in his gaze. Roland lowered his dark head, his lips seeking her breasts, gently circling them with his tongue, the light tug of his lips so loving, so tender, making her body arch, trembling with the delicious thrills he created. The enchantment he wove around her senses made her whisper his name over and over like a litany. Heart to heart, pulse to pulse, their breaths mingled, heated by a sacred calling as ancient as birth.

"I love you," Roland whispered against her ear as he lifted her and carried her to the perfumed and flower-decked bed. From breast to thigh the hair-rough texture of his skin against the smooth satin of her own was exhilarating, intimately sensuous. Beneath the masterly touch of Roland's caresses, Eloise was melting, enslaved by the passionate kisses which were rousing her body to a storm of blissful magnitude, swirling her senses into a vortex of pleasure. Each kiss was an accolade of their love, each caress an affirmation of constancy. The earthly world blurred as she surrendered in avid abandon. Senses revolved faster, spiralling them upwards to heavenly heights as mind, body and soul finally blended and became one. Their joining was the union of twin souls, binding them until eternity. The explosion of sensation when it came was hallowed by their love, transporting them beyond dreams, beyond paradise.

As the world steadied back on to its foundations, Eloise sighed. Roland was gazing at her as though he had just discovered the Grail itself. He smoothed back a damp tendril of hair from her brow.

Smiling with contentment, she put a finger to his lips which were swollen from their lovemaking. She moved languidly beneath him, savouring the heat and touch of him lying so intimately against her. "Throughout the years you and Alaric were prisoners of the Moors, it was your image I carried in my heart. It was you I fell in love with on that long-ago wedding day, not Alaric."

Roland smiled. "I adored you, my love, from the moment I saw you walking towards me in the village that first day of my return. You were so beautiful, but so unattainable, that I refused to acknowledge the hold you wielded over my affections. And it was not until the time I came to your room when you were singing that I admitted to myself that I loved you. I realised that I loved your goodness, your loyalty, your sense of justice and the way you defend those less fortunate than yourself. Now you are mine forever. And I will love you until the end of my days."

Epilogue

Three years to the day of Roland's return to Penruthin as a pilgrim, the rebuilding of the castle was complete. The newly-cut limestone was pale as golden wine in the summer's sunshine. The skyline of Penruthin had changed. No old-fashioned keep dominated the landscape. The castle, although capable of being defended by its battlemented walls, was now a fortified manor, in the style which was becoming more popular with the nobility. Each room had its own fireplace, a large oriel window brightened the Baron's Hall and large glazed windows replaced the old arrow slits in the main chambers.

Eloise stood on the parapet of the square watchtower over which flew the new Standard of Penruthin, the black lion on gold, quartered with the twin silver dragons of Eloise's family on its own background of azure. Her eyes strained to the distance where a fanfare announced the arrival of her husband's return from Court. The trumpet was distant and she waited impatiently for the cavalcade to appear through the wood before they approached the thatched and lime-washed cottages of the village.

Not only Penruthin had flourished since her marriage; Whytemead was also prospering and on this special day both villages had come together to pay tribute to their lord's return.

This time it had been only two weeks since she had seen Roland but, even so, her heart fluttered with the anticipation of their reunion. In the years since their marriage Roland had served the King, keeping his vow to win his own fortune. Their third child kicked in her womb. It would be born in a month's time and Roland had been too concerned for Eloise's welfare to allow her to accompany him to Court.

A month after their marriage the King had recovered from the malady—which many had declared to be insanity—from which he had suffered since losing his domains in France. They had been summoned to Court. The King, impressed by Roland's tales of his pilgrimage and captivity, had appointed him an emissary to strengthen his allegiance with foreign powers on the Continent. The partings had been hard for them both, but the reunions had been wonderful, their love growing stronger with each year.

A tugging at her skirts made her smile as she bent to lift up two-year-old Edgar, and she kissed his dark hair. Already he was the image of his father. His sister Clothilde, at a year, was asleep, watched over by the children's nursemaid.

When the first bright colours of livery could be seen through the trees, Eloise left the watchtower to welcome Roland at the Gatehouse. She was dressed in a gown of sapphire velvet with a matching hennin headdress. She had ordered the courtyard to be draped in garlands of flowers to mark this very special home-coming.

Her heart was full and tears of pride were blinked rapidly aside as Roland rode under the portcullis. The Penruthin Standard was proudly carried by Sergeant Maddock at his side. Roland was in half-armour, which gleamed in the sunlight; the blue and gold ostrich feathers adorning his steel helmet bobbed jauntily as he dismounted. The people roared their cheers, but Roland's stare was fixed solely upon his wife.

With disregard of ceremony he snatched off his helmet and pushed back the chainmail hood beneath and, bare-headed, strode to her with unconcealed impatience.

"There will be no more partings, not for some time, my love," he said excitedly, uncaring of the villagers watching as he embraced her with unrestrained passion.

The people cheered louder, delighting in the loving reunion between their lord and lady.

"When I heard the news, I ordered the grandest feast Penruthin has known." Eloise stared up at him, her eyes bright with love and adoration. "You have achieved your ambition. The King has rewarded you handsomely with lands in Sussex."

He grinned and ruffled Edgar's hair before taking her arm and drawing her aside within the seclusion of the doorway for a moment's privacy. "I did not tell you all. You are now a Countess. His Majesty created me Earl Mountjoy for my humble work in sealing the secret alliance with the French noblemen and their allies.''

Eloise knew that for the rewards to be so high and to please the King so greatly there must have been danger in Roland's work and his achievements far from humble. She was so proud of him, so full of love.

''An appropriate name,'' she said, smiling into his eyes. ''The French *montjoie* means a cairn set up to mark a victory. And in the *Song of Roland* it was the heroic Charlemagne's warcry. You have won a great victory to achieve so much.''

''But it was you who inspired me to aim so high. When Edgar was born I was so proud of you. I wanted to repay you for all the happiness you had given me. I wanted to make you a Countess. Knowing that you loved me...'' He broke off, his ardent kiss telling her more profoundly than any words how much he loved her and how his pride had driven him to win lands and a title of his own.

He put a hand below her heart on her swollen stomach and grinned as the child within kicked him. ''Penruthin's wife no longer, but Countess Mountjoy, the most beautiful and exceptional woman in all Christendom.''

Then his mouth was again on hers. Outside, a linnet serenaded them and the midday sun cast its golden aura on the home of the lovers whose destiny of a rich and rewarding love was unassailable.

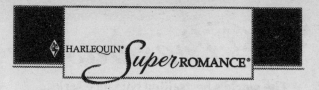

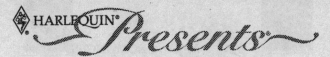

HARLEQUIN®
INTRIGUE

WE'LL LEAVE YOU BREATHLESS!

If you've been looking for thrilling tales of contemporary passion and sensuous love stories with taut, edge-of-the-seat suspense—then you'll love Harlequin Intrigue!

Every month, you'll meet four new heroes who are guaranteed to make your spine tingle and your pulse pound. With them you'll enter into the exciting world of Harlequin Intrigue— where your life is on the line and so is your heart!

THAT'S INTRIGUE—
ROMANTIC SUSPENSE
AT ITS BEST!

HARLEQUIN®

Makes any time special ®

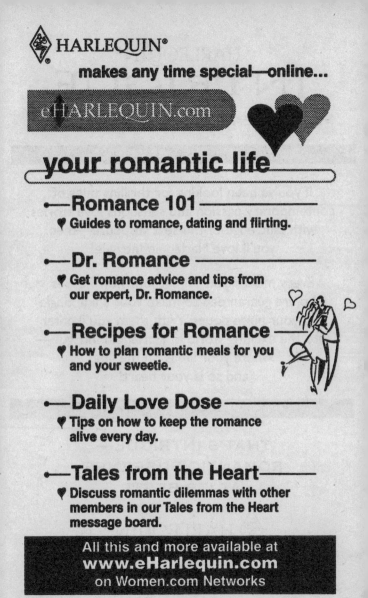